mr. swoony

Piper Rayne

Cover Design and Illustrator: Buerosued

1st Line Editor: Joy Editing

2nd Line Editor: My Brother's Editor

Proofreader: My Brother's Editor

about mr. swoony

Hockey players were never my type.

At least, that's what I thought—until I met Conor Nilsen. In truth, I didn't know he was the goalie for the Chicago Falcons when he struck up a conversation the night of my bachelorette party.

He proved he wasn't just some hot guy looking to score when he helped me get my drunk bridesmaid safely back to our hotel. That's when he discovered my 30-before-30 bucket list —a list I hadn't managed to check a single item off.

What was meant to be innocent stargazing turned into so much more. The chemistry between us was undeniable, and after one night together, I started to question everything— especially my upcoming wedding to a man I wasn't sure loved me.

Fast forward to my wedding day, and just as I'm standing at the altar, Conor bursts through the church doors to object. And now, somehow, I'm his roommate. Yikes.

Mr. SWOONY

one

Eloise

THIS IS NOT THE BACHELORETTE PARTY I HAD ON MY vision board.

I should be in a mud bath getting a head massage or being rubbed down with aromatic oil in a dim room. At the very least, sweating the toxins out of my overly stressed-out body in a steam room. I should *not* be sitting in a nightclub with a stained pink bride-to-be sash snug around my chest and a T-shirt with a QR code printed on the back for people to scan and buy me a drink.

But no, two days ago, the spa called to say that a pipe had burst, and the whole place flooded and could no longer accommodate our party. Sure, they felt bad and offered us some complimentary gift cards, but it still left my bridal party SOL. Then to top it off, my maid of honor, Jade, got stranded in Holland because of some issue with the airport's computer software so everything was grounded.

That left my college-roommate-slash-bridesmaid, Penelope, to organize my bachelorette party in less than forty-eight hours. I'm sure it was no easy feat, and I appreciate all she's done, but tonight has shown me a few things. The biggest one being that Penelope and I don't have a lot in common these days. She clearly enjoys the club scene while I'm more of a "nice restaurant, a few glasses of wine, and in bed by ten" kind of girl. This is what happens when you're scrounging up bridesmaids due to your fiancé's inability to not ask every damn person he's ever met to be a groomsman.

Penelope's taken most of the shots that men have bought for me through the QR code. Not that I'm complaining. She can have the shots and the attention for all I care. It's disgusting how many men have some lame pickup line about how it's my last night of freedom, and I should spend it riding their big dick. Give me a break. Does that shit actually ever work?

One thing about Penelope, though, is that she's resourceful. After being denied the VIP section, she flirted us in. Her flirting has now taken her from tipsy to drunk, meaning I need to stay sober to make sure she makes it safely back to our hotel.

She's on the dance floor with the guy who had to convince his friends to allow our party to crash theirs. His two friends are entertaining women on the rounded part of the booth. And when I say entertaining, I mean they're on their laps in a make-out session, glancing in my direction every once in a while as if I'm a killjoy.

I lean back onto the black vinyl couch and cross my legs, sipping my water bottle, biding my time until Penelope returns, and I can drag her into an Uber. I glance at the adjoining VIP section, which is mostly filled with guys, and I half wonder if it's a bachelor party celebration. Where is their groom-to-be with his sash and QR code T-shirt? If I had to guess, I'd think it's probably the blond-haired guy with a girl on either side of him. I can see from here that he's a charmer.

One of the guy's heads rocks back with laughter at something another guy says, and when his head straightens, our eyes catch for a moment. He brings his glass to his lips and sips, his eyes never leaving mine. Oh, he's good. His lips part, and he smiles, showing off his perfect white teeth. Inch by inch, his gaze flows up my body but stops on my sash for a moment before he raises his eyebrows when our eyes lock again.

He's got trouble written all over him. His dark hair has fallen across his forehead a little from being in the club, but it looks as if maybe he meant to style it that way. His shirt pulls across his broad shoulders and chest. But mostly, it's his alluring eyes and his perfect smile with a hint of cockiness that would draw in any woman. He knows how good-looking he is.

I pull my gaze away from him and glance back at the dance floor to find Penelope with the other bridesmaids, who are really more my fiancé's friends than mine. They've been drinking but not to excess like Penelope. I'm probably being a party pooper, but I've never been that crazy girl who can put my inhibitions aside and let loose, which is why I wanted a spa weekend for my bachelorette party.

Movement in my peripheral vision grabs my attention, and the guy I locked eyes with is talking with the two guys from this VIP section we crashed. They shake hands, and one guy opens the rope for him. He nods and thanks them before coming over to me.

Why am I nervous? I'm an engaged woman.

"Aren't you supposed to be the one out there?" His eyes are a light brown and laced with mischief that makes good girls do bad things. But not this good girl.

"Sorry, I'm not looking for some guy to show me what I'll miss out on by getting married." I sip my water and turn my attention back to the dance floor.

He sinks down on the couch beside me. "I don't pick up taken women." He sets his drink on the table in front of us and turns his body, blocking my view of the dance floor. He puts his hand out between us. "I'm Conor."

I glance down at it, then look back at his face. Seeing his eyes up close brings a feeling of familiarity I can't place. I slide my hand into his. His large hand swallows my smaller one, and the roughness and callouses along his palm are something new to me. "I'm not interested."

He chuckles. "Me either."

I shake my head and pull my hand back, biting my lip to not smile at his flirtatiousness.

"No name then?" he asks.

I place my bottle of water next to his glass. "No name." I straighten my back. "Listen, maybe you're genuinely just a nice guy, but you clearly see this." I circle my hand over my sash and T-shirt. "I'm not here to pick up a guy. I don't want one more fling before I say I do. I'm just waiting until my friend is ready to leave so I don't spoil her night and can go back to the hotel."

"I am."

I lean around him so I can try to find Penelope on the dance floor again, hoping she's coming back. "You're what?"

"A genuinely nice guy. Ask anyone over there." He nods toward his VIP section.

"Yeah, I'm sure your friends will vouch for you."

He chuckles again, and I hate that I like the sound. "True."

"Why are you here?" I attempt to get him to give me a straight answer.

"I don't want to tell you." He sits back and crosses his leg so his ankle rests on his knee, getting even more comfortable instead of leaving, which is what I wish he would do.

"Trying to pique my curiosity?" I arch an eyebrow.

"I'm vulnerable." He flags down the waitress, and she

saunters over in a short micro dress that doesn't leave much to the imagination.

"What can I get you, Conor?" she asks in a sultry voice that implies, as I assumed, he's the player type.

I scoff, and Conor turns to me but talks to her. "Two bottles of water." Digging into his pocket, he pulls out a fifty and places it on her tray of empty glasses without his eyes ever leaving mine.

"Be right back," she says.

"So, you're a regular, huh?"

"I've been here twice."

"The bottle girl knows you by name. She must be really good at her job then." I scootch up on the edge of the seat. "It was nice meeting you, but I'm gonna go get my friend."

"Really?" He sits up straight. "You're just going to leave after I came all the way over here?"

I laugh. "Well, I'm sure it's a foreign concept for you that a woman isn't interested but think of it as an opportunity for some character growth."

He smirks and shakes his head. "And I thought I was cocky."

I tilt my head and narrow my eyes. "Excuse me?"

"You assume that I was hitting on you."

"Weren't you?"

"I told you I don't go after taken women, so unless this whole bride thing is a façade, I'm not interested in pursuing you." The waitress comes back with two waters, and he grabs mine, holding it out toward me. "Want me to open it?"

I nod, and his forearm flexes as he opens the water bottle and hands it to me.

"Thanks," I mumble. "And I'm sorry, it's just been a shitty night."

"I figured." He glances at the stain on my sash. "I came over because I'm a fixer."

I choke on my water but manage to swallow it before spitting it in his face. "That's your profession? A fixer?"

"Not my actual profession. But it's who I am to my core. I like to fix people's problems."

I nod and screw the cap back on my water bottle. "Well, no worries here. No problems." I wipe my palms together and hold up my hands. "Go back over and enjoy your party."

His eyebrows scrunch, but he moves to stand. "All right then. My conscience is clear."

"Yep, you can sleep well tonight." I stand before I blabber all my problems to this guy.

Penelope stumbles into the area with the guy she was dancing with, laughing as they fall onto the couch's other side.

Just when I thought I could make my getaway.

two

Eloise

"Lulu!" Penelope slurs, using the nickname she gave me in college. She only uses it when she's drunk, or when she's whining for me to do something I don't want to do.

"Lulu, huh?" Conor asks.

Penelope perks up as if she didn't see this gorgeous hunk of a man next to me. She probably didn't, or she saw two of him. That'd be something if he had a twin. The universe would've really been working overtime if that were the case.

"Actually, it's Eloise."

"I like Lulu," he says, his gaze fixed on mine.

His attention is slightly unnerving.

"You're hunky," Penelope says, trying to sit up straight but failing miserably.

"Hey, you're going to make me jealous," the blond guy Penelope has been dancing with all night says.

"Are you ready to go?" I ask her, raising my eyebrows at the guy behind her. I'm sure he'll fight me to take her home, but it's not happening.

"Lulu," she whines and slides closer to me.

Thankfully, the blond guy stays put and talks to his friends. All of them are whispering and looking at Conor. I'm starting to think I missed something.

"You're drunk, and it's time." I really don't want to ruin her night, but she's about a sip away from some bad decisions.

"I'm sorry." She lays her head on my shoulder but picks it up immediately, concentrating on Conor. "It's her bachelorette party."

"I see that," Conor says with a nod.

"And I'm the world's worst bridesmaid." Penelope's bottom lip trembles.

Oh no, not the tears and the crying. Shit, I forgot she gets emotional after a lot of drinks.

"No, you're not." I put my arm around her shoulders.

"I am. Your maid of honor wouldn't be drunk at your party while you're sipping... what is this?" She picks up the water bottle as if we're nineteen again and sneaking vodka into our water bottles. She takes a swig. "Water?"

The pain in her voice says she's going to lose it, and I'm going to have a basket case on my hands soon.

"Come on." I stand and look over my shoulder to see the rest of our bridal party huddled with a group of guys.

Penelope falls down on the couch, rolling to her back.

Conor raises his brows at me and looks back at Penelope.

"Are you a model?" she asks him.

Conor chuckles. "No."

"Some finance bro?" she asks.

Not with those calloused hands, I think.

"No."

"Where did you come from?" she asks as though he's been conjured up via some science project.

Conor points toward the VIP area next door.

She gets up on her knees and peers over. Looking over her

shoulder at Conor, her eyes widen, and her mouth hangs open. "There?" She points.

Conor nods.

Her eyes narrow, and her gaze drags down his body and back up. "Oh shit."

"What?" I look between the two of them, clearly missing something because Conor's cocky smirk only gets wider as if he's answering her silent question.

"Good looking. Cocky. Strong thighs. She doesn't even know it, does she?" Penelope giggles—which is kind of annoying because it's clearly at my expense, but I'll take it over tears any night.

"What am I missing?" I ask.

She points at the other VIP area. "That's Tweetie Sorenson."

I shrug and follow the direction of her finger to the tall guy with blond hair cut to his chin who is laughing with three other guys. "That's his name? Tweetie?"

Conor laughs but doesn't answer.

"No, it's his hockey nickname. I'm not sure I even know his real name, actually." She turns to Conor.

He shrugs as if he doesn't know either, or he's not going to tell her.

"He's your friend?" Penelope asks him.

Conor nods.

"Teammate?" Penelope's brows lift.

Conor nods again.

"Holy shit! Are you serious?" Penelope slaps the top of the booth cushion. "You don't even know it, do you?" She flips around and slides down on the vinyl couch, catching herself before her ass slips right off, and she lands on the floor.

"Know what?" I ask with irritation.

"You're sitting next to a Chicago Falcon." She shakes her head and glances at Conor.

"Really?" I ask because she could be too drunk, and these guys may look like them, but they can't actually be professional hockey players.

"Yeah."

The blond guy on the couch slides over next to Penelope with two shots in hand. He whispers something in her ear, and she downs one.

I need to get us out of here. "Wait here, I'm going to tell everyone we're leaving."

I stand and stare at the dance floor, but the rest of our party is on the other side, and I really don't want to walk through all those sweaty bodies. I could send them a text. I mean, they're here out of obligation, but they took time out of their lives to come here and celebrate me, even if I think most of them don't like me very much. When I'm around them, I always feel as though I don't belong.

A calloused hand falls onto mine. "I'll take you," Conor says.

I ignore the flutter in my stomach. What the fuck is that about? I'm going to be a married woman in a week.

He tugs me forward, but I stop and look at Penelope, tugging her up by the hand and making us a chain of three. The blond guy protests, but I put out my hand.

"Stay. She's done. It's been fun," I say.

Penelope's head lolls to the side. We only have a short amount of time before someone will have to carry her out of here.

"Bye," she mumbles and waves to the guy, who thankfully doesn't follow us.

Conor weaves us through the crowd, and I'd be a liar if I said it wasn't hot the way people part for him. I think maybe I was the only one in this club who didn't know who he is.

We stop in front of the other bridesmaids, and the guys they're with corral around Conor, competing to shake hands with him first. Each of them fawns over him as though he's The Bachelor, and it's episode one. I tell the other bridesmaids I'm taking Penelope back to the hotel, and they offer to come back too, though I say no. They're having fun and should stay. Plus, this way I can get Penelope settled and have some peace to myself instead of them thinking they have to entertain me.

Penelope grows heavy behind me, tugging my hand down, and I know from our days in college that I'm on borrowed time. I say goodbye, wrap my arm around her shoulders, and walk us along the dance floor's perimeter toward the front door, leaving Conor with his wannabe entourage members.

As I'm about to walk out the door, a big body comes along behind me, pushing it open.

"Let me." Conor's breath tickles the nape of my neck.

Penelope and I stumble through, and Conor joins us on the sidewalk, flagging down a cab. I stand on the sidewalk as Penelope sinks further into my hold.

"Why are you still here?" I ask.

"You already forgot?" He moves his hand from left to right on his chest. "I'm a fixer."

"The earth is spinning," Penelope whispers. Her eyes fall closed, and her body goes limp right before she sways.

Conor rushes over, catching her before she crashes her head onto the cement.

I'm not sure what I'm supposed to do now. I can't possibly carry Penelope around once it's time to get out of the cab. I consider calling Tristan for only about half a second. He'll be pissed if I interrupt his bachelor party with the guys, regardless of the situation.

Conor opens the cab's back door and gets Penelope inside. Though I try not to, it's impossible not to notice all those muscles he has to use to push her to the other side. Then he straightens beside the car and holds the door open for me. "Your chariot awaits."

"I have always dreamed of a yellow taxi, thank you." I cover my heart with my hand and slide in. "Really though, thanks for helping, and I hope you have a great season next year."

I reach forward to grab the handle of the door, but he rounds the open door and moves to slide in next to me.

Panic flares in my chest. "What are you doing?"

"Coming with you." He says it simply, as though it's obvious he would.

"No, you're not."

He chuckles. "How else will you get her to your hotel room?"

Though I know he's right, I still put up a fight. "I'm resourceful."

"I think I'm going to throw up," Penelope pats the window with her open palm over and over again. "Open! Open!"

I reach over her to press the window down button, and Conor uses the distraction to sit beside me and shut the door.

Once Penelope's head hangs out the window like a dog with her tongue out of her mouth, though without the excited car trip energy, I turn back to Conor. "You're not coming to our room."

"Where to?" the cab driver asks.

"Hurry," Penelope groans.

Conor raises his eyebrows at me. I growl and give the hotel name, then the cab driver moves away from the curb into the Chicago nighttime traffic.

"Just so you know, I know Henry Hensley," I say, interrupting the silence.

"You know Daddy?" he asks.

My forehead wrinkles. "Daddy? Is that another hockey name?"

"Yeah… Daddy." His shoulders lift. "How do you know him?"

"He's my maid of honor's soon-to-be husband."

"Jade?" His voice goes up a few octaves. "Now I *have* to help you."

"I have it handled." *Liar.* I feel as though I don't have anything about my life handled these days.

He leans forward and inspects Penelope. I follow his line of vision to find her eyes closed, and she's completely still. Unless I use a luggage cart, there's no way I'm getting her up to our room. "Do you really think so?"

I huff.

He laughs. "Listen, I'm not going to lie, you're hot as shit. But I get that you're about to marry some lucky bastard, so I'm not here to convince you to give me a shot. Hell, I'm not a relationship guy anyway, and I sure as shit wouldn't want to ruin someone else's happiness. Henry's a great friend, and I love Jade, so let me help you get your friend to your room. Then we'll part ways, and maybe I'll run into you at a wedding or baby shower or something, and we'll share a laugh about tonight. But you don't have to worry about me trying to get in your pants. I'm honestly here just to help."

I lose the fight inside me because I'm defeated in more battles than just getting Penelope up to the hotel room tonight. Somehow, my life has spun out of my control, and I'm not sure how to right myself. Lately I feel as if I'm on the teacup ride, and it just keeps spinning and spinning, and there's no chance to get my bearings. Maybe it's just wedding jitters, and once it's over, and we're on our honeymoon, all this dread and anxiety will go away. I sure hope so.

"Thank you. Really. I appreciate it, and I'm sorry for taking you away from your friends at the club."

He shakes his head. "You're not taking me away from anything."

For the rest of the ride, I watch Penelope and the cab driver's GPS, eager to get to the hotel and out of the small confines of the cab because Conor's thigh is pressed to mine, and those butterflies aren't going away. They shouldn't even be fluttering. I'm marrying Tristan. *He* is the love of my life. Right?

The cab pulls up to the hotel, and Conor files out first. I nudge Penelope, and she mumbles something but falls on the seat. In the end, Conor picks her up and puts her over his shoulder. The three of us walk through the luxurious hotel lobby, pretending to ignore the stares from the reception staff.

"I really hope I don't end up in the gossip blogs for this," he says as we enter the elevator. "One girl slung over my shoulder with another at my side in a bride-to-be sash going up to a hotel room isn't a good look."

"You? My upcoming marriage would be over."

Right before the doors slide shut, a young girl pops into view, holding out her phone, and the flash goes off.

three

Conor

"Oh my god!" Eloise turns to me, her mouth hanging open.

The doors slide shut, leaving the girl with the phone on the other side. I'm thankful she didn't jump in and join us.

"That didn't just happen." She flings her body across me, her finger pressing the lobby button, but the elevator is already ascending. The tip of her finger turns white as she presses the button nonstop. "I have to get that phone."

"Is your hubby a hockey guy?" I ask, repositioning Penelope on my shoulder. Damn, it's been a long time since I've carried a woman over my shoulder. Especially one who's not coming to my bed.

There's no way Eloise would have been able to handle her friend. She's completely dead weight.

"Football mostly, but he watches all those sports channels." Her hands twist in front of her.

I can't help but laugh, although I feel bad. Eloise looks so panicked she's probably about to scale the wall and try to find her way through some vent to find that girl and destroy her phone. "I'm sure he's not on the hockey blogs. That picture might be passed around to her friends and her social media followers, but I doubt your hubby will see it. And if you want me to talk to him—"

"God, no. He'd never understand this whole situation." She circles her finger between us. Why do I love the way she's so animated?

"He wouldn't understand a guy helping a girl out of a bad situation?" Sounds like her fiancé is a dick.

She stares at the wall, watching the floor numbers as we approach their floor. "You're telling me you would be if I were your fiancée?"

"If I were ever to get married, I'd trust my fiancée. I would have hoped she'd called me—"

"It is his bachelor party tonight," she cuts me off, and I get the sense she's used to making excuses for him.

"I wasn't implying anything."

"I would've called him. It's just..." She doesn't finish her sentence—either because she doesn't want to or because the elevator stops, and the doors open on her floor.

It's good she didn't finish, because I don't want to become more invested in the reason why she sat all alone in the VIP section and sipping water during her bachelorette party. It wasn't my place to get involved, although I inserted myself because I pride myself on being a nice guy. Now that I know Jade is her maid of honor, I know I was right in helping her.

I deny the urge to ask more questions and instead follow her out of the elevator.

I noticed Eloise the minute I arrived at the club and entered the VIP section filled with my teammates. There's no denying she's hot as fuck. Her ass in her black leather pants is a sight all on its own. But when I saw the sash and the QR code, it stopped my mind from envisioning her topless and on her knees in front of me. I'm not the kind of guy who tries to steal another guy's girl away. Even if she looks like Eloise. But that doesn't mean I can't admire a beautiful woman.

Eloise swipes her keycard and opens the hotel room door to reveal a suite. "If you don't mind putting her in the bedroom..."

She walks through a door, and I follow, seeing one king bed. Eloise pulls back the covers, and I place Penelope on the bed, then she takes off her friend's shoes and tucks her in, ensuring she's positioned on her side with a pillow lodged behind her back so she doesn't roll over.

The way Eloise takes care of her friend is admirable. I've always thought there was a correlation between how a friend treats a friend and how they treat their significant other. I bet she loves them with all her heart and cares for them more than herself. I just hope that her fiancé isn't one of those douchebags who take advantage of her giving nature.

"I'll walk you out," Eloise says, pulling me from admiring her.

"No need, I can see myself out." I turn to walk out of the room.

She follows me. "Want a snack from the mini bar?"

I stop and turn around in the living area of the suite.

"For the road, of course," she quickly adds before I can say anything.

A laugh slips from my throat because I'm starting to like her as a person.

"I wouldn't have thought otherwise, but I'm good, thanks." I'm hungry, but I need to get the hell out of here before I try to fix any more of her problems.

She holds out a piece of chocolate. "At least take Penelope's pillow chocolate. It's the least she can do to pay you back."

I take the chocolate, and our fingers graze one another's. I ignore the softness of her touch. "Not really, but I've got a sweet tooth, so I'll never deny chocolate."

"I wouldn't have pegged you for a sweet tooth kind of guy."

"What kind of guy did you peg me for?" I hate how curious I am to hear her answer.

She looks me in the eye, long and hard, causing me to stare into her gray ones. How rare is that? I'm not sure I've ever seen someone with gray eyes. They look like cloudy skies with a hint of mystery, but they're still layered with warmth.

"Beef jerky."

My attention is pulled back to our conversation.

"I like jerky, but I'd pick sweet over salty every time." I unwrap the chocolate and plop the goodness into my mouth. Damn, it's tasty.

"You're enjoying it."

I swallow the chocolate and smile. "It was really good."

"Then let me give you mine." She shifts to walk back into the bedroom, but I grab her hand.

"Believe me, you want yours."

She stops and looks at my hand on her wrist.

I drop my grip. I'm starting to wish she wasn't engaged, and that is a problem. "Honestly, you're going to love it."

She nods, which surprises me, and eyes the door again. Got it. I'm overstaying my welcome.

"It's been fun, Lulu." I walk backward.

She rolls her eyes and shakes her head. "Thanks for all your help tonight. I hope you score a lot of... whatever they're called this season."

This girl pulls more laughter from me than my teammates do in the locker room. I'm starting to feel like one of those annoying giggling girls who approach me at a bar but are too nervous to have a conversation without acting as if everything I say is so damn funny.

"Goals, but I don't score them."

Her head tilts, and her forehead scrunches. She's fucking adorable.

I need to get the hell out of here.

"I'm the goalie. I stop the goals."

Her storm-cloud eyes widen. "That's scary." Her gaze flows down my body, and I realize that I like it a little too much.

Dipshit, open the door and get the fuck outta Dodge.

"Good thing I excel at what I do."

She nods. "And there's that cocky hockey guy."

"Excuse me?"

"Jade used to drag me to Henry's games, and afterward, we'd wait for him. So many of his teammates wouldn't even bother with a good pickup line. They'd just assume I'd be into them because they play hockey. Your egos are huge."

I widen my stance and cross my arms. I don't miss the way her gaze lands on my biceps for a second before popping back up to my eyes. "Because we play the toughest sport."

"Bodies are flying all over the place in football."

"Are you kidding me? We have to skate *while* hitting a small puck with a stick *while* checking players into the boards."

"Not you though. You stand in front of a net." She smiles.

I raise my eyebrows at her. "You calling me out?"

Her smile fades. "I didn't mean it like that." She holds her hands in the air. "Sorry."

"Don't be." I shrug.

Her gaze goes to the door again. "Well, good luck stopping all those goals this season. I'm sure you're a great blocker."

"The best," I say, grabbing the cool metal doorknob. "Good luck with the marriage thing. I'm sure you're a great…" I stop, and we both laugh, our minds going somewhere dirty. "Wife. I'm sure you'll be a great wife."

"Thank you."

I twist the doorknob and open the door. Three girls are waiting, all poised with phones, ready to capture another photo. I slam the door shut.

"Seriously?" she says, pushing me out of the way to look out the peephole.

"Ugh, mine is all blurry," one says.

"Damn it, mine was on panoramic," another one comments.

"We're going to camp out here until he comes out," the third one says.

Eloise falls down onto her heels. "They're sitting along the wall waiting for you."

"Who do you think she is?" one asks the other.

Eloise cringes and rises to her tiptoes to get another look at them. I'm not sure they understand how loud they're talking.

"You sure you don't want my chocolate? Because you're staying until they're gone." She points at the door.

"In that case, let's raid the mini bar." I step toward the small snack area, knowing this is a very bad idea, but I can't find the willpower to stop myself.

Sure, I could call security and ask them to remove the girls, but I'm enjoying myself more than I have since I got traded to Chicago last year, so I'm going to stick around. Not because I'm trying to get Eloise in bed, but because I enjoy her company. No harm, no foul.

four

Eloise

I CANNOT BELIEVE I'M HOLED UP IN A HOTEL SUITE with a professional hockey player. If Tristan catches word of this, he'll go ballistic.

Conor walks over to the mini bar and takes out a candy bar. He wasn't joking about his sweet tooth. The way he ate that chocolate earlier, the little moan that slipped out right after he swallowed, damn, I definitely wasn't thinking about my fiancé.

He sits on the sofa, tucking himself into the corner. One arm lies across the arm of the couch, and the other is along the back. He's a big guy. His half-eaten Snickers bar is in his hand. Those girls outside the door would die if they saw him right now.

"So, what do you want to talk about for the rest of the night?" he asks before taking another bite of his candy bar.

I grab a bag of chips and two bottles of water and join him on the couch. I keep my distance, sitting at the far end of the couch, but slide his water over to him. "I don't know."

He looks at the coffee table and spots my wedding planner. He leans forward and reaches for it, but I'm faster, leaping forward to swipe it away.

"What are you hiding?" he asks, reaching down to the carpet and picking up a piece of paper.

Oh no. Dread weighs in my stomach like a lead weight.

"I'll take that." I hold out my hand, but he doesn't hand it over.

I watch him scan the paper, his smile indenting more and more the longer he reads.

"Conor." My voice is pleading because this is embarrassing.

"Thirty before thirty bucket list?" He looks up from the paper, and my cheeks heat faster than if I was standing in front of a bonfire, and someone doused it with gasoline.

"It was just something I made when I was twenty-five. I found it this morning." I reach forward, but he holds it away from me. "Can I have it back please?"

"I could get down with this bake-a-cake-from-scratch thing."

"Conor," I plead.

"Sorry, I'm an older brother and tend to do asshole things. I didn't mean to invade your privacy." He holds it out to me, and I take it back.

"It's nothing. Just a list I wrote when I felt a little lost in life." I stare at it and think about how different I feel now than I did when Jade and I sat down on a beach at dusk and made the list, wanting to make sure our lives weren't wasted.

"I think it's pretty awesome. Do you mind if I ask you a question?"

I place the list in front of me on the couch cushion. The planner wouldn't have even been out had Tristan's mom not called me to discuss seating arrangements. Again. Seriously, my people-pleasing tendencies are approaching the edge of a massive cliff when it comes to her.

"Go for it."

"Why isn't anything crossed off? Isn't that the point of the list?"

My stomach hits the floor.

God, he's right. There's not one check mark or line through any of the thirty items. How have I gone four years without trying to accomplish these things?

"Life, I guess." I shrug. "I forgot about it until I was moving out of my apartment and found it in the bottom of my underwear drawer."

"Why was it at the bottom of your underwear drawer?" He crunches up the Snickers bar wrapper, tosses it on the table, and grabs his water. Again, those corded muscles in his forearm flex as he twists off the cap. Then I watch his Adam's apple bob as he swallows.

I've never once thought it was sexy when I watched Tristan take a drink, so why the hell am I fascinated watching Conor do the same?

After he finishes, Conor eyes me, and I realize he asked me a question while I ogled him like girls used to do to Henry back in the day. I never was a huge athlete girl. Their schedules are so grueling all the time. But I'm starting to see the appeal with Conor.

"I'm sorry, what did you say again?" I ask.

"Underwear drawer. Why wasn't the list posted on the fridge or the bathroom mirror to remind you?"

He has a point. I track my memory back to why I thought I needed to hide the list. "I'm not sure. I think... Tristan—my fiancé—was coming to my place for the first time, and I think I thought it made me seem lame. I don't think he'd understand something like this."

Why am I so ashamed of this list? I wrote down these

things because I wanted to experience them before I turned thirty.

"Why?" He sounds curious and interested, not at all judgmental, which makes it easy to answer him.

"Tristan comes from a wealthy family. I'm unsure what would be on his list because he's experienced everything."

He places his water on the table. "So, he's made a cake from scratch before?"

My shoulders slump. To explain Tristan to someone like Conor makes me feel a little ashamed for some reason. "Tristan would think it's a waste of time because he'd say, 'Let's just find the best bakery and buy one.'"

He nods, and I see judgment on his face. His hand moves toward the paper I set on the couch. "Do you mind?"

At this point, who the hell cares? At least it wasn't my other secret list that fell out, the embarrassing one with the sexual experiences I'd hoped to have. Thank God for small favors.

"Go ahead."

He scans the paper, and the wider his smile gets, the more my stomach flutters, as if he's approving of some of the things he's reading. "Tristan's not a hot air balloon kind of guy? No trips?"

"More like jumping out of the airplane type."

He nods as if he's starting to understand the type of guy Tristan is. "Not a guy for tattoos?"

I shake my head. "And mar his beautiful skin?"

He chuckles and sets the paper down, surprising me by not asking me the obvious question about why I haven't crossed fall in love off my list. It's not like I could give him an answer. I'm not even sure myself.

"Can I ask another question?"

Here it comes.

When I don't say anything, he says, "What is it about Tristan that made you want to marry him?"

I get up from the couch and take a jar of nuts out of the mini fridge, holding up another candy bar for him.

"Nah, but I'll take a bag of chips."

I toss him a bag and return to my spot on the couch. "It's a long story."

He opens his bag and tosses a chip into his mouth. "Good thing I have time."

I sigh, but talking to someone on the outside of my life feels nice. I've been drowning in Tristan's world, becoming who I feel I need to be. "I am the product of a one-night stand."

He eats another chip, not saying anything.

"My parents were from very different worlds, and they never got married. My dad was from Tristan's world—wealthy, entitled, and never accepted the answer no. My mom wasn't poor but didn't come from my dad's world. Anyway, they somehow made it work for me. I saw my dad maybe once a month when he'd pick me up and take me to my grandparents' house—or more like a mansion. Sometimes there was more time in between."

"I'm sorry," he says, and I feel as if he understands the frustration of my parents not getting along.

"I knew no different. My mom married Sam, who's a great guy and was more of a father to me than my own." I stop for a second. "My dad would get jealous of that and take me on shopping sprees or throw me a huge sixteenth birthday party, things like that. Throwing money at me was his way of showing me love. He was always going to some country or another, and he'd return and introduce me to girlfriends I'd never see more than a handful of times at most.

"Three years ago, he returned to Chicago, bought a condo in the city, and said he wanted to reconnect with me. I think a small part of me always wanted to know him better, to find out why I wasn't enough for him to stick around and be a constant part of my life, so it started as monthly dinners but turned into weekly ones after a few months. Then he asked me to go to my grandparents' country club for Sunday dinner with them. That's where I met Tristan. I guess you didn't need to know all that, but it ties into why I'm with Tristan."

Conor crumples the chip bag and waits patiently. He's a great listener.

"My dad loved Tristan. He always said he wanted me to find a place in his world. That it would give me financial security. So, although Tristan wasn't my type, I agreed to go on a date with him. You said you were a fixer. Well, I'm a people-pleaser." I run my hand over my chest like he did as if I'm wearing a T-shirt that has the moniker on it.

"It's got to be tough fighting that."

"I'm not sure I do, which is the problem." I eat a nut and take my time to chew and swallow.

"Anyway, we just kept dating, and in the beginning, he was really attentive. Surprising me with gifts and flowers. Amazing trips."

"Then?"

I look at the bedroom where Penelope is, hoping she's still passed out. I haven't told anyone this. "You can't tell anyone. Like, take it to the grave."

His eyebrows lift, but he holds out his pinkie. "Pinkie swear."

It's then I notice that the top part of his pinkie is missing. He still has a nail, but he's been injured in some way.

I wrap my pinkie around his. "What a night. I share my bucket list and a pinkie swear with you. I feel like I'm thirteen again."

He laughs. "Hey, pinkie swears are sacred."

The room grows quiet, and it's time for me to share what I've told no one else. "I'm sure it's like this in many relationships, but there's no more spontaneity. He always wants to go to dinner with his friends, and rarely are we alone. I think the real issue is I don't ever feel like I come first." I bite my lip. "But he has a lot of pressure on him. He's being groomed to take over his family's company one day, making for a lot of traveling. And I don't want to put more stress on him." Conor says nothing, so I ramble on. "After my dad died a few years ago, I just… I don't know."

Wanting to make my dad happy doesn't feel like the correct wording, but I fear it is why I'm about to marry Tristan in a week.

"I'm sorry," he says.

"Yeah, well, with his lifestyle, it's not all that surprising."

"Still, losing a parent…" He shakes his head. "I can't imagine."

"It sucked, especially since I finally felt like I was getting to know him as a person and not the person he wanted me to see him as over the years. He was always in competition with Mom and Sam." I shrug. "I can't believe I'm telling you all this. Even Jade doesn't know some of this."

He covers his heart with his hand. "I'm honored. And no judgment. I have family issues. But you still haven't answered my question. Why did you agree to marry him?"

"I'm making him sound bad, but he's not." I don't feel the truth of the words when they leave my mouth, and I don't know why.

"I didn't say that." He pushes off the couch and goes to the mini bar again, snatching up an array of items and tossing them between us.

"I'm sure it's just all the expectations and pressure of a big wedding. Social media makes it seem like there shouldn't be any arguments or distractions between couples who want to pledge their love to one another. After the wedding, it will all go back to normal. I'm sure of it."

He sips his water. "Yeah, I'm sure you're right."

But I don't think he believes me. Hell, I'm not sure I believe myself.

He tosses the chocolate-covered pretzels at me. "Here. Sweet and salty, the best combination."

I open the bag. "You have to tell me something personal now."

Conor stares at me for a beat and fidgets in his seat. Will he open up the same way I did?

five

Conor

I'M NOT GOING TO TELL HER, BUT HER FIANCÉ sounds like a complete douche. I'd love to question her more on the whole "he doesn't make me feel like I come first" comment. Or the fact he wouldn't want to spend an afternoon with her baking a cake or surprising her with a train trip. See the tattoo she'd pick out and hold her hand when the first needle pricks her skin. How could he pass up seeing her smile when it was all done?

If I were honest with her, I'd tell her that I think hiding her list in her underwear drawer so he didn't see it should've been her first red flag. I'd never want my girlfriend, fiancée, or wife to feel that way about me, and I pray whoever I decide to marry, if I ever do, knows that I'm her sidekick in whatever crazy thing she wants to do.

"There's not much to talk about, but you were so honest with me, I'll be honest with you."

She puts a chocolate pretzel into her mouth, and I watch

her reaction while I tell her something I talk to no one about, not even my sister.

"My mom and dad divorced last year. My mom was cheating on my dad, but it wasn't her first time. I'd witnessed her with another man before and told no one. I never told my dad. I never told my sister. I believed my mom that night when she said it was over. Because of me, my sister had to endure the same crushing blow I did years later when she caught our mom with someone else."

The guilt still eats at me, and I think maybe it's why I was so difficult about Kyleigh being with my teammate and friend, Rowan. Now, they're happy together, and I feel like a total dick over my behavior.

"Is that why you're not a relationship guy?" She puts another pretzel in her mouth. I shouldn't feel so happy that she likes the snack I picked out. What the hell is that about?

"Who says I'm not a relationship guy?"

"You." She chuckles and holds out a pretzel for me. "Here."

"We'll get back to the whole no relationship thing, but why are you offering me a pretzel?" I hold out my palm, and she places it in the center.

"You're watching me so intently I figured you wanted one." Her smile lights up the room even with the gloom of me reliving my parents' shitty past and how twisted it got with Kyleigh and me involved.

If she only knew why I was watching her so intently. It's because she's so beautiful, I'm having difficulty keeping my crush on her at bay. "I just liked watching you enjoy them."

Her cheeks flush pink, and she says nothing, so I quickly change the subject so as not to make her uncomfortable.

"Seeing my mom in the hotel bar messed me up, and I was just getting into a relationship with someone at the time. That crashed and burned because I spiraled, thinking there's no such thing as monogamy, and we aren't meant to love only one person our whole life. I've gotten over that disbelief for the most part. I'm not opposed to a relationship, but I keep thinking when I meet her, I'll know. But I'm not sure it will happen while I'm playing because it'd be hard to be a part of my life. My schedule is a lot during the season, and the fans aren't easy, especially some of the women." I stare at the door. Reason number two is exactly why I'm still here with her now, although I wouldn't change it for anything.

"I used to go to games with Jade, and I remember some of the girls being so nasty to her. I can't imagine what it's like on a professional level. She hasn't said much about it since she and Henry got back together." She eats another pretzel and holds another one out to me.

I accept it and place it in my mouth, chew, and swallow. "Well, Henry isn't the normal hockey player. Sure, there are probably women who want him, but from what I know, he was never the clubbing kind of guy."

"Not like you?" She raises her eyebrows.

"I can't deny that I go out a lot, and you might not believe this, but there are a lot of nights I go home alone."

She laughs. "I'm not judging."

"In the early years, the fame and women can get to you. If you're having a great game, you feel invincible, but I'm thirty now." I pick up her list again. "So now I have to do a forty before forty bucket list." I look at the one line that struck me as odd—To fall in love. Why hasn't she crossed it off? Is she not in love with Tristan? I'd never ask. She's taken, regardless.

"Are you making fun of my list?" She retracts the offered pretzel and tosses it in her mouth, her smile a little wicked, which only makes the pull to her increase.

Fuck, I'm in trouble. I want to taste that chocolate off her lips.

"No." I shake my head. "I probably shouldn't tell you this,

but I wish things were different. I wish I could help you cross at least one of them off your list."

"Oh." She bites her lip, hands me the rest of the bag of pretzels, and stands. "I have to go to the bathroom."

While she disappears through the bedroom door, I walk over to the suite door to look out the peephole. I see the three girls sitting across the hall, their legs stretched out, each one of them asleep.

"Are they still out there?" Eloise's voice sounds from behind me.

I turn to face her and see that she's replaced her T-shirt with a sweatshirt that hangs off one shoulder. Jesus, she's killing me. For the first time in a long time, I want a woman I can't have.

"How's Penelope?" I change the subject because if I tell her they're sleeping, she'll probably want me out of here.

"She seems okay. Still on her side and no vomit, thank goodness." She crosses her fingers as she makes her way across the room to look out the peephole herself.

"Want to go on a walk?" I blurt, afraid our time together will end, even if it's not destined to go anywhere.

She stops and bites her bottom lip, which I've noticed she does when she's thinking something over. "Um..."

"It's three in the morning. Not a lot of people out who will know or care who I am. We'll grab a cab or Uber to Lakeshore and walk the path." I reach for the list. "And you can cross stargazing and maybe even watch a sunrise off your list."

She seems to think about it for a moment more, then nods. "Okay, let me leave Penelope a note in case she wakes up."

She disappears back into the bedroom, returning in sweatpants with her long blond hair thrown up into a messy bun.

Fuck, she's beautiful in anything she wears. But I need to keep my dick in my pants and my tongue in my mouth.

"I nudged Penelope awake, and she swatted me away. Ready?"

"We have to be quiet." I open the door.

Eloise slinks out and tiptoes down the hall, moving toward the elevators. I follow and close the door quietly. Eloise has already pressed the elevator button, and I jog to catch up and step into the elevator with her. The doors slide shut, encasing us in the small space. If I thought the hotel room was close quarters, this is worse.

Somehow, we make it downstairs without my mouth getting me into trouble. We cross the lobby, and I stop at the front desk to tell them about the three girls outside her room, so they won't be there when we return.

After we walk through the sliding doors to the outside, Eloise says, "Why didn't you tell them about your fans earlier?"

"Because then I would have had to leave." I'm truthful, which I know I shouldn't be, and her cheeks redden again. I'm slowly becoming addicted to garnering that reaction from her. "I'm sorry. I'm not trying to make you uncomfortable."

The doorman flags down a taxi, and I tip him, allowing Eloise to slide in first.

Once I'm in the cab, she turns to me. "I know you're not. This is just a weird situation, right?"

"Weird in what way?" I'm not sure where her head is.

"That I like being with you when I shouldn't." Her teeth bite her lip again, then she cringes, and her eyes squeeze shut. "I'm a horrible person."

"No, you're not. And we're not doing anything wrong. We're just crossing an item off your list."

She nods, but she doesn't believe my lie any more than I

do. No matter what though, this thing between us doesn't go any further than tonight.

six

Eloise

CONOR PAYS THE CAB DRIVER, AND I CLIMB OUT onto the dark sidewalk beside Lake Michigan.

"God, it's beautiful." I stare at the sky filled with stars above the water. "What a clear night."

"And you've waited how many years to cross this off your list?" He quirks an eyebrow and nods toward the vacant pathway.

I follow him, and he guides us to a park bench. I have no idea what I'm doing here. Why did I agree to come here with him? Strike that, I do know, and it's not good. It's not as if I plan to hook up with Conor. I would never do that. But I'd be lying if I said I didn't feel this... pull to him.

What I can't figure out is whether this is cold feet. Conor is so different from Tristan and I'm enjoying it. Tristan never would've wanted to leave at three in the morning to see the stars. I probably wouldn't even get him out of his house, let alone get him to take a cab to the lakeshore. It's more than that though. I'm trying not to notice how Conor listens to me as if he finds my thoughts interesting and can't wait to hear what else I have to say. Tristan can be dismissive. Half the time I'm not even sure he hears the words coming out of my mouth.

Conor waits for me to sit on the bench before he slides on next to me. His one arm is slung over the back of the bench, and it feels intimate, though I don't think that's his intention. I think it's just Conor and his warm personality—he can't help but be in close proximity to the person he's giving his full attention to.

"Do you know any of the constellations?" I lean my head back and stare into the dark sky.

He lowers his arm and does the same, but his pinkie grazes mine, and an electric zing runs up my arm. "Right now, I wish I had paid more attention in school so I could impress you with some facts about astronomy."

I laugh and turn my head to look at him. The moonlight looks good on Conor, showcasing his strong jawline and sharp nose that looks as though it's been broken at least once. "I only know the Big Dipper, so I'm useless too."

"I could probably find an app to help us out." He turns to face me, and our eyes lock.

I quickly face the sky again to calm the nerves firing through my whole body. "Let's just enjoy it like this."

"I agree."

We sit in silence for a moment. I can't speak for Conor, but the big sky makes me feel so small. It makes all those decisions about linens and chair covers and flowers feel so foolish and trite. What does any of it matter? It's one day out of my life, yet it has consumed my entire world for more than a year.

"A shooting star would be pretty awesome right now," he says.

I think it would be a sign that this feeling of rightness in being here with Conor is legit. That I'm not imagining this sensation creeping up on me as if he was meant to walk into my life tonight.

"I've never seen one before," I say.

"Me either. Maybe you should put it on your list." I can hear the smile in his voice.

"That's not really up to me if I see the shooting star though."

"You just need to go stargazing more."

"Yeah." My voice holds longing because I have a terrible feeling that if I ever stargaze again after tonight, I'll be doing it alone. And if I see a shooting star by myself late one night years from now, will it be just as exciting? Or will I always remember this moment with Conor and wonder what if?

"Make him take you," he says, interrupting my thoughts.

I don't respond immediately because I'm unsure how.

"He's not a bad guy," I finally murmur.

His hand covers mine. It's not meant to be sexual or intimate but comforting.

"You don't have to stick up for your decision to marry him." His voice is also low, as if he's afraid to speak too loudly for fear someone will overhear, and tonight is a secret only we share.

"I just don't want you to leave tonight thinking..."

"That I missed out?"

I suck in a deep breath. "Don't go there, Conor." I straighten and lean forward, putting my head in my hands.

"I'm not. But I'd be lying if I told you anything other than the more time I spend with you tonight, the more I wish I had met you first."

I peek at him out of the corner of my eye. "Why now?" I stand and walk closer to the water.

"Why now what?" he asks, joining me, his shoulder brushing mine.

"Why am I meeting you now? A week before my wedding.

I'm not supposed to feel a pull to someone else. I'm in a committed relationship." My voice wobbles.

"I don't know." He shoves his hands in his pockets. "I don't believe in love at first sight."

"Neither do I."

"We don't even really know each other," he says. "Maybe it's just hormones."

I turn to face him and stare into his eyes. "Do you believe that? That it's just a physical attraction?" I can't tell if I'm hoping he'll say yes or no. My head is so messed up.

His chest rises and falls with a deep breath. "I am attracted to you."

"But?"

He sighs, and his vision strays to the water before returning to me. "It's more."

I suck in a breath and close my eyes because he's right, it is. "If I truly loved Tristan, I shouldn't be open to feeling this way for someone else, right? Especially after one night. That's crazy."

"Maybe we're meant to be best friends." He shrugs, knowing it's not the truth. There's an unexplained chemistry between us that's impossible to deny.

"I'm not this person. Yeah, I'm sure people always say that, but I'm really not. Most of the time, I do as I'm asked, what I should be doing, and I never rock the boat. I want people to be happy. I shouldn't be stargazing with a guy I met the night of my bachelorette party."

"You overthink what you should and shouldn't do." He steps away from me. It's the first time he's pulled away from me all night, and I don't like it. "Live life for yourself, Eloise. What do *you* want?"

I throw my hands in the air. "Is that your way of getting me to cross the line between us? Because I can't act on whatever this thing is between us."

He nods. "I know. I do, but fuck…" His head rocks back, and he stares at the sky. "I don't want to kiss you." He sounds like he's saying it more to himself than me, but I react anyway.

"You don't?" Disappointment shouldn't be seeping into my bones.

"I wouldn't be able to do it, knowing you'll return to him."

"God, Conor, what are we doing?" I wrap my arms around my chest. "I don't even know you."

"I meant what I said. I don't believe in love at first sight, but I don't want to say good night. I want to talk to you all night and learn more about you, even though it somehow feels like I've known you for years. I've never felt this before, and I'm trying to navigate these new feelings, but I feel lost in the middle of the woods without a compass."

I go back to the bench and sit down. "We should walk away now."

He sits beside me. "We should."

As I stare at the water, a tear slips down my cheek, but I try to brush it away discreetly. How did I get myself into this situation? Did I rush into my engagement with Tristan?

He stands from the bench and holds out his hand. "Come on. I'm taking you back to the hotel."

I glance at his hand then up at his eyes. "What about the sunrise?"

"The sunrise is the start of a new day. I'm going to claim tonight as ours. Our secret that only we understand."

I slide my hand into his and get up.

We walk to the road, and Conor flags down a cab. Both of us climb in. On the way to the hotel, neither of us says anything. There's nothing really left to say, is there?

Once the cab parks along the curb, we step out, but Conor asks the guy to wait.

"Can I hug you?" he asks, and I nod.

His arms wrap around me, and I greedily suck in his scent.

"I had a great time tonight. You might not believe me, but I do wish you nothing but happiness in your marriage."

I snuggle into his chest. This was a bad idea, but I couldn't say no. His strong arms squeeze me tightly, and I inhale the scent of his cologne again, wanting to never forget this moment. He pulls away too quickly, and there are so many things I want to say that I can't.

He keeps his hands in mine on either side of my hips and stares into my eyes. "Go watch the sunrise with Tristan. Fight for the relationship you want, Eloise. Expect more from him and leave him if he can't put you first. I'm not saying leave him for me but find someone who will love you how you deserve."

I nod as a tear slips down my cheek, and he releases my hand, brushing away the tear. "Okay."

"Promise?"

"Promise." I nod again.

"Thanks for a great night. I'll never forget it." The corners of his lips rise, and I commit his cocky smile to memory.

"Thank you."

"Hey, maybe I'll see you at a baby shower for Jade and Henry one day."

"Maybe."

He releases my hands, and I step away. The hotel doorman opens the door for me. I walk through the doors and look over my shoulder right before turning to the elevators.

Conor stands by the taxi with his hands in his pockets, and I can't help this dreadful feeling that what happened tonight has been an eye-opener for me, but I have no idea what to do.

seven

Conor

It's been three days since the night with Eloise, and I can't stop thinking about her. It's as if she's become an obsession, constantly on my mind.

Unable to sit in my condo any longer with thoughts of the woman I can't have rolling through my brain, I head to the workout facility my agent rents for his Chicago clients, my three closest teammates on the Falcons included.

"Look who finally decided to work out in the offseason?" Tweetie, our left wing, flexes his biceps as if I should be jealous he hasn't stopped his workout regimen since the season ended.

"Well, some of us still have youth on our side." I drop my bag and sit on the mat to change my shoes.

Tweetie is the oldest player on the Falcons, but he's still on the first line, and his game is on point. I've never asked, and he's never mentioned retiring, but we both know he's on borrowed time. I never want to stop playing, so I understand why he's been at the gym every day so far this offseason to make sure his playing days don't come to an end.

"I can still kick your ass." He picks up some dumbbells, sits on the bench, and starts his curls.

I decide to stretch because I have slacked a little more than I usually do during the offseason, for no reason other than I feel unsettled lately.

"Where the hell did you go the other night?" Tweetie asks, stopping my thoughts from floating back to Eloise.

"The clubs aren't doing it for me anymore," I answer. They aren't, but I'm also not sure Tweetie is the person I want to talk to about this Eloise situation.

Tweetie keeps his cards close to his chest as far as his romantic past. Since I played in Florida before being traded here, I heard rumors of him getting serious with some woman named Tedi. But I heard that after he was traded from Florida to Nashville, they broke up. No one really knows who initiated the breakup or why it didn't work out, but he's implied a handful of times that she might have been the one who got away. He ignores that fact, though, and continues acting as if he's getting some kind of fulfillment from the women who flock to and fawn over him, which is enough to tell me he's not the one to go to for advice on this matter.

"Just a blonde with a tight ass in leather pants does it for you now?" He smirks at me in the mirror.

"Fuck off." I stand to do the cardio I desperately need before weights. "I was helping her out."

"Help her out by being her last hook-up before she walks down the aisle?"

Why did I think Tweetie didn't notice where I was and who I was with the other night?

"I helped her because her friend was wasted and could barely walk."

"Always the good Samaritan." He grins at me.

I press the button on the treadmill, and in the mirror, I catch Rowan walking in.

"We could have shared an Uber! Why aren't you fuckers texting in the group chat?" He drops his bag next to mine and toes out of his street shoes.

"You spending so much money on my little sister that you can't afford an Uber?" I ask.

Rowan, our center, fell in love with my little sister while I was still playing in Florida, and now I have to watch him touch her all the time. Since they got together, there's apparently never enough seating anywhere because she's always on his lap. All in all, I love to give them a hard time, but he loves my sister and treats her how he should, so I'm good with it.

"Want to compare endorsements?" He smirks at me in the mirror.

I increase my speed on the treadmill to drown out these guys and their bullshit.

"He's in a mood," Tweetie says. "I think it's about the blonde from the other night."

"What blonde?" Rowan asks.

"Oh, that's right." Tweetie drops his weights and acts all dramatic. "You don't go out with us anymore."

"Kyleigh and I just went to the club with you guys last week."

"So, it's an every other week thing? Good. This week, we're on the list for that new club on Rush." Tweetie gets on the treadmill next to me. "Want to race, sunshine?"

"We have a wedding this weekend, sorry." Rowan stretches on the mat in front of us.

I've always thought I was flexible—I have to be, given that I'm a goalie—but damn, Rowan must be doing yoga with Ky or something.

"Your ass is doing that hot yoga shit, aren't you?" Tweetie asks before I can call Rowan out.

"Jealous?"

"Fuck yeah, hook me up." Tweetie pumps up his speed higher than mine and shoots me a cocky smirk.

I increase my speed and up my incline, working my thighs.

"I don't want you staring at Kyleigh's ass in class," Rowan says.

"I stare at her ass all the damn time," Tweetie says.

I reach over and lower his speed, and Tweetie almost trips over his feet and falls down on the treadmill. Of course, he barely fumbles before recovering and pumping up the speed again, shooting me another ego-driven grin.

Rowan reaches over and presses the button to go faster over and over, making Tweetie have to jog then run.

"I'm kidding, asshole," Tweetie says. "I stopped looking once you got all serious, and I found out she was Pinkie's sister."

Rowan continues to stretch. "Back to the blonde?"

Oh fuck, I'm not sure I want to have this conversation with anyone here.

"Ah, the blonde bride-to-be who Conor ruined for her soon-to-be husband."

"Jackoff, I didn't fuck her." I stop my treadmill, annoyed and frustrated.

"You wanted to," he says, stopping his treadmill too and following me to the benches.

Fuck yeah, I did, but I'm not telling them.

"You got with a bride-to-be?" Rowan asks.

He looks as confused as I am because he knows I'd never cheat on anyone or be the one they cheated with. He saw Kyleigh and me through our parents' divorce.

"No. I helped a bride-to-be get her drunk bridesmaid into her hotel room. End of story."

"Except." Tweetie lifts his hand then points at me. "You didn't get home until five in the morning."

Rowan's eyes shoot up and glance between us.

I shake my head. "It sounds bad, but honestly, I didn't do anything. And how do you know when I got home?"

"I have eyes everywhere," Tweetie says with a shrug.

"Sounds like you're holding out on some details," Rowan says, bending his body practically in half.

"Hell, what is my sister doing to you?"

"She's getting me in shape. In more ways than one." He winks, and both assholes laugh. "Now, stop deflecting. Give us the details."

I lean my forearms on my thighs and stare at the floor for a second. "Have you ever met someone and instantly felt like there's something between you? Not to sound stupid, but a spark that just feels different. A familiarity?"

"No," Tweetie says—a little too defensively.

"You don't want to hear this, but I felt something similar with your sister." I blow out a breath, but Rowan continues. "I wanted to see her again, and then I wanted to talk to her, and then I couldn't get enough of her. But if you really want to know, that first night at that wedding, I was completely obsessed with her before we ever left the venue."

It's the affirmation I was looking to hear. That you can find a connection with someone you've just met. But there's one problem—the woman I felt chemistry with is marrying someone else.

"Well, it was a one-night thing, and it's over." I shrug.

"Except you're all in your feelings about it," Tweetie says.

"Man, that sucks. She's marrying some other guy? Do you think she's happy with him?" Rowan joins us on the benches.

"Funny thing is, Jade is her maid of honor. I guess they were high school friends?"

"Are you talking about Eloise?" Rowan asks, mouth agape.

My head rears back. He knows her too? How has she met

two of my teammates and our paths have never crossed until now? "You know her?"

"Kyleigh designed her dress."

I stare blankly at him. He's got to be kidding me.

"So, during this magic moment between you two, it never came out that your sister designed the dress she's going to wed another man in?" Tweetie asks.

I ignore Tweetie. "What else do you know?" I ask Rowan, desperate to find out more details because... what? I'm going to stop the wedding if she's not happy? I'd never do that. Maybe I just like to torture myself.

He shrugs. "Henry probably knows more than me. I saw her at Kyleigh's shop last fall with Jade. She was trying on a wedding dress. I wasn't paying attention because I had brought Kyleigh an iced coffee, and we were in our little bubble."

"Surprise, surprise," Tweetie says with an eye roll.

Rowan flips him off without looking in his direction. "But she left abruptly, and Jade chased her, then Henry chased Jade. That's about all I know. That, and the fact that I have to go to her wedding on Saturday. I'm sorry. I'm not sure what I would've done had Kyleigh been about to marry someone else when I met her."

"It's okay. It's not like there's a future for us or anything. It was one night, and I'm probably making it bigger than it was. I need to push Eloise out of my head. Don't say anything to Henry or Jade, okay? I don't want this to be a thing. Plus, I'm sure Eloise wants to keep it a secret." I go over to my bag, change my shoes, and put my bag over my shoulder.

"You're the dirty secret," Tweetie says, laughing.

Rowan watches me carefully.

"Pinkie, you need to work out, at least to rebound off this blonde who's got you all fucked in the head," Tweetie says, but I just wave and walk out the door.

I'm half tempted to follow them to the wedding Saturday and hide in the shadows. Maybe when I see her marrying another guy, I'll finally know that anything between us is out of the question. But I'd never ruin her day, so I'll torture myself until there's no hope left.

eight

Eloise

I insert my shiny new key into the lock of Tristan's front door. We're only days away from marrying one another, and I'm moving out of my apartment this week, but I'll stay with my parents until we're official because of his grandpa and grandma's demands that we don't live together until after the I-dos.

"Tristan!" I call, getting no response.

The kitchen and family room are empty. I drop my purse on the counter and head to the back door, hoping he might be outside by his pool.

Tristan recently moved from his downtown condo to the north suburbs to be closer to his parents and grandparents. Mostly his dad and grandpa, since he has to spend so much time shadowing them to take on a larger role at the company at some point. I had looked forward to choosing a house together, but one day, he surprised me by driving me here and telling me it was ours.

I shouldn't complain. It's a beautiful four-bedroom, three-bath custom home on a private street with many families. When I mentioned raising our kids here though, Tristan was adamant that we'd be in a bigger house by the time we have kids.

The backyard is empty, so I grab my phone from my purse and go to the fridge to get a drink while I wait for him. I dial him up, and he answers on the first ring.

"Hey, baby, sorry, I'm on my way home now. Merrick asked me to stop for a drink after work. His dad is on him about that Paris getaway he took Ashley on last weekend." He laughs. "But I'm just pulling down my street now. Be there in a second."

He hangs up, and it isn't until I open his fridge, which holds nothing but beer, white wine, and ten takeout containers, that I realize I never even said a word to him. And that he referred to the street as his, not ours.

I hear the garage door open, and Tristan walks in the door down the hall, still wearing his suit from the office.

"Thank God I'm not Merrick. He's getting his ass raked over the coals about taking off." He tosses his keys on the counter, wraps his arms around my waist, and buries his head in my neck.

"Why? Those two are always going out."

He pulls back and goes to the fridge, grabbing a beer. "His dad told him he'd better marry her if he's going to spend that type of money on her." He unscrews the beer cap and raises his eyebrows. "I told him he should be smart like me. Let's go out on the patio." He walks by me to the French doors, and I follow.

"I was thinking, how about we go to the store and grab some things to make dinner here?" I sit on the patio furniture he bought a week after moving in. I'm not a huge fan of the hard iron, but his mom picked it out.

He stretches his long legs out and rests his feet on the chair across from him, tipping back the beer. "I'm supposed to go out with the boys tonight."

I frown. "You were just with Merrick."

"Yeah, which is when we decided to live it up before we're both chained down." He chuckles again, and when I don't, he sighs. "Oh, come on, it's a joke."

"Well, you make it sound like I'm going to be cramping your style."

"You're so sensitive. This wedding has made you lose your sense of humor."

"There didn't have to be a wedding. I wasn't the one who got on bended knee, or was it your father demanding you marry me to make you a company man?"

He alluded to that once when he was drunk, and when I asked about it the next morning, he said he didn't remember or know what I was talking about.

"Damn, baby, you've been different since Saturday. Did the bachelorette party really go that badly?"

I stare at him, but he's too busy pulling his phone out of his pocket to notice. "I told you about my night. Penelope was drunk. The drink I had poured on me."

He laughs and drops his phone on the table, exchanging it for his beer. "Oh, yeah, how much did that QR code make us? Will it cover the liquor cost for the wedding?" His head rocks back in laughter. "Fucking Penelope."

"She did what she could in the small amount of time she had."

He rolls his eyes. "Ashley told Merrick the whole night was a mess."

I hope Ashley didn't tell Merrick about Conor because I don't want to explain anything about him. I'm not even sure I could if I wanted to. I'm still confused about everything.

"It was fine. Wait here, I want to show you something." I

stand from the chair to head inside, wanting to change the subject.

"Not another wedding question. I'm tapped out, baby. Just call my mom."

"It's not wedding related."

I head through the French doors and grab my list out of my purse. He's back on his phone when I return, and I take a moment to watch him from behind. Tristan is attractive. He's tall and lean but muscular. He's always put together and turns a lot of eyes when we're out. But he's different than Conor. Where Conor holds a cockiness in his stance, Tristan is more arrogant. Although Conor is way more well-known in the world, Tristan thinks everyone should know who he is when he walks into a room.

Jesus, what am I doing comparing the two? This is madness.

I stop by the side of his chair. "Is this seat taken?" I ask, eyeing his lap.

He mindlessly wraps his arm around my waist but still concentrates on his phone.

"Tristan?"

He shuts off the screen and tosses the phone on the table again. "Sorry, work thing."

Does he think I can't tell it's his friend group chat?

He lowers his feet to the ground, and I sit on his lap.

"So, I have something I want to share with you, and I was hoping tonight... well." I open the sheet of paper.

"This is cryptic. Are you about to tell me some secret about yourself?"

I ignore him because I'm so scared to show him my list, and I don't know why, except that Tristan likes to poke fun at my expense quite often. "When I was twenty-five, Jade and I wrote these lists on a girls' trip."

"Oh, this should be good." He laughs, but it's not a good-natured one. In fact, it comes off as patronizing.

"It's a bucket list. Of things I wanted to do before I turned thirty." I hold out the paper to him and bite my lip, waiting for his reaction. I watch him read it over, my heart beating faster with each second.

"You want to smoke a cigarette?" he asks, raising his eyebrows. "Adopt a puppy? You know I'm allergic, so that's never happening." He frowns.

"I want to cross some of these off. What do you think?"

"I think you turn thirty in November, so it's not going to happen. I'm good, but I'm not a magician. There's not enough fairy dust to get this done."

I take the list back, and he willingly gives it up. "I'm not asking for all of them to be done, but I think it would be fun to do a couple. Like, we could get tattoos together." I hate the note of hope I hear in my voice.

"And have my dad disown me? No, thanks."

"How about dying my hair? I could be a brunette."

He twirls my hair around his finger. "You know I love blondes." He grips the edge of the paper. "I could get down with this one." He's pointing at the line that says, "say yes to everything for a day."

"When do I ever tell you no?" I roll my eyes.

"Last Thursday."

I'm not going to get into an argument again about not having sex with him last Thursday when I wasn't in the mood because my entire bachelorette party was combusting.

I lean back into him, and he holds me, his hand splaying across my stomach. "How about we watch a sunrise tomorrow morning? You're off work for the week, right?"

He guffaws. "So I can sleep in. This wedding is stressing me out."

"You? Your mom has been on my ass, and I've done most of the planning."

"You both keep dragging me everywhere. I don't care about the cake or the meal. As long as the liquor is top shelf, I'm good, and my mom knows to make sure it is, otherwise she'll have to deal with my dad." He kisses my temple. "Let me change then we'll go eat so I can meet up with the guys."

I sit up. "You're really going out with them?" I fold up my list, disappointment settling in my chest since he's clearly not going to help me cross off anything.

He nudges my hip to get off him, which I do. I don't want to sit on him anymore anyway.

"Baby, you have me for the rest of our lives. This is my last week."

"So, you won't be hanging out with the boys after we get married?"

He laughs, leaves his beer on the table, and walks toward the house. "No, I'm chained to you, remember?"

I follow him, grabbing the bottle off the table. "Tristan, you know I don't like the whole chain reference."

In the kitchen, he turns around and tugs me toward him. "I'm just joking. I'd be glued to you if I could be because I love you." He bends his neck to kiss me, and I pull back.

"This list is important to me." I hold up the folded piece of paper between our mouths.

He blows out an annoyed breath, and his shoulders sink. "Fine, we'll cross off that 'say yes to everything for a day' on the honeymoon, okay?"

"Seriously, Tristan."

He scoffs. "I hope your sense of humor comes back after the wedding." When I don't say anything or move, he acts all dramatic by rolling his eyes and moving his body as though he's losing strength in his muscles. "Fine. You pick some out, and we'll do them on the honeymoon. But no dogs and no hot air balloon ride, baby, that's so cliché. You should pick more extravagant ones. Like a trip on a private jet to Italy or having a wine named after me. You're marrying a Somerset, after all." He kisses me quickly and releases me before jogging up the stairs. "Stay the night. I want you in my bed when I get home," he calls on his way to the bedroom.

It's like I'm only a warm body for him to lose himself in when the mood strikes. He only wants me here to have sex, and he cared nothing about my list or how important it is to me.

Five minutes later, he barrels down the stairs in jeans and a V-neck T-shirt, his hair freshly styled and with more cologne on. "I'm sorry. Your list is great. Wait up for me, and we'll lie down on the chairs tonight and stargaze. Maybe you could wear that lingerie I bought you last month that you've yet to show me." He kisses my cheek, swiping his keys off the counter simultaneously.

He says stargaze, and my mind veers to Conor and our one night together.

"We'll see. I should clear up some of the pending wedding items."

"Let me know, because if you're not staying, I won't rush home." He gives me a chaste kiss and walks toward the garage. "Oh, and hire a decorator if you want. I know how much you hate the white walls."

I don't respond because he's not waiting for an answer, which the garage door shutting moments later confirms. I tuck my list back in my purse and look at the beautiful kitchen, willing myself to imagine Tristan and me in this space, living as a couple in love. The image won't materialize, so I grab my purse and leave.

Surely this is just me nitpicking him because of Conor. Or wedding jitters. Everyone says they're natural. I'd be insane to call a wedding off this close to the big day.

nine

Conor

My condo feels like a jail cell because I cannot stop thinking about Eloise and the fact that she's getting married today. I walk out of our security gate, seeing a new sign plastered there. The Nest is written in girly script with notes and phone numbers from puck bunnies who know this is where three of the Chicago Falcons reside. I really should be plucking off a number and calling one of them to get my mind off who will soon be a married woman.

Instead, I walk into Peeper's Alley, the bar under our building, and find the usual group of regulars there. Every bar stool is occupied by an older man with a beer mug in his hand and both eyes glued to the televisions above him. By the night's end, two or four of them will end up in some heated argument about the Colts since Chicago baseball is in season right now.

"Hey, Rubes." I bypass the owner, who reserves a backroom for us Falcons and whoever we're with.

"Why are you here so early?" She eyes me the entire way to the backroom.

I don't bother answering, instead shutting the door behind me. I grab the remote and turn on the television, sitting at the big round table in the middle of the room. The door opens behind me, which I expected.

"I'm not serving you any alcohol," Ruby says, standing at my right.

"Fine. I'll have a water."

"Fine."

She doesn't argue. That's not Ruby's style. She just tells you how it is.

I watch the Colts for a bit, thankful it's an away game because we live across from the baseball field. I would not have the patience to deal with all the fans today. Easton Bailey ties up the game with a double to left field, and I hear the guys in the bar cheer.

A bottle of water is placed in front of me. "Here's your water."

"Thanks, Ruby."

She slides the chair out next to me and sits. "Okay, I was going to let you sit here and stew about whatever's up your ass, but Kyleigh told me I need to be nicer." She leans back and crosses her arms.

"Shouldn't you be watching the bar?"

"Please, those guys would never try to take something for free. They know I'd cut off their fingers." She waves. "So, let's have it."

I blow out a breath. "It's just woman bullshit."

"Oh no, you too? First Rowan, then Henry, and now you. Pretty soon, you're all going to leave, and I'll have to train a whole new group of entitled athletes. I'm not sure if you've noticed, but I don't like new people."

"You'll always have Tweetie." I crack open my bottle of

water and down a third of it.

"Nah, eventually he'll get his head out of his ass and get out of his own way. I don't have all day here, so let's go. Tell me what the problem is." She crosses her legs and grabs the remote, muting the television. "If you don't start talking, I'm gonna turn the damn thing off."

I huff and spin my water bottle around. "I met a woman last weekend, and I'm sure you don't believe in this, but I felt an instant connection with her."

"Oh, that." She pats my shoulder and stands from the chair. "It's lust. It's just your dick talking, forget it."

"Rubes," I plead because I need someone's advice on this matter.

I've already ruled out my friends, and Kyleigh is way too close to the situation for me to talk to her about it. She's just starting her brand, and then one of the first dresses she designs, her brother steals the bride? Not a good look. And that's assuming Eloise feels the same way about me.

"Oh, fine." She sits back down. "Instant chemistry. Like the movies?"

I nod.

She blows out a breath, and her eyes roll back. "Okay, well, go after her. I know she's your sister, but your boy Rowan chased Kyleigh hard. Showing up here and interrupting our time with iced coffees every day? That's what you gotta do. Show her the good guy you are."

"There's a catch." I twirl my bottle again.

"Always is." She huffs.

"She's getting married today." I turn to face Ruby, and her face shows no reaction. There's no expression other than her usual boredom. "Did you hear me?"

"I already don't like her." She puts her hands on her knees to stand.

"You'd like her. She's Jade's friend."

She sits back down. "Jade and Henry are okay with you pining away for their friend who's getting married today?"

"They don't know."

She nods slowly. "That makes more sense." Ruby pushes her chair back and stands. "My advice is that you sit in this room all night. I'm sorry, but you lost out. Maybe you'll find out she canceled the wedding. But if she marries that guy, you move on. It means she wasn't meant for you." She pats me on the shoulder.

"Rubes, do you believe in soul mates?"

She laughs, her hand resting on the door. "I wouldn't own this bar if I believed in soul mates. What kind of shot do you want? On the house."

"So I can drink now?"

"I always serve broken hearts." She walks out, and I assume she'll pick the shot for me. "Oh, great, you three can cheer this guy up," I hear her say.

The three rookies who think of this room as theirs walk in.

"Hey, chipmunks," I say.

"Water? What is this? We're not even in season." The guy we call Alvin sits down next to me.

The other two, Simon and Theodore, follow suit. These three are more attached than Rowan, Henry, Tweetie, and I are. But it's good to have close friends in the league.

None of my friends are around. In fact, two of them are attending Eloise's wedding today. So, I'm going to seek the advice of these younger, fresh-faced players.

A half hour later, Ruby hasn't just brought me one shot, but four—with the encouragement of the chipmunks—and now I'm babbling about Eloise as if she was mine at some point, when, in reality, it was only one night that we shared.

"Where is this wedding?" Simon asks.

I saw the invitation on Henry and Jade's fridge when we

helped them move furniture around earlier this week. Talk about a punch to the fucking gut. "It's up in Winnetka."

"And Henry's there?" Simon asks.

"Yeah. And Rowan."

"We should go to the wedding," Alvin says.

"Hell yeah, we should," Theodore adds.

"I'll call an Uber." Simon picks up his phone off the table.

"Nah, guys, she's obviously happy with the asshole. Let her marry him."

"Are you sure?" Simon asks, holding up his phone.

"Yeah, but I'll take another shot," I say.

"You got it." Theodore stands and heads out of the room.

I lean back in my chair. "She was fucking beautiful though..." I shake my head, reliving that night for the umpteenth time.

"We saw her. She was." Alvin pats me on the back.

"Not helping." I lift the drink one of them got me at some point. I think it's my second. Maybe it's my third. "But this will help me forget." I down it in one gulp.

Theodore comes in with another tray of shots, then Simon gets the next round ten minutes later.

"You're getting him up to his place," Ruby says, delivering another round of drinks a half hour later.

"I'm just upstairs," I say, feeling buzzed but not completely smashed.

I pick up my phone at some point and see that Jade has posted a pic on her social of her and Henry dressed for the wedding. At the wedding where she'll walk down the aisle before Eloise.

"You know what?" I put down my drink. "What's the harm, right?"

"What?" Alvin asks, probably sick of listening to me by now.

"Going to watch her marry him. It'll do me good." Yes, this is a great idea. It'll solidify the fact that she's not mine. Really drive the point home. Then I can move on.

"You should go in there and stop the wedding," Alvin says. "If she means that much to you, and you're this upset, I'd say it's justified."

"I second that. You'll be saving her from a lifetime of misery." Simon nods.

"Go get your girl. You can't ignore these connections. That's how people end up like my parents. Unhappily married and yearning for other people," Theodore says.

We all look at him because that's some deep shit.

"He's right. I saw this psychologist on my feed the other day, and he was talking about how many sexless marriages there are. Usually, people are married but still in love with someone from their past, but since they couldn't get them, they settled. You don't want to settle, man," Alvin says. "Neither of you should. You owe it to her if you care about her!"

They're so right. Why didn't I see it before now? I need to stop this wedding!

I down my drink and stand. "You're right. I'm Conor fucking Nilsen. And I'm not stupid. I know she wanted me just as much as I wanted her. I'd be saving us both." I drop the glass on the table.

Tweetie comes into the room. "What are you assholes doing here midday? And why is Ruby letting you all get smashed?"

I pat him on the chest. "I gotta go."

"Where are you going?" he asks.

"This is gonna be epic. We're coming with," one of the chipmunks says, but I'm not sure which one.

I'm already halfway across the bar.

"Where are you fuckers going?" Tweetie asks, following.

"I already ordered the Uber." Simon raises his hand, and a car pulls up along the curb.

We all file into the Uber and head to the church.

Is this what a white knight feels like? Because I feel badass.

ten

Eloise

I'M STARING AT MYSELF IN THE MIRROR, DRESSED IN my wedding gown. Jade stands behind me, ready to help me with my veil.

"Guess what I found the other day?" I say to her.

"Do I want to know?" She's careful to put the comb part of the veil on top of my bun, securing all my hair away from my face except for a few wispy pieces.

"My bucket list." I bend forward to give her better access. She secures it with a few bobby pins.

"Really? I wonder where mine is. God, I feel like a totally different person than when we wrote those."

I smile in the mirror at my best friend. "You're engaged and a mama now."

I'm super happy for Jade. I was worried about her for years, but she returned to Chicago and reconnected with Henry.

"Sometimes I can't believe I'm here."

I'm envious of the radiance she has now, as if every day is better than the day before. "You deserve it."

She positions the tulle from the veil around my bare shoulders. "And so do you." She looks at me in the mirror over my shoulder. "You're happy, right, Eloise?"

Jade really is a great friend. Since the day I ran out of the bridal shop when I first tried on a wedding dress, she's been asking me the same question. The problem is that I haven't been a good friend because I haven't been honest with her. Still can't be honest for some reason. "Yeah."

She stares at me long and hard. I know she sees it. She knows me too well not to guess that I'm having doubts. Have been having doubts for a while now.

"It's just this wedding. I mean, look at me." I pick up the big skirt and drop the stiff layers of tulle.

"You look beautiful, just like Cinderella." She smiles at me.

I nod. It's not my style, but Tristan's mom was pretty firm about what she felt was best. I think it's because she views her son as a prince.

"So, tell me what was on your list," Jade asks, leaving me to stare at my reflection. She opens her purse and grabs her lipstick.

"A lot of things I've never done. I should have traveled with you."

"I was running away," she says before puckering her lips in the mirror.

I wouldn't mind running away right now.

"You know that you don't have to do this," she says. "I'll get Henry's keys, and we'll sneak you out the back door."

I turn away from the mirror, hoping that gets rid of my nerves. "No, silly, it's just jitters. Do you mind if I have a moment alone though?"

"Eloise..."

I raise my hand. "I'm okay, Jade. If you could keep Tristan's mom out of here, I'd appreciate it." I run my hand down her arm to reassure her.

"Okay, I'll be your bodyguard outside the door." She keeps giving me that look that says, "I'm ready to run if you want," and I appreciate it.

"Thanks."

She leaves me alone in the bridal suite, moments before the ceremony starts. Standing in front of the mirror again, I gaze at my reflection.

"Do I even know you anymore?" I whisper to myself.

This isn't the dress I wanted to wear. Last fall, when I first met Kyleigh at the dress fitting, and she insisted I try on a dress she felt was perfect for me, I freaked out because I saw a glimpse of my old self in that mirror. It was the first time I realized I'd morphed into someone I didn't even recognize. I really wish she had just allowed me to try on what I'm wearing now, the Cinderella dress that everyone expects me to show up in. Then maybe all these mixed feelings inside me wouldn't be brewing. Perhaps I wouldn't have found some refuge with Conor.

Turning away from the mirror, I dig out the list from my bag and read over it again.

To fall in love.

When I first found the list, I should have been able to cross that off, but something stopped me from doing so.

A knock sounds on the door, and I fold the list and tuck it back into my bag.

Jade peeks her head in. "It's your mom."

"Oh, okay."

My mom walks in, and Jade shuts the door after her. Mom stands there for a second and takes me in. I've been on borrowed time with my mom. She's been giving me looks for months, but today is the big day, and she's not one to let things happen without a conversation.

"You look beautiful, but I had no doubt you would."

"Thanks, Mom."

"I just wanted to have a quick word. I know the ceremony is going to start soon." She takes my hands. "This is what you want, right?"

"Why do people keep asking me that? I'm here, aren't I? I'm dressed and ready." I slide my hands from hers, upset with myself for losing my patience.

"Because you don't look happy. Listen, sweetie, I know your dad wanted—"

"This isn't about dad," I argue, knowing there's more untruth in that comment than truth.

"Fine, if you say so, but I want you to know one more thing. And then I'll go sit in my pew and be quiet. Your dad wanted you in this world, his world. He wanted you to want for nothing in life. And Tristan can offer that to you. No one can deny that fact." She places her hand on my cheek. "But he'd also want you to be happy. And believe it or not, your dad wasn't always happy in his world. I think he chose to forget that in his later years, but sometimes he felt caught up in it, as if he was on the hamster wheel and couldn't get off. I'm not sure. Before I leave you here, I want you to know that you can walk away. You have the option not to marry Tristan, and it's okay. Yes, people will be upset, and yes, people will be nasty, but it's okay. You're not a monster for changing your mind."

Her hand drops, but I take it before she can walk away. My eyes fill with tears, but I swallow them down, not wanting to ruin my makeup. Is it a mother's gift to have some sense of what their children need to hear at the exact right moment? "Thanks, Mom."

She squeezes my hand. "You're welcome. I know there are a lot of big and powerful people in that church, but you have an army behind you too, Eloise. An army of people on your side."

"I know."

"I love you."

"I love you too."

Her gaze remains on me until she nods and leaves the room.

I wait for the door to shut to blow out the breath I've been holding. I head to the window and stare at the street, watching a few late guests arrive. I wonder where Conor is right now. Was our connection real, or was it infatuation? Was it just my subconscious looking for an out?

Jade peeks her head in again. "Eloise, it's time."

I turn away from the window and pick up my bouquet off the stand the florist left it on. Jade holds the door open, and I walk over to the main doors that lead into where the ceremony will be held. The wedding planner who did Tristan's sister's wedding is at the doors, organizing everyone to walk down the aisle.

Jade keeps glancing over her shoulder at me, checking that I'm okay. I wish I had put my foot down and had Sam walking me down the aisle, but my grandma said she couldn't bear to see a man other than my father escorting me. It would make her so sad on what should be a happy day, so I obliged and said I'd walk by myself. But I feel like Sam would give me great words of encouragement right now.

Then again, he might feel the same as my mom. She's always hated this world. She never liked it when I went with my dad for a weekend. I overheard her once talking to Sam after the engagement party, telling him how horrible they all were to her, treating her as if she was less than them when she was pregnant with me.

The music starts, and the doors open. My chest tightens as the first bridesmaid gets into position.

"Hey, Jade," I whisper and wave for her to come closer, away from the other bridesmaids and the flower girl.

"What's up?" she asks, giving me that same expression she's had all day, probably ready to call Henry out of his pew.

I shouldn't ask her, especially now, but I have to know before I do this. "Conor Nilsen? He plays for the Falcons, right?"

She draws back, questions lingering in her eyes. "Um... yeah. Why?"

I bite my lip but release it, not wanting to ruin my lipstick. "Does Henry know him? I mean, I know they play on the same team and stuff, but..."

"You've met him?" she asks, eyes wide.

"I never met him." I shake my head. "I mean, I did, but not with you."

She looks around and leans in closer. "Eloise, why are we talking about Conor Nilsen right before you walk down the aisle to marry Tristan?"

"I just wondered what kind of guy he is. Like a Henry kind of hockey player or like a real hockey player?" The second bridesmaid begins her march down the aisle. "You know, like a playboy or the settle-down type?"

"Eloise..." I see the confusion on her face. I'm sure this is all coming out of left field.

"Just answer me."

She looks over her shoulder and sees most of the bridesmaids have already started their walk. "He's a good guy. Not really a good dart player though."

I huff and roll my eyes, wishing she'd be straight with me. She probably would be if I told her what happened last Saturday and how Conor has been the only thing on my mind this week whenever I'm alone.

"Jade," the wedding planner whispers.

"Playboy or not?" I ask, eyes wide. I need this answer before I walk down the aisle.

Jade's eyes lock with mine as if I'm a puzzle she's trying to figure out. Or maybe she doesn't want to answer.

"Playboy," she says, and my heart sinks to the depths of my stomach.

Was I completely wrong about him? Are my instincts that off? Trusting him felt so natural and easy. But was it all just an act for him? A game?

"It's your turn." The wedding planner touches Jade's shoulder.

"Eloise..." Jade's tone is the same one she's used all day with me. She knows me the best, so I'm not stupid enough to think she doesn't see what's happening with me.

I shoo my hand at her. "I'll see you down there." I plaster on my smile for the day.

Jade doesn't turn around.

The wedding planner taps Jade again, and her voice has more urgency. "Go."

With a sigh, Jade leaves. Then Abby, Tristan's niece, walks down the aisle, sprinkling flowers along the runner.

The music shifts to the bridal march, but I don't move. I can't. I'm frozen solid.

How many times have I dreamed of this moment? Marrying the man I love and who loves me. All the times I imagined this day, I never thought I'd have this doubt inside me.

"Darling, it's time," the wedding planner says.

"Sorry, just a minute." I stare at the door leading out of the church then back at the doors leading toward Tristan.

"It's becoming awkward now..." the wedding planner says through gritted teeth.

I nod and step into the doorway, my grip on my bouquet tight enough to crush the stems.

The movement of everyone shifting in their seats, ready to watch me walk down the aisle, makes my heart beat faster. My eyes seek out Tristan as if he's my life preserver in the middle of the ocean.

He is my future.

But he's joking around with Merrick, his attention not on me, and for the first time today, I can't mask my disappointment under a fake smile.

"Darling, go," the wedding planner whispers in my ear.

I scan the pews. Tristan's mom's lips are stern and unwelcoming. Already, I can hear her judgment about my makeup or hair, although it's what she wanted. I'm like a doll she's dressed up.

My mom's smile is forced and probably looks like mine.

The wedding planner nudges the small of my back, and I step forward. I can't even hear the wedding march over the sound of my heartbeat thrumming in my ears. My breaths are shallow, and a cold sweat breaks out on the back of my neck.

Halfway down the aisle, Tristan finally looks at me. His lips part in a big smile. I'm sure he has some love for me, but I doubt it's enough to ever put me first. Sometimes I think he likes the idea of me and the fact that I make things easy for him most of all.

Fight for the relationship you want, Eloise. Expect more and leave him if he can't put you first.

Conor's words from that fateful night run through my head again.

I look straight ahead as I walk the rest of the way down the aisle, my panic growing with every step until I feel as if it might burst out of me.

On autopilot, I hand Jade my bouquet. She whispers something to me, but I can't make it out over the thoughts running a mile a minute through my head, so I turn to face Tristan.

The officiant has everyone sit down and starts the ceremony. We go through all the typical wedding steps. Tristan cracks jokes and his side of the congregation laughs, with Merrick laughing louder than anyone else.

He's paid more attention to Merrick than to me during this ceremony. And that's the way my entire marriage will be.

I can't do this.

My eyes shift to his mom again. She's sitting next to his grandma. All prim and proper, back straight, ankles crossed and tucked under the chair, her hands clasped in her lap. Was she once a vibrant woman who was pushed down by her husband's mother? Is that going to be me in twenty-five years?

I need to say something.

Say something.

But there's been so much money spent.

So much time arranging everything.

Important people have taken time out of their busy schedules to be here.

They've bought presents.

There's been an engagement party, a wedding shower, a bachelorette party.

It will be so embarrassing for everyone involved if I put a stop to this.

Everyone's expectations weigh down on my shoulders until I feel as though I want to scream.

The officiant asks whether anyone objects to this union, and I open my mouth to put an end to this, but the church doors burst open. Everyone turns in the direction of light pouring in at the end of the aisle.

Conor.

He bends over and heaves for breath before raising his hand.

He searches me out, and when our eyes lock, a smile creeps

up his lips, wrapping around his face as though I'm his sunshine after a destructive storm. "I object!"

eleven

Conor

"Where the fuck are we going?" Tweetie asks.

"You wouldn't understand," Alvin says, elbowing Simon, who elbows Theodore. I guess none of them are going to tell Tweetie.

I sure as shit am not going to say anything because he'll stop me for sure, the commitment-phobe he is. He wouldn't understand.

"You didn't have to come," Simon adds.

"We had this handled," Theo says, the three of them having some nonverbal communication with one another. They're like creepy triplets or something.

It's almost comical seeing Tweetie in the dark. "What the fuck? Winnetka? I'd hoped we were heading to a bar crawl or something. And why is Conor shitfaced?"

Tweetie turns around from the front seat of the Uber XL, but all three of the chipmunks shrug. He blows out a breath. I know he'll only take being out of the loop for so long, but our driver asks him if he's Tweetie Sorenson and if I'm Conor Nilsen, which retargets his attention.

"Yeah. You a fan, or are you going to criticize us?"

Leave it to Tweetie.

"I know the Cup is yours this year," the driver says. "Last year was a hard break, but that first line is too good not to come through this year."

"Fuck yeah, we are," Tweetie says, looking over his shoulder. "And we got one helluva goalie."

The driver looks through the rearview mirror at me. "You are a wall, man."

"That's why he's got his nickname." Tweetie winks at me. "Another brick in the wall."

"I thought it was from your pinkie?" Theo asks.

"No, asshole, he was Pinkie way before the injury." Simon shakes his head as if he's embarrassed for his friend.

"It's just a coincidence that I have two reasons for them to call me that. One for the Pink Floyd song, 'Another Brick in the Wall,' and then the pinkie injury happened." I shoot Theo an expression to say don't sweat it.

The injury could've been so much worse. Taking a blade to the tip of my pinkie. Most people don't notice it unless they're staring at my hands, but it does suck that I've got nerve damage. Thank God, it's only my pinkie.

"That's a killer nickname," Theo says.

"Thanks."

I'm proud of my hockey name. I've worked hard to become one of the best goalies in the league. So hard I've pushed anything personal to the back burner, but damn, Eloise makes me second-guess that decision. Because she's marrying some other guy right now.

I lean over to check the time on the car dash. In five minutes, my opportunity will be gone.

We pass the sign that says we're entering Winnetka, and my heart hammers.

Alvin pats my shoulder from the seat behind me and holds out a flask. "Liquid courage?"

Theo smiles next to me, and I accept the flask, downing a few swigs.

"Thanks," I say, handing it back to him, but Theo snatches it and downs a shot worth.

I watch the GPS on the Uber's dashboard, which says we're only two minutes away.

"We're getting close," Simon says, running his palms together.

Alvin puts his hands on my shoulders, massaging me as if I'm getting ready to enter a boxing ring. "You're fucking Conor Nilsen. This is your moment."

Simon and Theo join in with encouraging comments, as if I'll be facing the heavyweight champion in a second.

"What the fuck is going on?" Tweetie glares at us over his shoulder.

We pull up to the church, and I open the van door, knowing I have little time left.

"Why are we at a church?" Tweetie shouts, getting out of the van. "Oh shit, no, Pinkie." He rushes in front of me on the sidewalk leading to the steps, putting his hand on my chest. "You can't do this." His gaze zeros in over my shoulder. "What are you assholes thinking?"

"He likes this girl. They had an instant connection. You can't stand in the way of true love!" Simon says.

"You thought you wanted that Aubrie girl last year. And where is she now?" Tweetie asks Alvin.

I use Tweetie's momentary distraction to get around him, and I jog up the church's stairs, pushing through the door. The entry area is quiet, so I burst through the next set of doors, bending over to catch my breath.

I hear some people gasp, and I hold up my hand for a second before standing straight and searching out Eloise. She's at the altar, next to who I assume is Tristan, the douchebag.

"I object!"

More whispers and yells surround me.

"Oh, fucking hell," Tweetie says from behind me.

Henry and Rowan push out of a pew and hurry over to me.

"Conor, what the hell?" Henry says.

"You let him come here?" Rowan asks Tweetie.

Tweetie raises both his hands. "Listen, I'll admit that something like this has me written all over it, but I swear I had nothing to do with it. It was the chipmunks. They got him shitfaced and talked him into it. Even I wouldn't let him do something this stupid."

"It's not stupid," I say, waiting for Eloise to respond.

She's still standing there, looking so put together like she should be on top of a cake. Her dress is big and puffy, and her hair is so tight in a bun that I want to release it and let her blonde strands fall over her shoulder. She looks rigid and cold. Not at all like the Eloise I met last week. They're like two completely different people.

I walk down the aisle, the flower petals crumpling under my shoes.

"Con—" Kyleigh steps in front of me "—you're drunk. What are you doing?"

I don't look at her. My eyes are solely on Eloise. "I'm sorry, Ky. I know this is a big deal for you, but I can't let her marry him."

"It's not your decision," she whispers.

Tristan hasn't even reacted yet. I know I'd be down those steps and knocking out the guy who's trying to steal my girl.

I place my hand on my sister's hips and pivot her out of my way. "Eloise?"

"I knew it! She's a whore!" A woman on my right points at Eloise.

"Excuse me?" A woman from on the left stands and steps into the aisle.

"Are you Conor Nilsen?" one of the groomsmen asks, hitting Tristan on the arm. "Shit, half the team is here. At your wedding, man."

I ignore them all. "Eloise?"

Her eyes soften, and there she is. I get a glimpse of my Eloise. Then her eyes narrow, she lifts the skirt of her dress, walks down the steps, and grabs my hand. "Come with me."

She pulls me down the aisle and out the doors.

This isn't exactly the reaction I was hoping for.

twelve

Eloise

"Who is that?" Tristan asks from next to me at the altar.

"Shit, man, I think that's Conor Nilsen," Merrick says, elbowing Tristan.

"Who?" Tristan asks.

"You know, the Chicago Falcons goalie. Big contract last year when he got traded." Merrick steps forward. "Are you Conor Nilsen?" He hits Tristan again as if he should be fanboying. Did he miss the part where Conor objected to our marriage? "Shit, half the team is here. At your wedding, man."

"Eloise?" Tristan whispers with accusation while Conor says my name in that sweet voice of his.

I must be in a dream. I mean, nightmare right now.

I weave past my mom and Tristan's mom as they argue about if I am, in fact, a whore, and grab Conor's hand, tugging him toward the door. "Come with me."

We pass Kyleigh, and she mouths sorry.

Henry and Rowan have their teammate with the longer

blond hair cornered, his hands up, and he keeps repeating that he didn't know.

Once we're out the church doors and in my bridal room, I flip the lock and whirl around. "What are you doing here?"

He smiles. Oh, that panty-melting smile he uses on all the girls. "I'm here for you." He says it as though it's obvious and perfectly acceptable.

I groan. "Conor, this is my wedding."

"Yeah, and that's why I'm here."

I lean forward and smell the alcohol on his breath. "You're drunk. You smell like a distillery."

"No." He shakes his head and seems to lose his balance a bit. "Maybe a little bit." He brings up his fingers and laughs. "But it gave me the courage to do what I've wanted to for the past week."

He was thinking of me the entire time I thought of him?

My shoulders drop. "Oh, Conor."

"I wasn't alone in my feelings on Saturday night. You know you don't want to marry him."

I stare at Conor, at how handsome he is, and he's right. I was there with him, but still. To do this?

"It's not up to you if I marry Tristan today." I throw my hands in the air. "Why does everyone think they can tell me how to live my life?" I rip the veil off my head.

"I thought—"

"You thought what? That I'd run down the aisle, and you'd catch me? That I'd link hands with you, and we'd run out of the church and disappear to some island?" My voice raises.

A hard knock lands on the door. "Eloise!" Tristan shouts.

"Kind of." Conor looks sheepish now.

My hands land on my hips. "Did I give you the impression I wanted you to come here and save me?"

"Eloise!" Tristan bangs again.

I pull bobby pins out of my hair, my scalp sighing with every single one I remove.

"Don't try to minimize it. You know you don't want to marry him." Conor points at the door.

"So what? You want to marry me because we shared one night with some chemistry between us? You want to step into Tristan's place on the altar?"

His face pales.

"Yeah, I thought so." I step forward with my finger in his face. "Go look in the mirror, Conor, because you don't want this." I take a break from pulling the bobby pins out of my hair and lift the skirt of my white dress. "You're used to getting what you want, and you couldn't have me, so you've convinced yourself that I'm somehow the girl for you." I step closer. "Tell me, Conor, what number am I on your list? But I'm supposed to believe you felt different with me?"

"I did," he says, not arguing about how many women came before me. "And you did too. I know it with everything inside of me. Sure, I'm not ready to marry you, but I—"

"You're just drunk, Conor."

There's more noise at the door, and I worry Tristan will break it down if I don't let him in.

"Just go home and sleep it off. I have a lot to handle here." I cross the room and open the door.

Stepping outside the room, I find Tristan's fist raised to knock again. He lowers his arm and glares at Conor behind me.

"What the fuck, Eloise?" Tristan lets me walk out into the foyer area of the church, and I hear Conor follow us.

Henry is there, talking to Merrick.

"Just let them talk," Henry says with Rowan, Tweetie, and three other guys at his side.

"Eloise, I want answers now!" Tristan shouts.

"Give her some breathing room," Conor snipes from behind me.

"Fuck you!" Tristan yells at Conor and grabs my wrist to spin me to face him. Then he decides better of it and turns us so his back is to Conor, lowering his voice. "You need to explain this—now. Nana is going crazy in there, and our moms are about to roll around in the rose petals."

"Get your hands off her," Conor says.

I shake my head at Conor and try to unwind my wrist from Tristan's grip, but he tightens it, leaning closer. "This isn't a fucking joke, Eloise. All my family's business contacts are in that room, which is embarrassing."

I hear Henry starting to argue with Merrick behind me.

"Let her go," Conor growls.

"Okay, bud, how about we go outside to get some air?" Rowan comes over and says.

"Fuck no." Conor dodges Rowan's grip and pushes Tristan to the side.

Tristan's shoulder hits the wall, and when he recovers, he eyes Conor as though he's going to kill him with his bare hands. He focuses on where Conor now has my wrist, inspecting it.

I wiggle out of Conor's hold. "I'm fine. You need to go," I say softly.

"I'm not going anywhere until we talk." He turns to me, blocking out Tristan. "Talk to me."

"This isn't the time." I shake my head.

"You don't want to marry this asshole. He only cares about himself."

Kyleigh breaks into our little circle. "Let's go, Conor. We'll go outside and let them get this all get sorted out."

Tristan stomps toward us and raises his fist, but when Conor ducks, Tristan's punch lands on Kyleigh's cheek.

"You're a dead man!" Rowan tackles Tristan.

Merrick breaks from Henry, trying to pull Rowan off Tristan while Conor grabs the back of Merrick's jacket. Soon, all the groomsmen and the Falcons are in a brawl in the middle of the church's entryway.

"Are you okay?" I ask Kyleigh, who is holding her cheek.

"Yeah, but I think I saw stars for a second there."

"Okay, I think I got the moms handled." Jade steps through the doors to the sanctuary and takes in the scene, her gaze zipping around the room. "What the hell did I miss?" She finds Kyleigh and me and rushes over to us. "Did you get hit?"

A few other guests enter the foyer, presumably hearing the fighting. It's hard to miss with all the cursing, punches, and expensive items falling to the floor.

As Jade takes care of Kyleigh, I slink away to the bridal suite, toss everything in my bag, and leave through the back door. I stop at the curb, still hearing all the yelling going on in the church, and close my eyes. I need somewhere to go and a way to get there.

Henry's restored vintage car pulls up along the curb, and Jade leans over from the driver's seat. "Get in."

I open the door and see Kyleigh in the back, still holding her cheek.

Climbing in, I look at the church and say, "Go."

I didn't think today would go as planned, but I've made a huge mess. All because I put everyone else's needs ahead of my own. No more.

thirteen

Conor

When the fights are finally broken up, I look around the room but can't find Eloise.

I run outside just in time to see Henry's car drive away with the skirt of Eloise's white dress hanging out the passenger window.

"She's gone." I push a hand through my hair.

"In my fucking car." Henry pulls out his phone and steps away from everyone.

I sit on the concrete steps of the church, blood dripping from my nose.

Tweetie argues with the chipmunks, and Rowan tells Henry to tell Kyleigh that she needs to put ice on her cheek.

Tristan is cornered, looking like a scorned teenager, by two older adults I assume are his parents.

This isn't how I thought this would go.

fourteen

Eloise

"Where do you want to go?" Jade asks, continuing to drive out of Winnetka.

"I feel like you two are Thelma and Louise up there, but who can I be?" Kyleigh asks from the back seat.

I turn to face her. "I'm so sorry you got hit."

She shoos me off. "It's my brother's fault. Can I tell you how sorry I am that he ruined your wedding?" She cringes.

"And do you want to explain exactly why Conor is objecting to you marrying Tristan?" Jade asks, side-eyeing me and pulling onto the freeway.

I keep my attention on Kyleigh. "You don't need to apologize. Something tells me Conor always does what he wants no matter who tells him differently."

"Truth." She rolls her eyes.

Turning around to face forward, I lean back into the seat. "I didn't want to involve you guys, but since you're in the getaway car, I'll bring you up to speed. I met Conor at my bachelorette party last weekend."

Jade makes a sound of frustration, and her hands tighten on the wheel. "I was so mad when the airline told us they couldn't do anything to get us home. I'm sorry. You had to wear that sash and shirt." Her shoulders sink further and further.

I shake my head. "You don't have to apologize. But I was alone in some random people's VIP section that Penelope got us into, and Conor was in the VIP section next to ours. He came over."

"Did he hit on you?" Kyleigh leans forward and peers between us. "What a sleaze. And now he ruins your wedding? Turn this car around. I need to give him a piece of my mind."

"Relax, killer," Jade says.

I shake my head. "He didn't hit on me. I think he felt bad for me. It was pretty easy to tell I wasn't having the best time, and he came over to cheer me up. Then Penelope got wasted, and he saved me from having to put her on a luggage cart to get her out of the cab and into our room."

"He went to your hotel room?" Jade asks. "How am I just hearing about this right now?"

I stare out the window, watching cars whizz by us. "I was embarrassed, I guess. I let him help me with Penelope, then these girls were camped outside the room trying to get a picture of us together. So, we devoured the minibar, and he found my list."

"List?" Kyleigh leans in farther.

Jade glances at her and back at the road. "Eloise and I wrote down a bucket list of thirty things to do before we turn thirty."

"Oh, I like that." Kyleigh smiles.

"And I found mine when I was moving out of my apartment. Conor read it and asked me to go stargazing with him." I bite my lip in fear of their judgment.

"And you went?" Jade asks with some hesitation.

"I did. Nothing happened between us. It wasn't like that. It's hard to explain."

Kyleigh's phone rings, and she pulls it out. "It's Rowan."

"Yeah, Henry's been calling me nonstop. Tell him his baby is fine." Jade pats the dash.

"Is that why we're driving so slow?" I shake my head at her.

"I have to be careful. Henry would kill me if anything happened to his car."

"Henry wouldn't care. There are two things he cares about —you and Bodhi," I say.

She smiles, and jealousy rakes up my spine. "True."

"Hey, we're okay. Henry's car is fine. I'll be in touch after we decide where we're going. You just worry about Conor." Kyleigh is so even keeled and matter-of-fact. There's no hint of anxiety in her voice, and I envy her feeling so solid in her relationship. I probably wouldn't have left the church if I'd felt the same in mine. "I'm okay, I don't need to see a doctor, and yes, I'll put ice on it. Okay, see you at home. Love you." She hangs up and slides between us again. "What did I miss?"

"How is it there?" I ask.

She waves me off. "That's not important. They'll handle it. You concentrate on yourself."

Jade laughs. "That's not Eloise's style."

Kyleigh touches my arm. "I can't imagine what you're going through right now. And I don't know what happened with my brother and why he would think it was a good idea to do what he did, but I'm assuming, since we're not at the church, that you didn't want to marry Tristan?" She poses it like a question.

"You'd be correct and..." I turn in my seat. "I can't ask Jade because she's been in love with Henry since she was seven, but with Rowan, how did you two get together?"

Jade pulls off the highway. I'm pretty sure she's going to her house.

"Oh, well..." Kyleigh's eyes meet Jade's in the rearview mirror. "It was a one-night stand, turned into more that turned into feelings." She and Jade exchange a look again. "Are you saying that you and my brother... I mean, was it love at first sight?"

"No, but there was a connection. Chemistry I haven't felt with anyone before. Not ever. Not even Tristan. Which is bad, I know." I cringe and flop back in my seat, bringing my hands to my face.

Jade pats my knee. Well, actually just layers and layers of my dress. "Maybe you should let this all settle and see how you feel after tonight. It's a new day tomorrow."

"You're probably right." I straighten and face the window.

"Okay, that's ridiculous. Listen, Eloise, I know I don't know you as well as Jade, but when you first came into my store, you said you were a people-pleaser. And right now, you're pleasing Jade by agreeing to let all these emotions settle. What do *you* want?"

"I hate to interrupt, but she just walked out on her fiancé. A fiancé she was very committed to." Jade pulls down an alley and presses a button to open the garage of the house they're renting until the renovations are done on the house that was her grandma's. "And don't worry, Bodhi is at my parents'."

"Exactly. She finally decided to live for herself. So come on, tell us what you want to do. Order a bunch of junk food and devour it? Want to take off the dress and burn it?" She holds up her hands. "I might tear up, but it's fine. I get it."

"I wouldn't do that to you." I huff out a weak laugh. Though I'd love to torch this thing. It represents all the power I handed over during the course of my relationship. Who gets married in a dress they don't even really like?

She reaches between the seats, grips an appliqué, and tugs, making beads scatter through the car.

"Okay, it's Henry's car, remember?" Jade turns the key in the ignition, shutting off the car.

"You hate this dress," Kyleigh says. "Let's just rip it apart."

Jade turns to face Kyleigh. "What is going on with you?"

"Come on, Jade, you know exactly how freeing it is to finally put everyone else's wishes and wants for you in the rearview mirror. Let's give that to Eloise."

Jade glances at me, and a smile creeps up her lips. "Did you love Tristin?"

"I thought I did."

"But? Is Conor the only reason why you called it off?"

I shake my head.

"I didn't think so." She pulls out her phone and holds it up to her ear. "Hey, yeah, you can't come home tonight. Yep. All safe in the garage." She laughs. "Oh, I'm good." She looks at me. "We're all going to be good. Go have a guys' night." She laughs again. "Love you too."

Hearing her and Kyleigh on the phone with their partners solidifies that Tristan isn't the man I want to be with. I don't want to live in fear of judgment whenever something doesn't go as planned.

"I'm jealous, girls. You have some great men." I sigh.

They turn to one another and nod. "We do," they say in unison.

Jade takes my hand. "And you will too. Now, let's go burn the dress."

She smiles at me, and we all exit the car, heading into Jade and Henry's rental house. I forgot how good it feels to have real friends who have my back.

"Wait," I say when we walk inside. "My mom. Sam."

Jade shakes her head. "I've got it. You go with Kyleigh, and I'll handle it."

"You don't have to do that."

"Hey, I'm the maid of honor. It's my job." She winks and heads to the staircase.

"Thank you."

"You'd do the same for me." She squeezes my forearm and walks up the stairs.

"All right then—rip it, burn it, or both?" Kyleigh asks, distracting me from my thoughts.

Although my mind is full of lingering worries about what the aftermath of my decision to leave Tristan will be, I push those thoughts aside and try to finally think about what it is I really want.

fifteen

Conor

SOMEONE NUDGES MY SHOULDER, AND I GROAN, rolling over. It feels as if my brain is sloshing around inside my skull.

"Get up, lazy ass."

I slowly sit up, taking a minute to get my bearings, and find Henry standing at my bedside.

"Put some clothes on and come out to the family room," he says before he leaves.

I wobble when I stand from the bed. My body aches as I throw on a pair of sweats and a T-shirt.

Rowan, Tweetie, and Henry sit in the family room. There's coffee on the counter along with some breakfast sandwiches from our favorite place. I pick up a coffee and sandwich before joining them in the family room.

"Did I really do it?" I squeeze my eyes shut for a beat because my head is pounding.

"Yep." Rowan pops the 'p' on the end of the word.

I groan.

"Just ran in there and said I object," Henry says with dad-like disapproval.

Tweetie just shakes his head at me.

I place my coffee on the table and open my sandwich. I'm starving. "You let me keep drinking when we got back here?"

"It was the only way to get you to stop fighting us. We had to cancel two Ubers," Henry says.

"You owe me a hundred bucks for having to pay for the ride you booked, plus extra." Rowan sips his iced coffee.

"I had a good night planned last night," Henry says. "Jade looked so sexy in her pink dress. We booked a hotel, and I had roses on the bed, champagne ordered. But instead, I got to pick you up off the floor at Peeper's and clean up your puke."

"Shit, I'm sorry, man. Truly." I ditch the sandwich and coffee, suddenly nauseated.

"Can we address the real problem here?" Rowan asks. "Why were you running into a church and stopping a wedding?"

I glance at Henry.

"I met Eloise last Saturday," I confess.

Henry nods. "You kept telling everyone who would listen the story last night. Then the chipmunks caught me up what they told you. But most people would at least try to talk to the person before they bust into their wedding and objected."

I turn to Henry. "What do you know about her?"

"According to you, the two of you have a shit-ton of chemistry, and she's your one. So, you must know her better than me."

I run my hand through my hair. "So, I might've gotten a little carried away. I was drunk. Where is she? I should apologize."

Henry looks at Rowan and Tweetie. All three of them sigh.

"You're just going to apologize and move on with your life?" Henry asks.

"No." I scowl at him.

"Please tell me this isn't a case of you wanting something you can't have and now that she might be attainable, you don't want her anymore," Rowan says.

I think about what he's saying, my hungover brain trying to catch up.

"Fuck, seriously? This is so messed up. Why are you pissing around in my pool of people? She's Jade's best friend." Henry stands and walks out of the family room.

"What is going on with you? You've been off since we lost the Cup. And now this shit?" Tweetie sits up and rests his forearms on his thighs.

"Henry and Jade are gonna have a lot of shit Eloise will be invited to. So, now since you're upset you couldn't bag her, you go and ruin everything like some toddler having a tantrum." Rowan leaves the room shaking his head, and I hear him and Henry talking in the kitchen.

"Hey," Tweetie says, pulling my attention off the coffee table and over to him. "I get it. Seeing those two so in love can make it seem like you want it for yourself. But finding what they have isn't for everyone. Not everyone gets to find their one. I'd go buy some knee pads because you have a lot of groveling to do."

He leaves me too.

I sit on the couch, wrapping my head around everything they're saying. The more their words rehash in my head, the angrier I become.

"You know what, assholes?" I stand from the couch and walk into the kitchen. "Fuck you. I know it wasn't my brightest decision to run into her wedding and do what I did, but what I feel for her is real. I'm not five and so jealous of some other kid's toy that I want to steal it away. You." I point at Rowan. "You said yourself that you had a connection you couldn't explain with Kyleigh. You just had the benefit that she wasn't getting married to someone else."

Rowan crosses arms but doesn't say anything.

"And you." I point at Henry. "Lucky bastard, you met the love your life at ten years old."

"Seven," Henry corrects me.

I shake my head. "Whatever. And you." I point at Tweetie.

"You got nothing on me." He huffs, stretching his arms behind him, gripping the countertop edge.

"I fucking played in Florida, Tweetie. I heard about Tedi."

His smile drops. "Don't go there. You don't know what the fuck you're talking about."

"Besides Tweetie, you both went after what you wanted. Why am I getting shit on for doing the same?"

They all groan.

"Because you ambushed her wedding," Henry says as though it's obvious.

I throw my hands up at my sides. "I'm sorry, I'm a little late to the game, okay? I had to process my feelings for her."

"And you were drunk." Henry's eyebrows raise.

"Fine. But the only person I owe an apology to is her. So, I'm going to your house, and I'm going to ask her to forgive me."

"And?" Rowan arches an eyebrow.

"That's between her and me."

Nobody fights me on my plan.

"Well, you'd better shower and get that horrible smell off you if you want her to forgive you," Rowan says.

Tweetie slaps me on the back. "I'll get your kneepads."

"I'm disgusted that you have kneepads," Henry says with disdain.

"I'm a gentleman. I want my girls to be comfortable." Tweetie winks.

We all groan, and I head to my bathroom to shower. As the warm water runs over my back, I consider what I'm going to say to Eloise to try to get her to forgive me. I can't believe I was such a selfish asshole. Hopefully she'll see that it was a moment of temporary insanity.

sixteen

Eloise

The door to the bedroom I'm staying in opens, and my mom stands in the doorway.

I slide up the bed and lean my back along the headboard. "Hi, Mom."

"I brought some donuts and bagels. There's coffee downstairs too." She sits on the edge of the bed. "How are you?"

I nod, tears welling in my eyes. "Did that really happen?"

She gives me a small smile. "Yeah, sweetie, it did."

I tip to the side and bury my head in a pillow. "I can't believe I did it."

"Technically *you* didn't. Can you tell me who this Conor boy is? Sam says he's some hockey player?"

Oh, my mom, she watches sports about as much as me. "He plays for the Falcons."

"Okay, but that doesn't tell me who he is to you."

She pulls the pillow out from under me, and I sit back up, grabbing it again and hugging it to my chest. "I have no idea why he came yesterday, but I met him the night of my bachelorette party. Nothing happened between us, not like that. He knew I was getting married."

"Something must have happened if he thought you might pick him."

I shrug and roll my eyes. "I liked him. Being with him felt comfortable, and it seemed like maybe we shared a connection. But I mean, it was one night."

She remains quiet.

"And I don't know. It was a nice night." I shrug again. Still she doesn't say anything, so I continue to fill the silence. "And he's a good listener."

Nothing.

"And he took me stargazing because he saw this list I made of things I wanted to do before I was thirty, and he wanted to help me cross something off."

"Nice." She smiles at me.

"He's got a sweet tooth."

Back to her silence.

"He told me not to settle. That I shouldn't come second."

My mom sighs. "Yesterday I hated him, but today I kind of like him. He's right. But..."

"I know. I'm not moving on from Tristan to him. I need to clear that up and figure some things out for myself." That's about the only thing I decided last night as we were ripping apart the beautiful dress Kyleigh made.

My mom takes my hand. "Was it a relief when he stopped the wedding?"

I nod, not wanting to tell her that I should have done it long before it got to that point. "I'm sorry, Mom."

She shakes her head. "Don't be. I only want you to be happy. I'll go through all the storms and be by your side as long as you come out happier. That's a mom's promise."

She opens her arms, and I fall into her embrace. "I think I

got a little caught up, and I didn't want to hurt anyone. All that money and planning. There was so much pressure."

Her hands run down my back. "I know, sweetie. It was a hard decision to make, but can we be honest and admit that your dad had a little bit to do with why you stayed for so long?"

She draws back, and I sit up. "I just... he really liked Tristan. Said we were a perfect fit. I kind of wanted to..."

"Please him?"

I nod.

Her hands land on my shoulders. "Now is time for a restart. Of course, this aftermath won't be fun, but after it's all said and done, you have a great opportunity to decide what your future looks like. No one can tell you what makes you happy but you. So, take control of it and to hell with everyone else's opinions."

"I know."

A knock lands on the door, and Jade peeks her head in. "Hey, I'm sorry to interrupt and no rush, but I just wanted to warn you before you came downstairs. The boys are back... Conor is with them, and he really wants to talk to you."

I nod. "Thanks. I'll be down in a minute."

She shuts the door, and my mom stands. "I better hurry. Sam's meeting him before me." We both laugh, but she sobers up fast. "You're okay though? No regrets or anything?"

"I just wish I would've stopped it before the wedding." I shrug.

"It doesn't matter when. Even if you'd married him and decided afterward, it would have been okay."

"I know."

"Okay." She pats my leg. "I'll see you downstairs." She turns but stops and circles back around. "Hey, there is one problem, and I feel horrible about this. But remember how Sam and I decided to do the renovations at our place?"

My forehead wrinkles. "Yeah."

"The contractor said it will go faster if we move out for a month or two, so we rented a one-bedroom apartment starting next week. You're of course welcome to the couch... oh, you know what, we'll just delay them. You should be home until you can find a new place to rent."

I force a smile. "No, Mom. You and Sam continue with your plans."

"We can talk about it later. Come and eat." She smiles and walks out the door.

I flip the blankets over me and swing my legs out of bed. Here goes nothing.

I dress and throw my hair in a ponytail. A shower never felt as good as it did last night, although I had to shampoo three times to get all the product out of my hair.

Bodhi must be back home because I hear his footsteps running downstairs.

I go down and find a kid's movie on, but no one in the room, so I venture farther down the hall, following the voices into the kitchen. Jade has Bodhi on the island, the two of them preparing something. I smell something baking in the oven. Henry is pouring a coffee for either himself or someone else, but he stares lovingly at Jade and Bodhi.

Kyleigh, Conor, Tweetie, and Rowan all sit around the table, my mom and Sam with them, drinking coffee and talking. Sam gets up when he sees me enter, and I'm thankful that Conor's back is to me. My stomach rumbles with nerves over how I'll feel when I see him face-to-face again.

"Hey, you." Sam pulls me into a hug and whispers in my ear, "I'm proud of you. It's not easy to do what you did."

"Thanks, Sam." I hug him harder, thankful to have him in my life, as tears sting my eyes.

"Always."

We part, and the table turns quiet, everyone taking little glimpses of me as if I'm a guard dog they can't stop watching to make sure I don't attack.

"Eloise, would you like some coffee?" Jade asks.

"Let me pour you a cup." Henry is quick to grab a mug and the pot of coffee.

"There are donuts and bagels," Jade says.

"Hi, Eloise." Bodhi waves at me. "We're making potato chip cookies. Jade said they're your favorite." He holds up a bag of potato chips. "I get to crumble them."

"Thank you. I do love a sweet-and-salty mix." I meet Jade's gaze, and we smile at one another.

"I can't promise anything. It's my first attempt at them." She holds up her phone because she must be following a recipe.

"Here you go." Henry holds a coffee mug out for me.

"Thanks, Henry."

"You're welcome."

I sip the coffee, feeling all eyes on me. A chair screeches on the floor, and in my peripheral vision, I see a large body coming toward me.

This is it. Conor's going to ask me to go and talk. Of course I'll accept, but what is he going to say? Does he feel obligated to date me or something now? Does he regret what he did yesterday? Oh god, this is such a disaster.

"I haven't had the pleasure yet. I'm Tweetie." A large hand lands in front of me.

I slide my hand in his. His blond hair is chin-length and wavy. The night of my bachelorette, I never saw him up close, but I can see why he had a woman on either side of him.

"Hi. Eloise. The runaway bride."

He laughs and squeezes my hand. "I like you. Got to laugh at yourself." He winks and steps away. "Okay, Conor, make your move."

Another chair screeches, and I glance over to see Conor standing and scowling at his friend and teammate. "I didn't realize we're in the seventh grade."

Just the sound of his voice makes my stomach flip. Especially as I concentrate on sipping my coffee as if he's not walking over to me.

His feet come into view, sneakers matched with jeans. "Hey."

"Hi." I look up and realize his eyes are the same as Kyleigh's. Now I know where the feeling of familiarity came from the night we met.

"Can we talk?" His voice is low, as if that will keep everyone from eavesdropping.

"Yeah."

"Front porch?"

"Sure."

He holds out his arm, waiting for me to lead the way.

"Don't take too long. The cookies are almost done!" Bodhi calls behind us.

"We'll be back," Conor says, reaching in front of me to grab the door handle and open the door for me.

"Thanks."

"You're welcome."

I walk down the steps and sit on the third one down. Jade and Henry have rented a typical house in Chicago. Narrow but deep with three levels.

Conor sits one step down from me and leans his back against the iron railing.

It's a sunny day, hot since it's August, but the light breeze makes it comfortable.

"I'm really sorry, Eloise," he says. "I was drunk and

listened to the advice of three rookies who were only thinking about me and not how that stunt I pulled would affect you. Actually, I can't blame them. It's all on me. I'm the asshole in this situation."

I wrap my arms around my legs and stare at the street. The neighborhood is so similar to the one I grew up in. One I thought, once upon a time, I'd raise my kids in. But had I married Tristan, I would've been in a more affluent area with large yards and sprawling streets void of parked cars most days.

"Is that it? You were drunk?"

Conor stretches one leg out along the stair. Nothing in his body language says he's anxious or nervous, whereas I feel like a kinked chain necklace. "I had a lot to drink, but I think it only aided in me acting on the thoughts that had been running though my head most of the week."

"I was about to call it off right before you came in." My confession is one I wasn't sure I wanted to share with him. I don't want to give him false hope.

He tips his head toward mine, and his jaw hangs open. "Really?"

"Yeah. I feel like it took forever for me to make that decision, but there was a lot of pressure."

He holds up his hand. "You don't have to justify your reasoning. It takes a lot of courage to leave."

"Yeah, I'm not sure I thought I ever would do it, but this weight I've been carrying around is finally off me."

He touches my knee. "I'm glad."

"But, Conor, I can't be with you right now. I need to figure myself out. You might be surprised to find out what a mess I am. I allowed Tristan to feel as if I was helpless and needed him. After my dad died, he just kind of took over. So, although I did feel our chemistry that night, and I thought about you all week, I can't start something right now. I'm really sorry."

He scootches up onto the step beside me, his strong thigh and shoulder touching mine. God, my body wants me to say screw it and tell him to make me forget all the shit in my head.

"I get it, and you don't have to apologize. Let me help you though. I feel as if I got you into this mess."

I shake my head. "I just need to figure a lot of stuff out. I've been living off my trust from my dad for a while because Tristan didn't want me to work. Well, his mom had these plans for me sitting on charity boards or something. And I moved out of my apartment to move in with Tristan. My mom and Sam are renovating and moving into a one-bedroom for a while." I lower my head into my hands. "And here I go again, complaining about my life. I promise I'm not one of those Debbie Downer types. You just keep finding me at the wrong times."

He wraps his arm around my shoulders, pulling me into his side. And I allow him—for the selfish reason that it feels nice. "I can't help you with all those problems, but I can help you with one. Move in with me."

He's got to be kidding, but when I draw back, I see that he's stone-cold serious.

seventeen

Eloise

"Are you out of your mind?" I ask, because on what planet is this a good idea?

"Probably. But I have a second bedroom. It's yours. For a night, a week, or however long you need it."

I straighten my back, and his arm falls off my shoulders. "It's a horrible idea."

"Yeah, it is."

I like the fact he isn't trying to rationalize it.

"You're taking that fixer thing to a new level." I lean my head on the iron spindle and think about his offer.

Conor chuckles. "Well, I guess you're learning to fight your people-pleasing habits, since you're telling me no."

"I didn't say no," I joke, although I'm about to.

"Listen, I'm behind on my offseason training, so I have to kick it into high gear if I'm going to be the stellar player I was last year."

"There's that ego again." I roll my eyes.

He shrugs. "I won't be home a ton is what I'm saying. So, you'll have your space. I'm not doing this as a fixer."

"Then why?" I'm genuinely curious why he would want me to move in with him when I'm not close to being ready to be with anyone.

"Because walking out on your wedding was a step toward a new future, and I don't want to stop that progress. It's admirable what you've done and... everyone needs a person who believes in them around to support them."

"You don't even really know me."

"Listen, take out all the shit people would say, since I know that's the reason you're resistant to the idea. You'll never find a place right away. Not a decent one at least."

"I could stay here." I motion toward the house behind us.

His eyebrows rise, and I know we're thinking the same thing. Henry and Jade are finally starting a life together, why would I want to intrude on that? I wouldn't.

I sigh. "Yeah, I couldn't do that to them. Plus, after I break off my wedding, I really don't want to live with the happiest couple I know."

He chuckles. "Try being around them *and* my sister and Rowan. Come live the single life with Tweetie and me over at the Nest." He knocks my shoulder with his.

"Conor..." I'm not sure how to answer.

"Don't think about what other people are going to say. What do *you* want? And I promise to keep my hands to myself... until you maul me."

I giggle and shake my head. Conor's right, I'll never find somewhere decent in a week. Nor do I want to sign a lease for an apartment when I don't know what my future holds yet. I've done enough settling lately, and when I woke up this morning, I loved the feeling that all my decisions were mine again.

"Are you sure?"

"It's up to you. You're the ruler of your life now. I'm just offering you shelter while you figure it out."

His offer is enticing. But my attraction to Conor is what scares me. How can I possibly be around him every day and not cross that line with him?

"I'm messy," I say.

"I have a housekeeper."

"I can't cook."

"I can."

"I'm moody."

"I'll make you a sign to wear around your neck that says don't talk to me today."

"You're positive?"

"I knew you liked the thought of it." His self-assured grin tells me once again how bad of an idea this is. But I can't seem to care.

"I admit that I do, but if it ends badly, we're going to make it uncomfortable for all of them." I nod toward the house.

"What if it doesn't end badly?"

He's right. Given the situation I just got out of, perhaps I am being a pessimist. Maybe that's what I like about Conor. His optimism.

He stands and steps in front of me. "This is your decision. If you say no, that's okay. It's an option, but I can't deny I wouldn't mind being alongside you as you start this new chapter. In friendship only... at first." He slides by me, stepping up to the front door.

"Conor," I say, not taking the time I should to make this decision, "I pay my share."

He chuckles. "Deal."

Shit, just like that, I'm moving in with Conor Nilsen. But it's temporary. A month at most. But it will be an experience, I'm sure.

"I'll see you inside."

I hear the door shut behind him, but I stay on the steps, unable to not wonder what people will think.

The door opens back up, and Bodhi comes out, sitting down next to me, and handing me a cookie on a plate. "I see why you like them. They're yummy."

"Thanks, buddy."

I accept the warm cookie and take a bite, Bodhi watching me the entire time. The salty and the sweet flavors mix together, and I swallow.

"I love it. You guys did a great job. I'm jealous. I wish I could bake like this." I finish the cookie.

He hops up and jumps down the steps one at a time then back up. "Jade says you can't perfect something the first time. That you have to learn from your mistakes before anything comes out the way you hoped." He jumps down the last two steps and lands on the sidewalk. "But I think she just wasn't putting enough glue on my school project when she said that."

I know it wasn't easy for Jade to give her heart to Henry again. The scariest steps to take are the ones where you can't guarantee the outcome.

The door behind me opens again. "Bodhi, Daddy needs you for the next batch." Jade sits on the step next to me.

He hops on one leg, and I can see he's trying not to step on the cracks of the sidewalk. "I don't want to bake anymore."

Jade sighs. "Remember, we have to finish what we start."

His head falls back, and he groans.

"If you go now, we'll go to the park later."

"Okay." He runs up the stairs but stops right in front of Jade. "She liked it."

Jade turns to me and smiles, raising her hand to Bodhi. "Way to go, sous chef."

He slaps her hand, and she shakes it out as he rounds us and heads inside. Seconds later, the front door slams shut.

I bump shoulders with her. "It's nice to see you happy."

"It's nice to be happy." She wraps her arm around me. "I heard a rumor."

"Can he not keep anything to himself?" I lay my head on her shoulder.

"Are you sure you want to move into the Nest? You can stay here as long as you want."

I love that she's not telling me I'm being crazy and is just supporting my decision. I've missed her all the years she was away. Sure, she was there for me to call anytime, and we planned get-togethers where I'd meet her in some exotic locale, but this is what I missed most. Living our lives day by day, side by side.

"You have a family now. I'd be in the way."

"Elo—"

"No, Jade." I sit up and turn to face her. "Thank you for the offer, but it's time I find my footing. I have no idea what I'm doing, but I'm excited too."

She nods. "Okay, but it's just roommates, right?"

"Yes."

She opens her arms, and we hug. "I'm always here, and that room is always yours."

"Thank you. And it's only temporary. You can help me try to find a place after I clear up this whole wedding mess with Tristan."

She cringes, and her gaze diverts to the street.

"What?"

"Tristan posted a picture on his socials this morning." She opens her phone and scrolls for a moment before handing it to me.

There's no caption—just a picture of him in front of an ocean with this arm slung around some hot blonde. I would've expected my chest to squeeze or for anger to heat my veins, but there's nothing.

"He went on our honeymoon. Why am I not surprised."

"Do you know the woman?" she asks.

I shake my head. "If I had to guess, I'd say he probably just met her and picked her up at the resort. Either because he's hurting, or he's trying to hurt me."

I understand that I ran out on our wedding, but when he didn't even try to contact me afterward, that told me all I needed to know. I feel bad about how everything went down, but a man who is heartbroken at his relationship falling apart would at least call you to find out why it happened, right?

"You're better off," Jade says, patting my leg and standing. "Come and eat when you're ready."

"Thanks, Jade. For everything."

"That's what best friends are for." She walks behind me, and the front door clicks shut again.

There's no point in wallowing. Tristan wasn't nearly as invested as I was in our relationship. He's made his choices, and it's about time I make mine.

I've got until November before I turn thirty, and I plan on finally crossing items off my list.

eighteen

Conor

ELOISE IS UPSTAIRS WITH JADE, BORROWING SOME OF her clothes until she can get her stuff from Tristan's. I haven't questioned Eloise as to whether she thinks there's a chance her stuff might not be there anymore. Supposedly, the movers took her stuff to his house on Friday morning before their rehearsal.

"Are you sure about this?" Rowan asks me as we sit at Henry's kitchen table.

"I wouldn't have asked if I wasn't."

"I get the whole instant connection thing, but moving her in after she just ran out on her wedding?" Tweetie shakes his head and downs the rest of his coffee.

"We're not going to date. She's not going to be sleeping in my bed."

Henry scoffs, pulling my attention to him. He's been quiet most of the morning.

"Speak your mind, Daddy." Tweetie holds out his hand as

if we're in some business meeting, and he's magnanimously giving up the floor.

Henry's eyes bore into mine over the rim of his coffee mug. He swallows and sets the cup down in front of him. "She's Jade's best friend."

"I know." I maintain eye contact.

"If you hurt her, Jade is going to be upset. If Jade gets upset, I'm going to be pissed off. Last year, you were concerned my feelings for Jade were gonna fuck up our team dynamic. How do you think it's going to be if you screw over Eloise, my fiancée's best friend?"

I sink back into my chair and run my hand over my face. "I'm not going to screw her over."

He twists his coffee mug in his hands. "I hope not. But don't go fucking around with her emotions. Crashing the wedding turned out to be a good thing. Tristan was a shitty fiancé from what Jade says, and Eloise wasn't happy. But to move her in with you is next level."

Tweetie and Rowan remain quiet.

"Daddy, I promise, we're roommates only. I'm not going to step over that line unless she tells me she's ready to. But I can't sit here and tell you I don't want to. I like her, and I know there's something between us. That said, I'd never try to get with her right now. I understand she needs time to heal."

He nods.

"Relax, Henry, I've never seen Conor so invested. I have a feeling he knows what he's doing." Rowan smiles at me.

"Thanks, man." I'm happy that a guy who knew me in college sees how different I am right now.

"Of course, that's what good friends do for one another. They vouch for the other." He widens his eyes, obviously calling me out for how I acted toward him when Kyleigh told me she loved him.

"You're an adult, and I can't stop whatever is going to

happen, but we thought last year was our year. We're only getting older…" Henry says.

We all look at Tweetie.

He raises his hands, flipping us off. "Fuck you all."

I raise my hand. "Don't worry. I got this handled."

"You better."

I let the topic go because I can tell Henry whatever I want, but it will be my actions that speak the loudest.

And I sure as shit don't want to tell him I'm a tad worried myself. I really hope Eloise doesn't wear skimpy pajamas or anything like that.

Thankfully, we hitched a ride back to the condo with Tweetie, Kyleigh, and Rowan. Coming back to the apartment alone with Eloise could have been hella awkward if we both just sat there in silence, digesting the arrangement we both just agreed to.

"If my brother's being an idiot, I'm just upstairs," Kyleigh says as Rowan tugs her toward their condo.

"Can you play darts?" Tweetie asks Eloise, walking backward up the stairs.

She shakes her head. "Afraid not."

"That's one thing you guys have in common then." He laughs and jogs up the stairs to his condo.

"Jade said you weren't very good at darts," Eloise says to me.

I key in the passcode for my lock. "I can hold my own. She and Henry are on another level."

Unlocking the door, I push it open for her to go first and grab the small bag to bring in for her. She walks in and looks around.

"This is very masculine," she says and twirls around, holding her hands in the air. "No judgment though."

I take her bag to the bedroom that will be hers. "You can judge. I'm a bachelor. This is your room. You have your own bathroom as well."

"So, I don't really have to see you, huh?" She joins me in the bedroom.

"Very boyish because this was Bodhi's room."

She spins in a circle, taking in what will be her space. "Would you be upset if I painted?"

I chuckle and put her bag on the bed. "It's yours to do what you want with."

She unzips her bag, and I head over to the door.

"Should we go over the bills now?" she asks.

"No. Get settled. If you need anything, let me know. I'll be around."

She stops taking clothes from the bag but digs into a pocket and unfolds a piece of paper. "I guess I don't need to hide this from you."

After walking over to the corkboard Henry didn't take with him, she pins it there. I push off the doorframe and walk over to read the list.

"I thought you were crossing them off?" I ask, seeing stargazing still on there.

"Oh yeah."

I leave the room and return with a pen, which I hand to her.

She bites her lip and takes the cap off the pen, holding it up to the paper. She puts a checkmark beside stargazing instead of crossing it off. "That felt good. I should have done that earlier."

Her blonde hair is swept up in a messy bun, and she's wearing a T-shirt and yoga pants that I'm pretty sure are

Jade's. Her ass looks amazing in them, which does nothing to help me remember that I need to keep this platonic.

"Let me know if you need my help at all." I force my feet to move in toward the door because she needs her space, not me hounding her.

"Thanks again, Conor. Your place is really nice."

I stop at the door. "Our place."

She grins and nods. "Not until I pay my share."

I ignore her and walk out of the room. I don't want her money.

I go into the family room, grab the remote, and turn on the reality show I've been binging lately.

I wasn't expecting it to be this weird, but she's the first woman I've ever lived with, and she's the first woman I've wanted who I couldn't have. Those two things together form a powder keg that will eventually combust. I just hope it's at the right moment.

nineteen

Eloise

"We're in, and we're out," Jade says, turning onto the street where Tristan's house is.

"I hope he hasn't changed the locks." I grab the key out of my purse.

We finally reach his house and find no vehicles in the driveway. Thank God. I can only imagine if I ran into his mother here.

"Well, your stuff isn't on the lawn. That's a good sign." Kyleigh clasps my shoulder from the back seat.

Jade parks in the driveway, and I stare at the house I thought I'd be returning to as a married woman. There's a box on the porch steps. I wonder if Tristan's car is in the garage.

"Let's get this over with," I say.

We all climb out of the SUV.

As I walk up to the front door, I wasn't expecting all these emotions. It's not exactly sadness I'm feeling. More like disappointment in myself for not speaking up sooner.

"Man, how rich is his family? This is a nice starter home." Kyleigh stands behind me at the door.

"He's a Somerset, so this is probably slumming it to them." Jade rolls her eyes.

I slide my key in the lock, and I'm surprised when it turns over. I thought for sure that if he didn't, his mother would lock me out.

"This is for you." Kyleigh picks up the package from the porch.

"Thanks. It's a sign I ordered to be delivered yesterday because we were supposed to come back here instead of a hotel after the wedding."

I step inside. In my head, I had envisioned rose petals strewn on the floor, champagne chilling in the fridge with a platter of fruit and cheeses for us to have in bed after we made love for the first time as husband and wife. But there's no sign of anything like that.

You were delusional. You probably would have been taking care of his drunk ass.

"Can I open it?" Kyleigh asks, holding up the box.

"Ky," Jade scolds her.

She shrugs. "I just wanted to see it."

"Go ahead." I open the fridge and see it still has the ten takeout containers and beer. I grab the bottle of wine. "This is coming with us."

"Good for you. What else do you want to take?" Kyleigh opens a drawer, making herself at home, and cuts open the package.

"Nothing is mine. It's all his. Fully stocked thanks to his mommy."

She pulls out the sign that reads The Somersets.

"Super cute." Kyleigh holds it up to Jade.

Jade nods and turns to me. "Let's get your stuff."

Kyleigh drops the sign on the table and follows us up the

stairs. I walk into the primary bedroom, assuming my stuff was put in there.

The movers were running late, and I had to be at the venue to talk over last-minute details, since it was an outside reception and rain was predicted. Tristan said he'd take care of making sure all my stuff got where it was supposed to go.

"Did he unpack you?" Jade asks, staring around the room like I am, trying to figure out where all my boxes are.

Kyleigh goes into the closet. "Just men's clothes in here."

The bathroom doesn't have my stuff either, the drawers on the one side empty except for a few things I left here when I spent the night.

"What the hell?" I rest my hands on my hips and look around.

Leaving the primary bedroom, I turn right into one of the spare bedrooms. Sure enough, all my boxes are here. I open the closet, and my clothes are hung on the rack.

"This is weird," Kyleigh says. "Why is all your stuff in this bedroom?"

"Because he's a jackass, that's why." Jade picks up a box and walks downstairs.

Kyleigh cringes at me, picking up a box. "Good decision on not marrying him."

She walks out, and I sit on the edge of the queen bed and close my eyes. The anger inside me rises like flames doused in gasoline. Why did I ever allow him to do shit like this? My fists clench at my sides.

"This isn't healthy. Let's just get this done and free you from him forever." Jade returns and fills her arms with my clothes.

She's right. Why sit here and feel bad over Tristan doing something insensitive—again? He acted like this our entire relationship, and I just made excuses for him. I've called it off, so this is my last step before he's out of my life. Especially after the pictures I saw him tagged in on socials this morning. I showed the girls on the way over.

They were from Tristan's bachelor party, and I have to assume that Merrick tagged him in an effort to stick it to me. In one, there's a topless stripper on his lap, and his face is planted between her breasts. The picture was taken from behind her, so I can only see her naked back and the thong she's wearing, but there's no other place for his face to have been. In the next picture, I can see his face because he's leaning back, and he's groping her. In the last, she's on her knees in front of him and undoing the zipper on his pants. I can only imagine what happened next.

Just like when I saw the picture of him on our honeymoon with his arm slung around another woman, I don't feel any hurt or anger. It only further solidifies my decision. I don't even care to know what happened the night of his bachelor party or to know if things like that had been happening all throughout our relationship. It helps that I had a physical right after the last time we were intimate, and it came back without any issues.

For the next twenty minutes, the three of us get all my things stuffed into Jade's SUV.

I go back inside to grab the wine bottle and see the sign on the table. I pick it up and stomp out of the kitchen into the backyard with it.

"Eloise, what are you doing?" Jade asks, following me.

At the edge of the pool, I fling the sign into the water and watch it sink to the bottom.

"You go, girl!" Kyleigh cheers, flipping off the water. "Fuck you, Tristan Somerset." She raises her middle finger in the air to any cameras that might be around.

I'm sure he has them. Plus, the house will probably go on the market now, and he'll move back to the city.

Jade puts her arm around my shoulders. "You deserve better, and you're going to find it."

I nod, and she squeezes me to her side.

Kyleigh comes to my other side. "He's an asshole who has no idea what he just lost, but he will one day. You made the right decision. Not like you need my permission."

"Thank you."

We stare into the pool for a bit before returning to the kitchen. I like this girl power thing we have going on.

"I'd burn the house down if I wouldn't get arrested for arson." Kyleigh laughs, picking up the box on the table. "But..." She takes all the food containers from the fridge and opens them on the counter. "How long was your honeymoon?"

"Ten days."

"This should be nice and ripe by then."

Jade shakes her head and laughs. "Does Rowan know this side of you?"

"It's what makes him fall in line." She laughs. "Kidding."

"Wait." I hold up my left hand, slide off my engagement ring, and admire it one last time.

"You should keep it," Jade says with a shrug.

"I don't want it." I place it on the counter. "Now he's really behind me."

We walk out of the house, and I lock up behind us.

Right before Jade pulls away, I take one last look, happy it's in my rearview mirror. Tristan wants a Stepford wife, not one with her own opinions and desires. And I want more for myself than being a yes person.

Ruby lets us park in the alley outside Peeper's Alley, and Rowan and Tweetie help us bring my stuff up, letting us finish in only one trip.

"Where the hell is my brother?" Kyleigh asks, hanging up the last of my clothes in the closet.

"I'm not sure."

Jade runs her hand over the walls, looking as though she's lost in some memories. "I loved this condo. Bodhi will be so happy you're in his room."

"Well, if he wants to see it like this, he better come soon because I'm redoing it this week." I slide my boxes into the corner to go through later. "Where are Rowan and Tweetie?"

"Down at the bar." Kyleigh rolls her eyes.

I hear the front door open, and we all step out of the bedroom.

"Oh, look who shows up right after all the heavy lifting is done. How convenient," Kyleigh says.

Conor looks beyond his sister at me. "How did it go?"

He'd asked to go with me, said he could help with the moving, but I don't want to become dependent on him while I'm here. Besides, if anyone from Tristan's side was at the house when I arrived, that would have been a real mess.

"The locks hadn't been changed," I say.

"And no one was there?"

"I had her back if someone was. Relax on the bodyguard thing." Kyleigh peeks into the bags he brought home.

Conor shuts them. "Mind your own business."

"Flour? Sugar? My birthday already passed, remember? But sweet of you to want to make me a cake." She slides onto a stool. "The boys are down at Peeper's."

"Shouldn't your alarm be beeping that you're too far away from Rowan then?" He arches an eyebrow.

I enjoy watching their dynamic with one another.

"Well, he fucked me so good last night, I'm sore, so I should probably keep my distance."

He scowls and points at her. "That's going too far."

She slides off the stool. "You make it too easy." She comes over and hugs me. "I'm upstairs if you ever need me. I can't wait to tell Rowan about the sign."

"Thanks, Kyleigh."

She winks just like Conor does and waves. "Bye, guys."

"Wait, I'm coming with you." Jade quickly hugs me. "I'm only a short Uber ride away." She points at Conor. "Behave yourself. You think Henry is scary, remember how good I am at darts." Her eyes fall to his crotch.

Conor covers his package.

She smiles. "Now you two behave and have fun." Her voice is so sugary sweet, you'd never guess she just threatened Conor.

The door shuts after them, and I peek inside the bags. "What's all this?"

"We're going to bake a cake from scratch." He unpacks the grocery bags, taking out all the ingredients. "What's this about a sign?"

I watch him for a second, not looking at me but pulling out each item just so we can bake a cake. My emotions bubble up and pour over until I wrap my arms around his neck and breathe him in.

"Thank you," I whisper.

His arms move around my back, but he doesn't pull me closer. "It's just cake supplies."

"It's so much more, and you know it." I tighten my hold before falling back down on my heels.

His cheeks are pink when I pull away, and it's the cutest thing I've ever seen.

"So you don't mind me helping you?" he asks. "You'll bake a cake with me?"

"I'd love to."

He pulls out a recipe. "I found this online."

This will be a lot harder than I thought. We're only on day one.

twenty

Conor

Is she trying to torture me, or am I torturing myself? Eloise's thank you hug threw me off guard.

She's probably just emotional. Today had to be hard for her, going back to the house where she thought she would embark on a life with the one person she loved most in the world. So, I figured the easiest way to keep her mind occupied would be to work on her list, and the easiest thing to cross off would be baking the cake. Plus, I don't want to assume she's going to include me in her quest to do everything on her bucket list, so I didn't want to choose one of the bigger tasks.

"I found this recipe, but you can search for one yourself if you don't like it." I hand her my phone, and she hesitates before taking it.

I watch as she reads it over. Her hair is down in light waves and veils her face, blocking her reaction to the recipe I picked out.

"I think this is good. We should definitely try vanilla

before we do anything fancy." She digs into her purse hanging off the breakfast stool.

"What's your favorite cake flavor?" I ask.

"Probably chocolate on chocolate." She uses both hands to push her hair away from her face and secure her long strands in a bun. "You?"

"Red velvet with cream cheese."

"Oh, that's a good one too. Maybe that will be our third cake." She chuckles.

I love the way she says our as if I'm on this adventure with her.

Her finger runs over the screen of my phone. "We have to get the butter soft and the eggs at room temperature."

I take out the butter. "How much do we need?"

She looks up online the fastest way to get butter and eggs to room temperature without waiting hours, and fifteen minutes later, we're blending the butter and sugar together.

"Do you mind if I inquire about today?" I ask while I measure the dry ingredients, and she takes care of the wet.

Eloise doesn't look away from the bowl. "It wasn't as terrible as I thought it would be. Weird, but refreshing in some ways. I'm still processing how I didn't see that I could never be happy long term with Tristan. For example, we were going to stay at the house the night of the wedding, instead of a hotel. I envisioned this whole thing of him carrying me through the front door and rose petals leading up to our new bedroom."

I grip the measuring cup more firmly, thinking about her in Tristan's arms.

"But there wasn't even a bottle of champagne in the fridge. Maybe I'm being presumptuous to think a guy would think of something like that. Maybe my expectations are out of line."

She turns on the mixer again, leaving me no time to tell her that a guy who loved her would have wanted to do something like that for her and wouldn't have to be told. That she just picked the wrong guy. But it's best I keep those thoughts to myself. She turns off the mixer, and I sift the dry ingredients into a bowl.

It felt as though I needed a million little things to make this cake, and of course I didn't have most of them at my place. Thankfully, the woman at the gourmet shop put together all the supplies. She thought it was cute when I told her I wanted to bake a cake from scratch, but there was a little disbelief in her expression when she wished me good luck.

"When we left, it felt good to have the weight of it off my shoulders, but it's embarrassing at the same time. Makes me second-guess all my choices."

"You probably got caught up in the whole wedding thing. It happens." I shrug. "My mom and Kyleigh have seen it a bunch of times."

She shakes her head with what looks like disappointment. "Kyleigh probably knew. Last fall, I stared at myself in this dress she picked out for me, and I froze. I knew then but didn't want to admit it to myself."

"You're being way too hard on yourself." I head over to her with the bowl of dry ingredients. "You ready for me?"

Her gaze lifts, and our eyes lock.

Damn, there's that chemistry between us again. If she was mine, I'd say fuck the cake and pick her up by her hips, prop her up on the counter, and strip her down. I'd lick the sugar right off her skin, and it'd only be sweeter as a result.

She clears her throat. "Not yet, I have to add the vanilla." Turning away from me, she snatches the bottle off the counter.

Eloise measures and adds the vanilla before flipping the switch on the mixer. Again, we're quiet. She's watching the mixing bowl, and I'm taking not-so-sly glances at her.

She's so beautiful—inside and out. I can't believe Tristan

didn't fight for her. That he just went on their honeymoon, probably with that jackass of a best man. I'd chase her to the ends of Earth to win her back if I were him.

"Okay, we're ready. We're supposed to add it slowly. You take control. Just a little bit at first and a little more and a little more. Well, you get the point."

Our eyes meet, and I smile. "I can do slow."

"Really? I figured you for fast and quick." She laughs.

"Quick?" I cover my heart with my free hand. "I'm insulted."

She turns on the mixer again, and I dump in a little bit of the dry mix, both of us watching it being incorporated into the wet ingredients. I add a little more and a little more. We're so close, I can smell her shampoo and what I think is her natural scent.

After it's all mixed, we pour the batter into two round cake pans I picked up and put them in the oven. She sets her timer on her phone. We clean up the mess together, her putting away the ingredients and me washing the dishes we used. I've never been like this with a woman besides Kyleigh, and I kind of don't mind it. Maybe domestication isn't as terrible as I assumed.

When we're done cleaning up, she slides on the stool. "Can we talk rent now?"

I chuckle and shake my head. "Let's do one thing at a time."

"Conor, don't baby me. I'm not some charity case. It's nice enough that you got all this stuff to bake a cake, but I'd like to pay you back."

It's not that I want to baby her. This is just in my nature.

"I don't know if you know, but I'm a helluva hockey goalie and signed a great contract last year." I wink at her, but she stares at me hard and long. Is that her mad face? I guess my attempt at humor didn't work.

"I have a trust fund, Conor, I'm not destitute."

"I didn't think you were."

"Are you sure? Because I feel as if you think I'm some woman who ran away from her rich fiancé and now has nothing." She leans back in the chair and crosses her legs.

"Trust fund kid, huh?"

She shrugs. "Kind of."

"You said you stopped working because Tristan wanted you to. What will you do now?"

Her mouth twists, and her cheeks turn a light apricot color. It's cute. She's embarrassed for some reason.

"I don't know." She holds up her hand before I can comment. "It's not what you think though."

"Who said I'm making assumptions?" I grab two waters out of the fridge, twist the cap off hers, and slide it over to her.

"Thanks." She takes a sip and screws the cap back on. "It's not that I don't want to work, don't want something for myself. I'm not content to just live off my trust fund, but I don't know what I want to do. I told you about my parents never being married. You met Sam, who is my stepdad. I didn't grow up like Tristan and his friends. My dad was still very absent most of my life. When he died, he left me what was more or less his trust fund. My dad was the guy who couldn't fall in line with what his father wanted. He never took over the family business but traveled and acted like a playboy most of his life."

"You don't have to explain this all to me. I think it's great if you don't have to work and can live off that money. It's a dream most people would probably want."

"Except that it's unfulfilling. After Tristan proposed, we discussed how I'd stay at home. His mom insisted that I would go with her to charity events and sit on boards until we had kids. My entire future was planned out for me." She points at me. "You're judging."

I hold up my hands and back off, leaning my back against the counter behind me. "I just can't imagine not playing hockey. Not doing what I love. But everyone is different. It's your life to live."

"I used to work in marketing for a large corporation, but on the side, I had this social media thing where I posted what I was wearing, where to get it, and stuff like that, but Tristan thought it was a dumb hobby and didn't like how it took my attention away from him so he pressured me into giving it up." She drops her head into her hands. "I sound pathetic."

"You sound like someone who got caught up in a life she didn't want and didn't know how to escape. And that's okay."

I round the island and put my arm around her shoulders. She turns to me, wrapping her arms around my chest. I rest my chin on her head, holding her close and wishing I could take away all her sadness.

"I think you're still processing everything, but maybe you need to stop dissecting everything from the past and start living for the now. I know it's only been a couple days but focus on who you are now and who you want to be."

She nods into my chest, and I squeeze her tighter.

The timer on her phone goes off, startling both of us. She turns it off, and we go to the oven, opening the door.

Eloise grabs the hot pads, and we both stare at the cake tin as she pulls it out because the cake hardly rose.

"Oh, boy, this is a disaster." She takes them both out and puts them on the cooling rack, both of us glaring down at it.

"I'm not sure what we could've done wrong." I scratch the back of my head.

She presses her thumb into one cake, and it bounces back as the recipe said it should, but it's really thin. "We did something wrong."

"We'll try again."

She sniffles.

I put my finger under her chin, bringing her face to mine. "Hey."

"What if I'm just a failure now?"

I shake my head. "No. This was our first try. We'll figure it out."

Her face is full of doubt. I hate seeing that because at some point in her life, someone told her the world wasn't hers for the taking. That mindset isn't going to change just because she left Tristan. She'll need a lot of support to change her view of herself.

"It will come," I say. "You're going to be okay. I promise."

She sighs but doesn't refute my promise. Although I still hope this roommate situation will grow into more, I have to set that agenda aside for now because Eloise needs to work on herself first. She needs to find self-confidence inside herself. Otherwise, we'd never make it anyway.

twenty-one

Eloise

I've been living with Conor for a few days, and he was right, he's barely been home. When I wake up, he's already gone but comes home about an hour or two later all sweaty from the gym. He takes a shower and heads out again, saying he's going to the rink. His tenacity is admirable, and I'm jealous of his dedication.

Leaving the condo, I push open the security gate and rear back when I see a group of women standing there.

"Who are you?" a brunette says, crossing her arms and looking me up and down.

I look over my shoulder. It takes a moment for me to realize they're talking to me, and they must be here for either Conor or Tweetie. At least, I hope they're here for Conor or Tweetie. I don't want to know what Kyleigh would do if some girl showed up here for Rowan.

"I'm no one." The gate slams shut behind me.

"You must be someone," the girl says.

I eye the piece of cardboard in one girl's hand and the

black marker in another girl's. I'm obviously missing something.

"No." I shake my head and move to go around them.

The brunette steps in front of me. "Are you here for Tweetie or Pinkie?"

"I don't know a Pinkie, and I'm not here for Tweetie. Sorry, girls." I step to the side again to get past them, and the girl purposely brushes my shoulder. What the hell is her problem?

I head down the street, glancing over my shoulder and seeing them pin the sign on the security gate. The brunette attaches a white note to it, and they all laugh, walking down the street in the opposite direction. But right before I turn around, the brunette tosses her hair over her shoulder and glares at me.

Is this what living here will be like?

The convenience store is only three blocks away. When I walk in, the guy says hello but never looks in my direction. A few construction guys stand in front of the prepared food area, rambling about the Chicago Colts. I open the cooler and grab a Diet Coke, biding my time for them to leave.

One guy puts something in the microwave, and another pulls an empty cup out to fill with a slushie. They obviously aren't going anywhere any time soon.

Whatever. I don't have to be embarrassed about what I want to do.

I go to the counter, and the guy behind the register scans my Diet Coke.

"Anything else?" he asks, barely making eye contact.

I lean in closer. "Can I have a pack of cigarettes?"

"What kind, sweetheart?"

I scan over all the options. "Um... whatever the most popular is." I pull out my credit card, prepared to get this transaction over with as quickly as possible.

"Sweetheart, just tell me the brand."

When I hear footsteps behind me, I glance over my shoulder and see the construction guys headed toward us. I don't know why they're intimidating to me.

"The yellow box, I guess." I point randomly.

"Are you buying these for someone else?" the cashier asks suspiciously.

The door chimes, and the cashier says hello to whoever walks in, but never looks over.

"No, they're for me, but I'm trying some brands out to see which one I like better."

He blows out a breath. "You know smoking is bad for you, right?"

"Yes, thank you, surgeon general."

The guys behind me laugh, and it eases the tension of buying something I know nothing about and making a fool of myself.

"She got you, Ike," one of them says.

"Holy shit, Conor Nilsen, what's up?" another one says.

I turn to my left, seeing Conor wearing shorts and a T-shirt, his hat backward and AirPods in his ears. God, he looks sexy.

He takes out his AirPods and shoves them in his pocket. "What's going on here?" He nods to the guy who works here. "You're not giving my girl problems, are you, Ike?"

His girl?

"She's yours?" Ike asks with an expression to say he doesn't believe it. And I'm pretty sure it's not because he deems me better looking than Conor, but more that Conor isn't known for having "a girl."

Conor looks at me as though he's asking how to answer, and I give him nothing since he's the one who said it. "She's my roommate. Eloise, meet Ike. Ike, this is Eloise."

"Pleasure," I say.

"Which pack do you want?" Ike sounds more annoyed than happy to meet me.

"Ummm."

"What are you buying?" Conor asks, leaning in and lowering his voice.

"Cigarettes," I whisper.

He raises his hand and points. "She'll take the silver ultra lights and hold up." He steps away. "Sorry, guys, I'll be a second." He returns with a water and a protein bar. Then he picks up and throws a lighter on the counter, which is good because I would have forgotten all about the fact that I have to light the cigarette. "These too. Put it on my tab?"

"Yeah, sure," Ike says.

"And these guys' stuff too. Thanks for waiting."

"Thanks, Nilsen. Can't wait for the season to start. The Colts are in a fucking drought, and I'm dying for more action," one of them says.

"Easton Bailey is carrying that whole damn team," another one says.

Conor talks to them about the Colts and whoever Easton Bailey is while Ike rings up all their stuff. I wait next to Conor, feeling very out of touch with all the sports talk going on around me. Conor shakes all their hands and leads me out of the store with his hand on the small of my back.

We head back toward the condo, walking along the sidewalk.

"Do you get that a lot?" I ask.

"Recognized?" He shrugs. "Sometimes. Usually if my hat is faced front, people can't tell who I am quite as much. It depends how big of a fan they are."

"You must feel like I used to at the country club."

"How is that?" he asks, tearing open his protein bar and taking a bite just like he did the Snickers bar that night in the hotel.

"Like you're in a fish tank. Everyone watching you. For me, I always felt like they were waiting for me to screw up or maybe wondering why Tristan was with me. But I'm sure not everyone is as nice to you as those guys."

He chuckles. "Yeah, when I have a bad game, I've been called some pretty shitty stuff. Your skin gets thicker the longer you're in the league. Doesn't bother me as much anymore."

"Most of the women my age were jealous because Tristan was a big catch in that circle. If I told you how many older men hit on me behind Tristan's back, you'd never believe it."

"Actually, I would believe you. The first night I saw you, I couldn't take my eyes off you."

My cheeks heat. Thank goodness for the distraction of having to dart around other pedestrians on the sidewalk. When we approach the security gate, I notice the sign still hanging there.

"Funny, when I walked out of the gate, a group of girls were hovering around. They put up a sign." I notice the letter with Pinkie written with curls at the end of every letter. "They were asking about Tweetie and a Pinkie? Is there another unit here?"

Conor studies me, a slow smile creeping on his lips. "I'm Pinkie." He points at himself.

"Pinkie? Oh, is this one of those hockey names?" I glance at his hand. "I noticed that the first night."

His hand clenches. "That's not why my name is Pinkie." He tears down the sign and dumps it into the trash can farther up on the sidewalk, not bothering to look at the note the brunette left for him.

I enter the security code, and he takes the handle, opening the door. "Am I in danger living here?"

He chuckles and waits for me to walk through. "Why would you ask that?"

"Those girls were asking me questions and were pretty aggressive. Especially this one brunette. She wanted to know who I was here for."

Conor's hand slips to the small of my back, and a rush of shivers runs up my spine. I like it a little too much.

"Kyleigh lives here, and no one has bothered her that I know of."

We go through the gate, and I sit on the stairs outside, ready to cross smoking off my list. "So, fill me in. Why does the sign say the Nest, and why is your name Pinkie if not for your pinkie finger?"

He sits next to me, stretching his arms behind him, tipping his head up to the sun. "Some of the fans refer to our building as the Nest. It used to be called the Den when some Grizzlies lived here. Actually, Cooper Rice owns the building."

"Cooper Rice?" I exclaim. "Seriously?"

"He you know, but me you had no idea. I'm wounded." He covers his heart with his hand, which I'm noticing is his thing.

I knock his shoulder. "Sorry, Tristan watched a lot of football."

"Then you should know, Damon Siska and Miles Cavanaugh also lived here." He dramatically opens his eyes and covers his open mouth as if he's fangirling.

I shove him with my hand, and he leans to the side before straightening. "Would you rather me be camped out at the security gate ready to jump you when you come out?"

"Yes," he deadpans. "Yes, I would."

I distract myself by pulling out the pack of cigarettes and the lighter.

"You sure this is what you want to do?" He sits up straighter, resting his arms on his thighs and looking at me.

"It's on the list." I shrug.

"You don't have to do everything on the list."

"Then what was the point of the list?" I sing-song, taking off the plastic and pulling out a cigarette. I run it under my nose and smell the tobacco.

He watches me intently, then his hand slides into mine, taking the lighter from my grip. I bring the cigarette to my lips.

"Have you ever smoked?" he asks.

I shake my head.

"This should be good then." He grins.

I bring the tip between my lips again, and he flicks the lighter with his thumb. The small flame heats my face a little.

"Inhale," he says when the flame hits the end of the cigarette.

His thumb lifts off the lighter, and smoke burns my lungs. I pull it away and cough and cough, unable to catch my breath.

"Happy now?" He takes the cigarette from my fingers.

My coughing fit continues, and he opens his water bottle handing it to me.

After I recover, he's still holding the cigarette between his fingers. "More?" he asks, holding it out to me.

I love that he's leaving the decision up to me, even though he clearly doesn't think it's a good idea.

"I think I'm good."

Shit, that was a very bad experience.

He brings the cigarette to his lips, holding it the manly way between his thumb and pointer finger. A curl of smoke leaks out of his mouth before he tosses it on the ground and steps on it.

My nipples pebble in my bra.

"Off the list," he says, standing from the step. He stills when he notices me watching him intently. "What?"

"Nothing." I rise from the step and walk to the door of the building.

"That look wasn't nothing." He grabs my wrist and twists me around.

"Did you used to be a smoker?"

He shrugs. "I've done it a few times, but it was never a habit. There's no way I'd have the stamina to play. Stop dodging the question. What was the look for?"

"It was just... I mean, you looked really..."

"Say it." He stares at me, and I have a feeling he'd wait all day.

"You looked sexy. Like a bad boy. It was swoony."

His eyebrows raise. "Bad boy? Is that your type?"

I pull my wrist from his grip and turn toward the door. "You're incorrigible."

He leans past me to press the code into the keypad, his hard chest pressing against my back. "I think I'm going to take up smoking."

The door opens, and we file inside, though by the time we reach his place, I'm still picturing how he looked with that cigarette. What is it about a bad boy that makes a woman want to lose all common sense?

twenty-two

Conor

I walk out of my bedroom after my shower to find Eloise putting her purse over her shoulder, ready to leave the condo.

"Where are you going?"

She stops and looks up, her gaze running up and down my half-naked body. "I think we need a rule about being dressed at all times."

I cross to the fridge and grab a water. For some reason, I've been dying of thirst all day. "Why? You like what you see?" I open the bottle and chug half of it.

Her eyes are locked on my abs, and I love the way her mouth is hanging slightly open. Nothing dramatic, but just enough to say she likes what she sees. "Should I prance around in a towel after my shower?"

"I wouldn't complain." I shrug. "And just so you know, those shorts are torture enough."

She's wearing short jean shorts and an oversized white blouse, along with all the jewelry she usually does, the gold necklaces and earrings and bracelets. One thing I've figured out since she moved in is that she's not a yoga pants and T-shirt kind of girl. Even her pajamas tops match the bottoms. I'm not complaining.

"My attire is clothing. Yours is basically a scrap of fabric."

"So are those shorts." Swiping my water bottle off the counter, I head toward my bedroom. "Hold up, I'll go with you."

"You don't even know where I'm going," she says from behind me.

"I'll only be a second." I disappear into my bedroom, keeping the door open a sliver so I can hear if she tries to ditch me.

"Who said you were invited?" she calls.

"I don't have anything going on this afternoon. Do you mind the company?"

I hear the breakfast stool slide out from the counter, and she huffs. "You're not going to like where I'm going."

"I'm not going for the *where*, I'm going for the *who*."

I throw on a pair of shorts and a T-shirt. I'd love to throw on a baseball hat, but not with my hair wet, so I hurriedly throw some product in my hair, add a spritz of cologne to my neck, and walk back out into our shared space.

"There was no need for cologne," she says, jumping off the stool.

"Are you wearing perfume?"

She stares at me, expressionless. "Yes."

"Did you ever think the cologne wasn't for you, but for others?"

She rolls her eyes while I grab my wallet from the tray by the front door and slide it in my pocket. She hasn't moved from the kitchen.

"Well, let's go. I don't have all day, Lulu." I purposely use the nickname that I love, but she doesn't seem too keen on.

She grunts and passes me, a waft of her flowery perfume floating up to my nostrils causing my dick to stir.

We walk out of the security gate, and there's another Nest sign with a similar note to the one before, addressed to me with the curls at the end of every letter. I tear it off and toss it in the trash as we head to the corner.

"Another letter. You have an admirer."

"Not the one I want." I raise my eyebrows, and she shakes her head, but I catch the small smile that plays on her lips. It hasn't been long enough for her to move on from her ex, but I'm enjoying this flirtatious relationship we're embarking on.

"What's it like to be so wanted?" Eloise leads the way, obviously knowing where she's going, but still yet to tell me.

"You would know."

A laugh bubbles out of her, and her perfectly shaped eyebrows furrow. "I don't. Trust me."

"You cannot tell me that men aren't hitting on you everywhere you go." I stuff my hands in my pockets to keep from touching her.

"Maybe I'm unapproachable." She turns into a building, and I look up to see us entering a café. "I need some caffeine."

I rush to grab the door for her. "I approached you."

"Thanks." She walks to the order line, and we stand together. "You approached me because you're a fixer, remember?"

I notice a few patrons take second glances at me, but thankfully—because of my goalie mask—I'm not as recognizable as some of the other guys, especially Rowan. That man can't disguise himself enough. Just in case, and because I don't want to be interrupted today with Eloise, I tilt my head down and away from those looking.

"Can I call you Lulu?" I ask, changing the subject.

The barista calls us up to place our order and Eloise ignores my question. "White mocha cold brew," she says, and when they ask for her name, she replies, "Lulu." She flips around and sticks her tongue out at me before venturing down the counter to wait for her order.

"I'll have a cold brew, black," I tell the barista. "Name is Lulu's sidekick."

Eloise can't fight her smile but tries to hide it by pretending to peruse the glass case filled with baked goods.

"Yeah, okay," the girl says, ringing us up.

I pull out my wallet, but Eloise presses her phone to the POS system, and it dings.

"Why are you paying?" I frown at her.

"You're my sidekick. You haven't let me pay a dime— today is my treat."

"Like a date?" I'm so tempted to touch her, but refrain. Instead, my hand nudges her along by her hip.

"Not a date."

We stand away from everyone else, waiting for our names to be called. "If you're paying for me, it's kind of like a date."

"It's not a date. And to answer your earlier question, you can call me Lulu, but I can't promise I'll answer to it."

Just then, the guy behind the counter calls her name and sets down her drink.

"He can, but I can't. So unfair," I say.

"Lulu's sidekick," the girl who made my drink says, sighing to her coworker before going to make another drink.

With both of our drinks in hand, we walk out of the café and down the street.

Eloise doesn't tell me where we're going, but I'd probably follow her wherever she wanted. All I think about is her, and it's been hard to know she's naked in the shower or wearing some barely-there pajamas to bed on the other side of the wall.

We cross a street, and she smiles at me as we walk up to a bookstore on the corner.

"Why did you think I wouldn't want to come here? You

assuming I'm a dumb jock?" I open the door, and she walks in.

"You don't have any books in your condo." She twirls around and walks backward. "Have you written your list yet?"

"No. But I'm thinking about it."

"We could each read a book." She twirls back around, and I admire her ass before she turns right and stops.

"If you want me in your bed reading you a goodnight story every night, just say so."

She chuckles. "I have a feeling I'd wake up, and you'd still be there, spooning me."

"Look how well you know me already."

Her head is tilted up, reading the genres on top of the shelves. "Maybe I'm just a good judge of character." She seems to find what she's looking for and heads down an aisle with purpose.

When she stops in the romance section, I ask, "Are you telling me something? I'm game if you want to read an erotica book and reenact the scenes."

She picks up a book and reads the back, ignoring me.

I walk around the section, checking out some titles like *Vow of Revenge*, about an academy for the kids of mafia bosses where apparently the dead fiancé from an arranged marriage shows back up.

"What kind of romance books do you like? The bad boys who push you to your knees or the sweet Prince Charmings on bended knee?" I lean my shoulder against the bookshelf to face her. "Something tells me you like a bad boy with a dirty mouth."

Her cheeks pinken. Fuck, I love earning that reaction.

"It's okay, you don't have to tell me." I push off the bookcase. "It can be our little secret."

"Why don't you go look at the sports biographies or something?" She shoos me away with her hand. "I'm sure you'll find a fan to fawn over you to keep you busy."

I walk over to a nearby table. "I like it when you fawn over me." I sip my cold brew. "Should we stop on the way home and pick up some cigarettes?" I quirk an eyebrow, and she groans, putting down the book in her hand and venturing down the aisle.

"Your ego seems to grow a little more every day."

"You love my ego, don't deny it." I see a title of a book and pick it up. "*Faking it with #41*? *Sneaking Around with #34*? Are these about athletes?" I flip it over and find out it's about a team of hockey players. Scanning the table, I realize it's all books about hockey players. "Is this a thing?" I hold one up to show Eloise.

She glances over. "Appears so."

"The entire table is covered in just hockey romance books. I knew we had women loving us because we play professionally, but I didn't know they're writing novels about us." I wave it at her. "Just think, you can have the real thing, and other woman can only read about having me."

She rolls her eyes. "Or I can just read the book and avoid the aggravation of the real thing." The corner of her mouth ticks up as she reads the back of another book she's pulled from the shelf.

"I wonder if the other guys know about this." I pick up another book, then another one, and realize that the majority of the time, the hockey player is a playboy. How cliché. "Do they write about other sports too?"

She returns the book she was reading to the shelf. "I haven't read in a really long time. Since reading a book is on my list to do before I turn thirty, that should tell you that I have no idea what's popular."

"I get it. Don't be jealous, Lulu. They can't get the real thing."

She grunts.

"Excuse me." A woman comes by, reaching for one of the books on the table.

"Sorry." I slide out of the way and watch her pick up a Piper Rayne book. "Can I ask you a question?"

She looks at me warily from the corner of her eye. "Sure."

"This is hockey romance... is it popular?"

Her eyebrows scrunch together. "Yeah, it's popular."

"It's what readers want?"

She nods.

"What about football or baseball?"

"Hockey is the most popular, I think." She seems confused as to why I'm asking.

I clap my hands together. "Thanks. That's awesome."

Eloise peeks around the corner. "You might want to get out of the way. He's about to blow up from an overinflated ego."

The woman just nods and takes her book, leaving the area.

"You scared that poor woman."

Eloise has two books in her arms. I hold my hand out, and she passes them over. None of them are about hockey players.

"This is disappointing. No hockey players?" I return them to her.

She walks by me. "Like you said, I have the real thing at home."

I follow her. "That you're not taking advantage of."

She giggles and walks toward the counter to pay.

"I can't wait to tell the guys about this," I say, following her.

She stops and checks out the display of bookmarks. "You are pretty giddy over finding out woman like to read hockey romance."

"It's cool, you know? I love my profession, and I know woman ogle me and stuff, but to be a hero in a book..."

"Technically, you aren't a hero in a book. It's not nonfiction."

"Okay, balloon popper, way to steal all my excitement." She hasn't, but I can't help ribbing her.

I'm still in shock about the whole hockey romance thing. I have a feeling the bookstore might be Tweetie's new pick-up place after I tell him about it.

"Well, you could go over and wear a sign around your neck that you're a real-life single hockey player."

"That's false advertising." I follow her to the checkout counter.

"You are a hockey player." She places her books on the counter, and the girl scans them.

"But I'm not really single."

"Yes, you are." She shakes her head at me.

"I'm taken. I'm just not dating her yet."

Eloise blows out a breath, shoots the cashier a smile, and pays for the books, ignoring me like she does when she doesn't know what to say.

I probably shouldn't be pushing and making it clear that I'm biding time until she's ready, but I can't help it. When I'm around her, I just want her to be mine.

Her phone dings, and it's on the counter face up from when she paid, so I can't help but read the text.

Tristan: I'm home. We need to talk.

I was wrong. It wasn't her popping my bubble, it was her goddamn ex-fiancé holding the pin.

twenty-three

Eloise

A knock sounds on the condo door, so I set down the book I bought yesterday and go to answer it. Rising on my tiptoes, I look through the peephole to see Kyleigh and Jade. Conor's been out all day, and I'm trying to pretend that him seeing Tristan's text yesterday isn't the reason he's keeping his distance.

I open the door. "Hi." I step to the side to welcome them in.

"We're going out shopping for fancy dresses and wondered if you'd come and help us pick them out?" Jade's gaze roams around the room, taking in the space. I can't tell if she's remembering her and Henry here, or if she's being a little protective and making sure there's no signs of us sleeping together.

"Of course. When am I not up for shopping?" I walk back over to the table, put my bookmark in the book, and set it back down. "Let me grab my purse."

"When did my brother become Betty Crocker?" Kyleigh calls from the kitchen.

I join her there to see her staring at the mixer on the counter. "Remember the other day with the flour and stuff?"

She leans her hip against the counter. "The day you moved in?"

I position my purse crossways over my chest. "He decided to help me bake a cake from scratch."

Kyleigh's nose scrunches, and she glances at Jade before looking back at me again. "Another item on the list?"

"I know what you guys are thinking, but he's just being kind. It's not a big deal."

Kyleigh shrugs. "If you say so."

"Come on, let's go." I wave them forward, away from the kitchen.

"How did the cake turn out?" Jade asks once we're on the concrete steps heading down to street level.

"A disaster. It didn't rise."

Kyleigh pushes open the security gate, and I'm thankful there aren't any women here today.

"Hey, guys, the other day I left, and there was a group of women hanging around here. Is that common?"

Jade and Kyleigh share a look and laugh.

"Unfortunately, yeah. Rowan always waited for me outside when we were dating."

"I had the security code from day one," Jade says with a grin.

"Oh, how nice for you," Kyleigh jokes, lightly pushing Jade's shoulder.

We wait at the curb for our Uber.

"What do you guys need fancy dresses for?" I ask.

"Well, Rowan and Henry's agent holds a big dinner for all of his hockey clients in August so it's before they start preseason," Jade explains. "We just need cocktail dresses."

"Anywhere specific you guys want to go?"

The Uber pulls up to the curb, and Kyleigh talks to the driver to make sure it's ours before opening the back door and climbing in. "We were hoping you'd guide us since you're the one with all the fashion sense. I just told the driver Michigan Avenue."

"You're a wedding dress designer," I say to her.

"Yeah, I can work on an elaborate bridal gown, but not cocktail dresses or even everyday wear. I can see why my brother is so smitten with you. You always look like you stepped out of a fashion blog."

Jade side-eyes me, and Kyleigh catches it, giving me no choice but to tell her.

"I used to do a little fashion blogging, but those days are over."

"They don't have to be," Jade says.

I sigh. "It would take me a long time to find followers again."

Thankfully, they let it go. It's something I can't think about yet. My future still feels very rocky, and my first step has to be settling things with Tristan and getting him out of my life. Which reminds me...

"So, Tristan messaged me yesterday. He's back from our honeymoon."

Jade's head whips in my direction, and Kyleigh leans forward with the same reaction.

"What did you tell him?" Jade asks.

"Nothing. Not yet at least."

Jade's hand falls to my knee. "Just get it over with and put him behind you."

"I know. I plan to, but I don't want to see him again."

"Make it a public place," Kyleigh says.

"And I'll go with you. I'll sit at the bar and wait." Jade isn't asking, she's telling me.

"I'm sure my brother would go." Kyleigh smiles wide.

I roll my eyes. "Yeah, I don't need another fight to break out."

"That's why I'll go. He won't even know I'm there." It's clear from Jade's voice that she won't take no for an answer.

I wouldn't mind some support for after I say goodbye to him. Not because I think I'll be sad—I'm sure about my decision—but I don't think I'll want to be alone. Even if I know it's the right call, thinking about how much time and energy I put into the relationship to have it not work out is upsetting.

"I'll let you know."

We arrive at Michigan Avenue and file out of the Uber. Kyleigh and Jade let me lead them to the stores I frequent the most.

"How do you know all this?" Kyleigh asks when I lead them into one of the smaller shops that I love but isn't nearly as popular as some of the others.

"She's probably been to about one hundred cocktail parties. She was going to marry a Somerset after all." Jade rolls her eyes.

"Stop it," I chastise her.

"I still remember when I went with you to spend the night at your grandparents' house because it was your dad's weekend. They made us go to the country club, and I had to borrow a dress from your closet there. I was in awe of all the dresses and shoes you had."

I nod, wondering what it will be like to leave that life completely. I'm sure my grandparents are more than upset. Their silence speaks more than if they'd reached out to yell at me. They're embarrassed by their granddaughter's actions, I'm sure. Another thing I need to deal with, but it's been so much easier to ignore it all.

"I always hated the country club." I sit on a chair while

Kyleigh and Jade try on some dresses that I picked out for them.

"You should have seen it, Ky. It was like she was like some princess, her grandma taking her around the room and introducing her as her beautiful granddaughter, Eloise. Oh, and this is her friend." She uses her best uppity rich accent. "No name or anything, like I was nothing."

Kyleigh comes out first wearing a black high neck halter dress stitched with a diamond beaded pattern. It falls perfectly over her body, showing off her beautiful figure. It stops midway down her calf with a slit up the back.

"Rowan is definitely going to have to thank me." I smile at her.

She goes to the three-way mirror. "I love it." She circles around to the see the back. "Yoga is doing my body good." She laughs. "I was skeptical about the length since I usually always wear dresses above the knee, but it's gorgeous."

"I'm glad you like it and that you trusted me with my rule to try on the dress I liked for you first."

We all laugh, since that was Kyleigh's rule when I tried on wedding dresses at her boutique.

Jade's dressing room door opens.

"Oh my god!" Kyleigh covers her mouth. "Jade..."

"I know, right?" She grins at us.

I smile, my chest warming at seeing them both so happy.

Jade's is a blush, off-the-shoulder dress that is ruched on one side. Her dress is also mid-length, but it flares a little more with a dramatic slit over her right thigh. She looks supremely elegant.

"Your boys both owe me big time." I clap my hands together in delight. They both look so beautiful.

They stare at themselves in the mirror, putting their arms around each other.

"It's our first year going to this thing." Jade's shoulders rise with excitement. "Thank you so much, Eloise. I never would have picked this out for myself."

"Well, we're not done, ladies. We have shoes and jewelry still to go." I shoo my hand at them to go get changed. "Let's get out of those dresses. We have things to do."

They laugh and take one last look at themselves before going into their designated dressing rooms.

My phone vibrates in my pocket, so I pull it out. A text from Tristan.

> Stop ignoring me. Call me.

My stomach sinks, but he's right. I can't just pretend this isn't something I need to address.

> Tomorrow night. Seven o'clock at The Urban Acre.

> You know I hate that place.

> Will you be there or not?

> Fine.

I click off the phone and tuck it into my purse, my belly filled with nerves. I want to take Jade with me, but at the same time, I feel as if it's something I should do on my own.

My friends come out of their dressing rooms, each holding their dresses. I love the way they're smiling and talking about how excited they are to have Rowan and Henry see them in their dresses. Somewhere along the line, I forgot what it was like to dress for your man. Was there ever a time that Tristan looked at me with awe when I stepped out to show him what I was wearing to a function we were attending? Maybe when you come from a world where dressing up is common, it's not as exciting, or maybe it's just because Tristan was always more worried about what he was wearing.

For a moment, I wonder what it would be like to walk out in a cocktail dress to show Conor. The space between my thighs hums because if it's like when I catch him staring at me when I walk out in my pajamas, I'd love to see his reaction to a dress he knew he'd be unzipping me out of later that night. Maybe one day.

twenty-four

Conor

I'M BACK AT THE GYM, AND THESE ARE MY FAVORITE kind of days because we're all here. Even Henry.

"I heard the girls went shopping," Rowan says to Henry.

"Yeah, it's our first time trusting Owen and Waylon to watch Bodhi. God knows what's going on over there."

I chuckle because Jade's twin teenage brothers are super competitive and always seem to be up to something they shouldn't be.

"Where's Mack?" Tweetie asks, referencing Henry's manny.

Henry blows out a breath. "He's on vacation. Before I forget, there's something I've been thinking about that I wanted to bring up. You know Jagger's dinner?"

We're all by the weights, doing different exercises. My agent, Jagger, gets all of his hockey clients together every August for a big dinner to kick off the season. This year he's having it in Milwaukee, so we only have to drive there instead of flying. Not that I'm opposed to flying somewhere, but I don't really want to be away from Eloise for long.

"What about it?" I ask, putting my weights down and grabbing my water bottle.

"I think we should go camping that weekend," Henry says.

Rowan and Tweetie stare at him as though he's just missed scoring on an empty net.

"Why would we do that?" Tweetie asks.

"I get that there won't be any girls there. Well, other than the ones we bring." Henry glares at Tweetie. "But you can survive for the weekend, I'm sure."

"You're bringing your women?" Tweetie lifts the weights to his sides, staring at himself in the mirror.

"They'd be with us for the dinner, so yeah... I think it will be fun. Something different." Henry's really pushing this.

I can't say it's bad idea, but I don't want to be sleeping in a tent with Tweetie and hearing my sister moaning my team-mate's name.

"I'm sure Kyleigh will be game," Rowan says.

I've never thought of my sister as the camping type, but that's for Rowan to figure out now.

"What about you?" Henry asks me.

I shrug. "You buy my earplugs, and I'm in, but I get my own tent." I eye Tweetie, and he scoffs.

"Like I'd want your snoring ass in my tent. I might bring someone if we're really going." He puts his weights down and sits next to Henry on the bench across from Rowan and me.

"You're going to bring someone?" I ask.

Tweetie shrugs. "Yeah, if I'm stuck in the woods with all you fools, I at least want to get laid at night." He laughs at me. "Sorry I can't be your wingman."

"What about Eloise? I think she's shopping with them today."

I startle. Henry waited until now to tell me that?

The thought had come to my mind about asking Eloise to be my date to Jagger's dinner, but I was afraid if word got out about the party, and my picture got taken... She flipped out so badly that night at the hotel, and I don't want to put her in a bad situation when things with Tristan still aren't resolved.

"She got a text from Tristan yesterday." All of them remain quiet, so I continue. "And I haven't asked what her plans are."

"You mean she might go back to him?" Tweetie asks with disgust.

I shake my head. "I don't think so, but I'm sure they have to talk. Which..."

"Fuck, you really like her." Now Tweetie looks horrified.

Henry elbows him.

"Where the fuck have you been? He ran into her wedding and objected." Rowan shakes his head.

"I thought it was a drunk thing." Tweetie shrugs.

"Yeah, and then he asked her to move in with him just because." Henry shakes his head and groans.

"Jesus, I hate this feeling inside of me. We were out shopping yesterday, and we were flirting the whole time. You know when you get those flutters in your stomach when she brushes up against you?"

Rowan and Henry glance at one another while Tweetie tries to act as if he doesn't have any idea what I'm talking about.

"Then the text came in, and it was like freezing cold water being dumped over us. I ended up retreating for most of the night. I was never adamantly against commitment, I just hadn't met anyone who made me want to, but I also didn't think I'd ever be stuck in this situation. She's nowhere near ready for a new relationship. Maybe asking her to be my roommate was a stupid idea."

"Ya think?" Tweetie gets up from the bench and picks up his weights again.

"It's a shitty situation you're in, no doubt, but it's her decision to make when she's ready," Henry says.

"He's right," Rowan adds. "You know how you hear those stories where a couple breaks up and then one of them is engaged or married to someone else, like, six months later? If she never truly loved Tristan, and it was something she felt forced to do, she might not need that much time to get past it. You might've stopped the wedding, but I saw her face when she stood at the end of the aisle."

Henry nods. "Yeah, I saw it too."

"What?" I look between them.

"She looked like she was walking to the electric chair," Rowan says.

"She looked at Tristan, but he was busy laughing it up with his best man. Her disappointment was clear before she put on a fake-as-shit smile." Henry brings his drink to his lips.

"And yet she was going to marry him," Tweetie says, lifting again while the rest of us shoot the shit.

"Because she was scared to call it off," Henry says, setting down his drink. "I've known Eloise longer than you guys, and she doesn't like to see people upset. Jade's alluded that her relationship with her dad was strained for a lot of years. Like Jade, Eloise was yearning for his attention. Then he dies after he tells her that he loves her and Tristan together and how happy seeing them together makes him."

"Fuck, really?" Rowan asks, pushing a hand through his sweaty hair.

Henry nods. "Give her some time, man, but I don't think you'll be waiting forever for her to get over Tristan."

I wonder if Henry could be right. I guess the only way to find out is to ask her.

Henry and Rowan stand and pick up their weights, spacing out to do shoulder raises.

"She sure is spending a shit-ton of time with you," Tweetie says. "What have you guys been doing?"

I stand and put plates on the bar. "We went to the bookstore yesterday." And then I remember what I wanted to tell them. "You'll never believe this, guys, but they write about fictional hockey players in these romance books. Like, there's a whole table of books with the hockey player as the leading male. I guessed they're called hockey romances. And there're so many books with the word puck in the title it's crazy."

Each of them stare at me in the mirror.

"No shit?" Tweetie says.

"Seriously, it's a huge thing."

I catch the door opening in the mirror and watch Easton Bailey walk in. He's a hot shot on Chicago's professional baseball team.

"What are you doing here?" Rowan asks.

"I just needed something different." He changes out of his street shoes and comes over to me. "I'll spot you."

"Thanks." I lower myself on the bench, positioning my hands on the bar.

"This season is shit, and no, I don't want to talk about it." Easton stands by my head, staring into the mirror at the other three guys' reflections.

"Well, Pinkie was just telling us how hockey guys are a big thing in romance books," Rowan says.

"Really?" Easton looks down at me. "What about baseball?"

I lift the bar off the handlebar. "Sorry. One lady told me it's hockey and football first. She didn't even mention baseball."

He grunts. "That's because we use our brains, and we

don't act like barbarians hitting one another into the boards and glass."

We all laugh.

"Don't be jealous because we're tougher," Tweetie says, flexing his muscles.

"We play America's pastime," Easton says.

"I'm not saying it's fair, but you guys better start charging the mound and throwing some fists if you want to rank on the romance book boyfriend lists." I put the bar back after doing my reps.

"I'll get right on that. Then again, if we don't start winning, it just might start getting ugly." Easton nods toward the bar for me to do another round of reps.

For the rest of the afternoon, Easton fills us in on the Colts and how they won't make the playoffs this year and how he can't wait for the season to be over so he can go back to his small hometown in Alaska to regroup. We gripe about how long our seasons are, both baseball and hockey spanning a good part of the year.

The entire time, I calculate a timeline in my head of how long I'll have to wait until Eloise might be ready to date, and I consider whether I can really start dating someone during hockey season. I've never done it, and I know it'll be hard as hell to balance the two.

Then again, Rowan did it with Kyleigh. Maybe if you want something badly enough, it's not that hard. First, I need her to put Tristan as far in her rearview mirror as possible.

twenty-five

Eloise

I walk into The Urban Acre and stop at the hostess. She's a cute little redhead who appears frazzled as if it's her first day on the job.

"I have a reservation under Corbin for two."

"Oh, your party is already here, but he said it should've been under Somerset." Her head tilts with an expression as if to say, "you're so silly."

I glance into the restaurant. Sure enough, Tristan is sitting at a table for two against the wall, his thumbs roaming over the screen of his phone.

"It's Corbin, and I see my party. Thank you."

I stalk across the room, reprimanding myself for taking out my aggression with Tristan on an innocent hostess.

"Tristan," I say, my hand landing on the chair across from him.

He looks up, pockets his phone, and shifts his body to stand.

I raise my hand and pull out my own chair. "I have it."

I'm sure it's only habit for him to pull out my chair at this point. A Somerset is raised to always pull out the chairs of ladies, after all. I sit in my chair and keep my purse tucked into my lap.

"Oh, I forgot, you're an independent woman now." He rolls his eyes. His skin is a darker bronze, and his hair is painted with more highlights than before the ceremony.

"Let's just have this conversation." I sit up straighter. "I'm sor—"

"Actually, I'd like to start."

I inwardly growl. "Fine." I hold my hand out over the table, motioning for him to take the floor.

"Why did a hockey player stop our wedding?"

"Tristan..." I sigh. "Shouldn't that have been your question, I don't know, before you went on our honeymoon?" I don't give him the satisfaction of bringing up the blonde in the picture.

The waitress comes over, and I order a white wine while he orders a scotch.

"After that scene, my parents demanded I go cool myself off and clear my head."

I huff. "Fair. But you didn't feel the need to know why I backed out at all? Doesn't that tell you everything you needed to know?"

"You embarrassed my entire family. You embarrassed your family. I deserved that getaway. Your grandparents have been apologizing profusely to my parents and said they..." He doesn't finish, but I have an idea what he's going to say. "Have you talked to them?"

I shake my head, and my chest squeezes. "No."

The waitress drops off our drinks and asks if we're going to order any food.

Tristan leans back in his chair and picks up the menu.

"I wasn't going to eat," I say.

He tips the menu down and his blue gaze lands on me. "You left me at the altar. The least you can do is share a meal with me."

A mouse-like sound comes out of the waitress, and I see her eyes are wide when I glance at her.

I pick up my menu and say the first thing I read. "I'll have the Caprese salad."

"Watching what you're eating so that hockey player can throw you around?"

The waitress eyes us both.

I scoot back my chair. "We're done here, Tristan."

He lifts off his seat, reaching his arm out to stop me. "I'm sorry. The anger is still there. Obviously." Without looking at the waitress, he passes the menu to her. "I'll take the garlic butter steak bites with the asparagus. Make sure there's extra garlic on the meat."

I look up at her, and she looks at him like she'd like to roll her eyes, snatching the menu from his hands and walking away.

"Let's try to be respectful, okay?" I know I hurt him and shocked him by calling off the wedding, but I won't sit here and take him disrespecting me. Not anymore.

He nods and lowers back down. I do the same and hang my purse on the back of my chair.

A woman crossing the room to the bar grabs my attention. She's wearing sunglasses and a big hat with a sundress, but there's something oddly familiar about her.

"I apologize, but you humiliated me, Eloise. Rumors are all over town about what happened. I can't even show my face anywhere."

My foot bounces under the table. "It wasn't my intention. I wasn't planning on what happened. I am sorry for that."

He takes a sip of his scotch and twirls the cup in his palm. "Want to tell me who he is?"

"He's a guy I met the night of my bachelorette party." I raise my hand before he can interrupt me. "Before you jump to assumptions, nothing happened between us."

It's a half truth, I know. Something did happen, but nothing physical, and that's probably all he cares about. I don't want to hurt Tristan any more than I already have.

"So, he didn't want you to marry me because what, you're such a great conversationalist?" He takes another sip of his scotch. Part of my wants to fire back a comment about what he might have been doing with the stripper from his bachelor party, but I somehow refrain.

"I like to think I can hold a good conversation. At the very least, I'm a good listener since that's all I ever did with you." My own annoyance with him shines through.

"Who's throwing the stones now?"

I take a deep breath, unwinding my silverware from the napkin and placing the napkin in my lap. "I don't want to go tit for tat, Tristan. I'm sorry for what happened. Yes, I met Conor the night of my bachelorette party, but all he did was help me with Penelope because she was so drunk."

"I should've known it was Penelope's doing." He sips his scotch again.

The waitress brings over a basket of fresh bread, but neither of us touch it.

"It's not her fault." I lean forward. "I was ready to call it off before Conor busted in."

"I just love how you refer to him by name now." He finishes his scotch and slides the glass onto the table.

There is no way this conversation will go smoothly if he's finished his drink in five minutes.

"I'm sorry I hurt you. I am. And I wish I'd had the courage to talk to you about how I felt before we were at the altar, but let me ask you something. Do you even love me? Think hard before you answer, Tristan. Would you die for me?"

He laughs so loudly some of the other guests peer over. "That's so cliché, Eloise."

"It's really not."

"Okay, I'd take a bullet for you," he mocks me.

"Fine. I'll put it this way..." I take another deep breath and clench my fists under the table. "I left you at the altar because I want more than you're willing to offer me. I want to be number one."

He rolls his eyes.

"I want to be taken seriously. My wants and needs weren't being met with you, and when I tried to talk to you about it over the years, you weren't interested in hearing me. You crushed me under that big thumb of yours our entire relationship, and I think you honestly thought it would work."

"What would work?" He picks up his empty scotch glass and wiggles it in the air to the waitress who's walking to a neighboring table. I absolutely hate when he does that. It's so condescending.

"Keep pushing me down. Keep putting me in my place. I wanted to make you happy, so I did everything you asked. I wasn't even the woman you fell in love with anymore."

The waitress brings over a refill, and he studies me. "You're not now."

"I am. What I'm doing right now *is* the woman you met. I was independent, had dreams and wants in life. Maybe it was a little here and a little here, I don't know, but at some point, the person I used to be was gone, and I didn't realize it until it was too late. Until..." I can't say that it wasn't until another man brought out a side of me I didn't know still existed. "I was standing in the doorway of the church about to walk down the aisle, and I knew that neither of us would be happy in the marriage. Do you even realize that you didn't look at me until I was halfway down the aisle?"

"I guess I didn't know that was the standard, the groom

watching the bride walk down the whole aisle. Merrick told a joke, and it was funny."

I sip my wine. More like drain half the glass. Nothing is going to be accomplished tonight. "I'm sorry, Tristan. You picked the wrong girl. I can't fit in your box. I can't slide into your life in the way that you want. I can't just be by your side as a decoration to dust off when needed. I want more for myself than to be Tristan Somerset's wife."

He tears off a piece of bread and picks up his knife to spread the butter. My gaze goes back to the bar, and the woman I noticed earlier is now talking to a man two stools down. He's wearing a baseball hat and a jacket with the collar up even though it's ninety degrees outside today. They almost seem to be in a heated argument.

"I turned down a lot of women who would've loved the life I was going to give you." He bites the bread aggressively.

"Well, maybe you can look some of them up now." I dig into my purse and pull out the key, sliding it across the table. "Here's the key for the house."

"Keep it as a souvenir, I changed the locks. Obviously after you left my takeout containers out to spoil. How childish can you get? And the sign in the pool? Grow up. Do I have to remind you that I was the one who was left at the altar?"

"I wouldn't have left you if you would have respected me." I'm seething, but there's no point in arguing with him about this. He's never going to see my side of things.

"My mom is sending the wedding gifts back." He ignores my comment.

"Fine. Thank her for me. I understand if your family wants me to pay them back for all the money that was lost—"

"Are you kidding me? The only thing worse than you ditching me at the altar would be people finding out that my family forced you to pay us back like we're paupers."

I have to clamp down my jaw, so I don't say something insulting back. I just nod. "Is there anything else?"

He puts the half-eaten piece of bread on the plate and sits back, his eyes on me for an uncomfortable minute. He huffs and lets out a deep breath, some of the tension leaving his shoulders. "I suppose you make some good points. Maybe I'm not ready for a wife."

"I should have spoken up sooner."

He shrugs. "I'm not sure I would have listened."

"You didn't."

"Okay, I was being nice, trying not to end up as enemies."

The waitress brings our dishes over and slides them in front of us.

I grab her attention before she leaves. "Actually, can I have a to-go container please?"

"You can't even have a meal with me?"

I look over at the bar again, seeing the man and woman glancing over their shoulders, their sunglasses not doing anything to disguise them. I can't believe they followed me here.

"I think it's best we end this as amicably as we can," I say.

The waitress brings over my takeout container, and I put the salad in it. I reach for my purse, and Tristan stops cutting his steak bites.

"I got it." He sets his silverware on the plate.

This is it. This is likely the last time I'll see him. I can't explain the sadness filling me like a vase with water being poured into it. I wanted this. I needed this, but Tristan was a big part of my life for so many years. He listened to the eulogy I wrote for my dad. He stood by my side at my dad's funeral as the casket was lowered into the ground. He held me for nights afterward, telling me everything would be okay.

I stand, and he slides out of his chair to stand in front of me.

The two fools at the bar are now watching us over their shoulders.

"Have a great life, Eloise." Tristan opens his arms.

I step into them and hug him back. It doesn't make me feel warm or safe. It's just a transaction, as if it's sealing the end to our relationship.

"I'm sure your Mrs. Tristan Somerset is out there somewhere."

"I think I'll be putting pause on that for a while."

I smile and nod, stepping back from him. "I'm sorry for hurting you. Goodbye, Tristan."

"Goodbye, Eloise *Corbin*." He winks.

I turn around, heading out of the restaurant. It's done and over, but I wasn't expecting this grief mingled with relief inside me. I hate the feeling of hope woven around a layer of failure, as if I don't deserve the opportunity of rediscovering myself.

I stop at a light post once I'm out of the restaurant, leaning my back on it and waiting until they walk out. "Hello, Jade. Hello, Conor. Enjoy your meal?"

twenty-six

Conor

"Relax, that's her goodbye hug."

I wasn't happy to see Jade walk in the restaurant right after me. I was here early enough that Eloise wouldn't see me. Tristan was early, and he doesn't appear to pay much attention to anything but himself, so I was able to change my seats to have the perfect view through the mirror on the back wall of the bar. Then Jade came in, and I saw Eloise track her journey across the restaurant.

"How do you know?" I ask, the two of us now glancing over our shoulders as if the reflection in the mirror has been skewed somehow.

"Her ass is out. It's a polite hug, not a 'let's get back together' hug."

Still, I hate seeing his arms wrapped around her. I shouldn't be here. I know this is Eloise's business to handle, and she doesn't need me. I'm still unsure whether it's protectiveness, or if I'm worried that he's going to talk her into getting back together.

"Oh, jeez, stop the jealous alpha thing." Jade slides off the stool. "She's gone."

I climb down from my stool, tossing some money on the bar top. "I'm not jealous."

"Sure, you are. Be prepared, I'm pretty sure she saw us."

"Because you came in late and wearing that ridiculous hat."

We walk toward the door.

"Have a great evening," the hostess says, waving.

We both mumble a thank you and goodbye.

"You're not even in disguise. You and the rest of your little gang think sunglasses and a baseball hat disguise you. That's ridiculous."

I push open the door for Jade, and she steps out.

"Should I have worn a Gumby costume?" I ask.

"Well, you could have left the jacket at home. Chicago's in the middle of a heatwave."

We fall in line on the sidewalk, but Jade stops, and I bump into her shoulder. I look up to see what's made her stop and see Eloise leaning against a light pole, waiting for us.

"Hello, Jade. Hello, Conor. Enjoy your meal?" Her eyebrows are raised.

I strip off my sunglasses.

"You know I can handle myself." Eloise pushes off the light pole and heads down the street.

Jade quickens her footsteps to catch up, and I follow, of course.

"I'm sorry, Eloise, I just wanted to make sure he didn't do something..." She shakes her head, tearing off her hat. "I wanted to be here for you in case he said some really shitty things."

Did he? If so, I might just turn around and break his fucking nose. Finish what we started at the church.

Eloise has to stop at a corner and wait to cross, so she studies both of us. "Look at you two. You looking like you came from the Kentucky Derby, and you"—she points at me—"are you trying to be James Dean with a baseball hat?"

I strip off the leather jacket I borrowed from Tweetie from when he dressed up as Danny from *Grease* at Halloween last year. My white T-shirt is close to being see-through from sweat.

"I can handle myself." The pedestrian sign blinks, and Eloise crosses the street.

Jade and I look at one another.

"We know that." Jade rushes and touches Eloise's arm to stop her once we're on the other side of the street. "But you don't need to do this alone."

Eloise moves out of the way of pedestrian traffic. "I'm sick of people thinking I can't survive without their help."

Jade sighs. "That's not why I went to the restaurant. I went because I'm your best friend. You were having a final conversation with the man you were supposed to marry. I didn't think you'd be skipping out of there, and I wanted to offer you a shoulder to cry on if you needed it." She thumbs in my direction. "I didn't realize I was going to have competition."

I point at my chest. "Are you blaming me for something?"

Jade scoffs. "If it was only me, she would've understood. She's only reacting this way because of you being all overprotective."

"Overprotective? I'm here for the same reason you are." I scowl at her.

"Let's remember you started a fist fight in the foyer of a church." Jade crosses her arms and raises her eyebrows.

"That guy is a douche. Don't tell me you didn't want to hit him too."

Jade struggles to fight the smile playing at her lips. "That's not the point."

"No, the point is..." Eloise sticks her head into our little huddle. "I'm a grown woman. I chose to end that relationship. I appreciate you both coming. I do. But I really want to be alone right now and reflect. So why don't you two go have dinner together or something?" She waves her hand between us, turns around, and walks down the street.

I start to follow, but Jade grabs my arm and tugs me in the opposite direction. "Don't follow her."

"I can cheer her up." I turn my body as if I'm not going to listen to Jade.

"You're coming with me." She tugs on my arm.

"Why?"

She raises her hand for a taxi, and one immediately pulls up along the curb. "Because you can't be trusted. You get some boy time with Bodhi tonight."

She opens the door of the taxi, and I take one last look at Eloise's back continuing down the street. Her legs look so fucking good in her summer dress. I wish she would've picked a burlap sack to wear to say goodbye to her no-good, asshole fiancé.

"Get in," Jade says.

"This is completely unnecessary." I climb in, and she gets in next to me, setting the hat in the middle seat. It's big enough to be another person.

"If I let you go home, you won't be able to control yourself. Trust me, Conor, if you want a chance with her, give her time to sort this all out on her own."

"But—"

"There's no but. If you go in there and try to fix it by crossing something off her list or bringing her ice cream or some other sweet gesture, you might end up just being the rebound guy. Now, if all you want to do is have sex with her, then I'll have the driver drop you off. Is that what you want?"

"Are you asking if I want to have sex with her?"

Her eyes bore into mine, and she inhales a deep breath. "Only. I meant do you *only* want to have sex with her."

"No." I shake my head, and my shoulders sag. "Just so you know, this is taking all the restraint I have. I'm going to listen to you, but if you're wrong... well, I'm not gonna be happy."

"Ask Henry. I'm never wrong."

She laughs, and I shake my head, rolling my eyes.

The cab drives away from my building and toward Jade and Henry's house. Probably a good idea for her to take me far away. The fixer in me wants so badly to step in and make Eloise feel better. But if this means I get an honest chance with Eloise, I'll grin and bear this discomfort. Hell, I'm a fucking professional hockey goalie. I've taken worse for far less of a reward.

twenty-seven

Eloise

It's been a week since my dinner with Tristan, and the sadness over the end of my relationship has slowly melted away, leaving only relief behind. Relief that I finally got up the nerve to say what I should have a long time ago. I feel as though I can finally leave that part of my life behind and discover this new version of me.

Conor has been giving me space ever since our little spat on the sidewalk, if you want to call it that. I'm kind of surprised honestly. Usually, Conor's MO is to cheer me up. The man hates to see people upset, I think.

I walk out of my bedroom as Conor is coming in the front door, obviously returning from working out.

"Hey," I say with a smile.

He stops and tosses a pile of mail on the table by the door. "Hey."

"Good workout?"

"I was training. I work with a guy before the preseason to

make sure my excellent skills remain intact." He doesn't crack a smile, just heads into the kitchen to grab a water. "What about you? What are you up to?"

Ugh, I hate this distance between us. More than I would have thought I would.

"I'm heading out to go do some random acts of kindness."

He peeks his head out of the fridge. "Include dinner, and I'm game." When he grins at me, my shoulders relax a bit.

"I don't remember inviting you." I turn and smile to myself as I grab my purse from the chair.

"You know it will be more fun with me."

He's right. It will.

This past week, I needed the time to reevaluate what I want my future to look like, and no matter what version I imagined, Conor was there. Maybe we won't last. Maybe we will. But I'm not going to be afraid to put myself out there just because it didn't work out with Tristan. I learned some lessons from how everything went down with him, and I plan to bring them into my next relationship. So, I'm done teetering the line with Conor. We need to figure out what side of it we're going to fall on. I'm not suggesting I'm going to tie myself to his headboard naked for his taking, but I don't want to ignore the chemistry between us either.

"You have about ten minutes," I say.

"I don't do a lot of things fast, but I can get ready in that short of time." He heads toward his bedroom, but stops and comes back over, standing at the back of the couch. "I'm sorry for last week."

I peer up from my phone. "You don't have to apologize. I just got defensive, because... well, you know. But I know you and Jade just wanted to be there for me."

He stays in place and holds my gaze. "I did want to be there for you in case he did something shitty, but... I was afraid too."

I drop my phone in my lap. "About what?"

"I was afraid you were going to take him back." He shifts his weight from one leg to the other, obviously uncomfortable. It's amusing that I can make this big, tough, successful hockey player uncomfortable. Scratch that, it's endearing.

"And had I, what would you have done?" I shouldn't ask. This line of conversation could twist us in a place we're not ready for.

"I'm pretty sure I would've interfered." Again, another shift of his body, his knuckles white along the back of the couch.

"Oh."

"That's it?" He arches an eyebrow.

"Well, it didn't come to that. Can I really get mad at you for wanting to fight for me?"

His gorgeous smile wipes away all the worry lining his face. I smile back and am relieved that things feel lighter between us now.

"I'll be right back." He circles around and heads into his bedroom.

Once the door shuts, I tip my head back against the cushions, repeating to myself to trust this feeling in my gut. If I'd done that in the first place, I wouldn't have ended up running out on my own wedding.

———

Half an hour later, after we've stopped to get some coffees, we're waiting for the light to change so we can cross the street.

"Okay, how many acts of kindness do you want to do?" Conor asks.

"Well, thirty total, but I have a few months. I was thinking I'd do a couple today."

He nods, looking around. "How elaborate do you want

them to be? Do we count picking up that piece of garbage as an act or opening a door for someone?"

"Garbage yes, but it can't be like thirty pieces of garbage, and we're done. One piece of garbage. Opening a door for someone..." My head bobs right and left. "Not for hot girls though."

Conor laughs and wraps his lips around his straw. He swallows, and his hand falls on my shoulder. "No hot girls and no hot guys then." He eyes me, looking for a response.

"Deal."

"Well, there's your piece of garbage." He points at an empty coffee cup on the sidewalk. Someone must have missed the garbage can or didn't even try to get it in.

"Okay..." I stare at the piece of garbage. "Let me get my wipes out." I shuffle over to the wall, out of foot traffic, and open my purse, taking out my wipes. "Here, hold this." I shove my coffee at him, which he takes with no complaint.

I grab a wipe, pick up the cup, and toss it in the trash can.

Conor leans against the brick wall. "Want me to get you a hazmat suit?"

I give him my sassy shut up look, which only makes him laugh. Taking out my sanitizer, I put it on my hands before taking my coffee back from Conor. We walk some more, and I rack my brain for what else we can do.

"Want to donate blood?" I ask.

"You're not afraid of needles?"

"Are you?"

"I'm not afraid of anything." He puffs out his chest and turns us to the right when we reach the corner.

"I don't believe you. Give me something." I take a sip from my drink.

He stops us around the corner of the busy street and pulls out his phone, resting his cup in the elbow of his arm against his chest. "No, there's nothing."

His thumbs move across the screen.

"You're lying. Snakes? Flying? Heights?"

Conor shakes his head, still looking at his phone. "Nope."

"Monogamy?"

He peeks up, and his expression says, "Are you really asking me that?"

After pressing more buttons on his phone and reading over the screen, he pockets his phone. "I hope you're not afraid of needles because tomorrow at ten, you're giving blood. There were no more appointments available for today."

"Just me?" I'm trying not to be disappointed that he's having me do it on my own.

"I'll be there. Good thing for you, I'm not afraid of needles. Nor am I afraid of monogamy, for the record."

I bite my lip. "It was just a guess. When was your last serious relationship?"

He leads us back to the main street. "College maybe, and even then, it was only a few months."

"Interesting."

He sips his drink, side-eyeing me. "My schedule has always been the problem. In high school, I had girls I went to dances with, and I had one girlfriend I dated for, like, six months. I rarely saw her. In college, I was too focused on making it to the professional league, and I wasn't willing to sacrifice my future for a relationship. I think over time, you just get used to going out with the guys and picking up women." He takes another sip of his drink. "As horrible as it sounds, early in my career, it was kind of a high. You go from a regular guy to women acting like you're a celebrity they can't believe they're seeing in the flesh. I probably took advantage of it truthfully."

An elderly man with a cane is walking down the street, and he turns toward the local tea shop. Conor hurries over and opens the door for him. He thanks him, giving him a double-take but enters without asking Conor if he is who he thinks he is.

"Hey, make your own list." I grin at him.

The door shuts behind the man, and we continue down the sidewalk.

"I did." Conor nudges me with a light tug on my elbow. "You inspired me."

"Are you going to share it with me?"

He tosses his cold brew into a trash can as we pass by, raising his fingers as if he scored a basket. Always the athlete. "I don't know."

"Hey. I shared mine with you."

He shrugs. "Technically, it fell out, and I found it."

"Come on."

"What's it to you?" he asks, grabbing my hand and jogging across the street before we miss the light.

I like the way my hand feels in his, but he drops it as soon as we've cleared the road.

"Tell me one thing from the list." I hold up a finger.

"All right. To go offline for a weekend."

"Oh, that's a good one. I want to add that to mine." I toss my empty cup in the next trash can we pass.

"Sorry, it's not thirty-one things before you turn thirty."

He stops at one of the businesses and opens the door for me. I go inside, not sure what this place is, but not questioning him.

"It can be whatever I want it to be. It can be thirty-two."

"When do you turn thirty?" He puts his hand on the small of my back to lead me farther into the store, and I memorize the shape and feel of it so that I can revisit it later.

"November."

"Do you really want to add to that list? I'm not sure you'll have time to finish yours before you turn thirty."

I stop and stare at him. "You're putting stipulations on it

like you're all high and mighty because you have, like, two years before you turn forty." I have no idea how I keep a straight face.

His forehead crinkles, and he narrows his eyes. "I'm not Tweetie. I have almost a fucking decade before I turn forty."

I stick my tongue out at him and giggle, finally looking around to see where we are. I realize it's a boutique that just opened that I've heard about and wanted to come check out.

"Why are we here?" Did he somehow know I wanted to see what this place has to offer?

"I meant to ask you before we arrived, but then you insulted me, and we got distracted. I have to attend a dinner my agent is hosting, and I'd really like you to be my date."

Excitement wars with nerves in my chest. I open my mouth to respond, but he shakes his head, holding my gaze.

"Before you answer, Jade and Kyleigh will be there, so you won't be alone. And Henry wants to go camping after, so it'll be a whole weekend thing. We can cross off camp outside, watch a sunrise, and spontaneous trip from your list. And if you really want to go for more, I'll even book us a train trip there."

"Um... and this?"

"I hope you'll allow me to buy your dress for the event, and for selfish reasons, I want to see you do a fashion show for me."

My stomach feels as if it has bubbles expanding and popping inside. "When is it?"

He tucks me into the corner away from everyone. "Remember that spontaneous part? It's next weekend."

"Okay." I nod.

"Okay?" he clarifies.

"Yeah, sure." I lean in close. "You pick out a dress, and I pick out a dress." I draw back and raise my eyebrows.

"Deal." He breaks away from me and peruses the displays.

I watch him for a moment. He really is something. I'm not sure Conor is even aware of how swoony he is. Under the disguise of playboy is a guy who will be one helluva boyfriend, fiancé, or husband someday.

twenty-eight

Conor

"Why do you have so much shit?" Tweetie asks, dropping his bag next to the SUV I rented.

"I have to take two of everything. Two tents. Two sleeping bags. Two blow-up air mattresses."

He brushes his blond hair away from his eyes. "Why?"

I load his bag, making sure to have enough room for Eloise's stuff plus whoever Tweetie invited. "We're not a couple. I'm not going to assume she wants to share a tent let alone an air mattress with me."

"Where are you guys staying tonight?" he asks.

Since we're not leaving for camping until tomorrow, we're booked at a hotel in Milwaukee. "I booked us a suite."

He sighs, widens his stance, and crosses his arms. "What is wrong with you?"

"You're judging me for being a gentleman?"

"I'm judging you for not seeing what's right in front of you."

I lean against the truck. "Let me guess. Your guest is

staying in your single room tonight and you'll be sharing not only a tent, but probably a sleeping bag with her?"

He shakes his head. "Nah, I'm riding solo."

"You said you were bringing someone?"

Henry pulls into the alleyway.

Tweetie chuckles. "That was just so you'd ask Eloise. Why would I bring someone for an entire weekend?"

I scowl at him. "I'm not Henry. I don't need to be tricked."

He shrugs. "Then make your move, Romeo."

"It's complicated." Tweetie doesn't need to know all the details of what's going on with Eloise and me, but now that it's over with her and Tristan, I'm having a hard time judging whether she's ready to start something new or not.

Ruby walks out on the loading dock from the back of Peeper's Alley, her apron secured around her waist. "This isn't your parking lot."

"We're just packing up for a trip. You can fill the back room because we'll all be gone," Tweetie says.

"That includes that blonde?" She eyes me.

"You have a problem with Eloise?" Tweetie asks, hitting me in the stomach with the back of his hand. "Your boy here is too scared to make a move."

"This is the runaway bride no one has brought down to meet me?" Ruby doesn't look impressed. Of course, when does she ever?

Maybe it's because the weather's been so nice, but we haven't been hanging around Peeper's as much these days.

"You haven't met her yet?" Tweetie asks, hitting me in the stomach again.

I step away from him. "Sorry, Rubes. She'll be down here soon. I'll introduce you."

She sits on an empty keg and lifts her chin at Jade and Henry when they step out of their SUV.

"Hey, Ruby," Henry says.

"Did you know Pinkie never introduced Eloise to Ruby?" Tweetie tattles as if Henry is our dad. I mean, his nickname is Daddy, but it's just that, a nickname.

"Oh, you'll love her," Jade says, walking up to Ruby. "She's my best friend."

"I'll be charmed then, I'm sure." Ruby sounds anything but excited.

Jade glances at Henry before sitting on another empty keg by Ruby. "You don't have to worry about these guys this weekend."

"Then can one of you tell those three young kids to stop coming in? They seem to think that room is theirs."

"The chipmunks?" Tweetie asks, pulling out his phone. "Are they giving you trouble?"

"No, but the girls they bring in." She shakes her head. "It's a younger crowd, and I don't like it or them."

"You don't like anyone," Rowan says, walking out of the private entrance from our condo unit to the alley. Both of his shoulders are filled with bags.

"Shit, Magic, you're pretty enough. What's all this shit for?" Tweetie asks with a grin.

"It's Pinkie's girl's. Maybe you should've helped?" He eyes me.

"It's mine too. Stop being so dramatic." Kyleigh slaps Rowan on the back. "Hey, Ruby," she says, beelining it right to her and Jade.

"Don't worry, I got it all." Rowan drops three bags by my car and takes the other ones to Henry's.

"Oh, we both know how much you love it when I dote on you for being so strong." Kyleigh and Jade look at one another and smile.

Girls and their games.

I round the truck, picking up Eloise's bags. Ruby talks

with Jade and Kyleigh about camping and how she's a city girl and doesn't see the sense in sleeping on the ground when there are perfectly good mattresses to be had. I put Eloise's tote bag on the top of the luggage since I don't know if she wants it up front with her.

"Shit, I forgot to pull out my charger." Tweetie's shoulder presses to mine as he moves Eloise's bag off his and digs inside for his phone charger.

Eloise's bag topples over, and everything falls out of the top. "Fuck, Tweetie."

"Sorry." He reaches to help me.

"I got it."

"Tweetie," Kyleigh calls him over, and he walks away.

I pick up Eloise's book, a notebook, her phone charger, her AirPods, and all the other stuff she had in the tote. I put the items back inside but spot a stray piece of paper between my duffle bag and one of the sleeping bags. It's another list in Eloise's handwriting, and it's not titled anything.

The first thing I read is "Watch porn together."

I look to my left, but everyone is talking, and no one paying me any attention.

I shouldn't be reading this, but I can't help myself, especially when I see "Have an orgasm by oral." What the fuck? Has she never come from a man's tongue on her pussy?

"Here she is," Kyleigh says, and I shove the paper back into the tote and pack it away. "Come here. We have someone really important to introduce you to."

"Sorry I'm late," Eloise says.

Stepping away from the truck, I join the group and take the rest of her bags.

"Oh, thanks," Eloise says.

"You're welcome."

She wouldn't be thanking me if she knew my dick was currently half chub from reading what I'm pretty sure is a rundown of sexual shit she wants to knock off her list. I place her bag in the truck, and I swear her tote bag is the only thing I see in the sea of bags. It's like Where's Waldo, and once you spot him, you can't unsee him.

Shutting the back door of the SUV, I huddle around Ruby with everyone else.

"So, you ran away?" Ruby asks Eloise.

Eloise glances at me and back at her. "I did."

"And this fool asked you to move in with him?"

She glances at me again. "He did."

"Well, I'm sorry you almost married an asshole. I can vouch for Conor. He's a great guy—when his head is out of his ass at least."

I scoff at her. "Rubes?"

"Why does she get the warm and fuzzy version of you?" Jade asks Ruby.

"Conor doesn't have a son whose young heart is at risk." Ruby's explanation makes sense. Henry had Bodhi to consider too. "If you have to hear it out loud, I like you. Does that make you happy?"

Jade nods enthusiastically, and Henry puts his arm around her shoulders.

"Oh jeez, get out all of you. I have a bar to run." Ruby stands from the keg. "Ladies, don't be jumping around scared of spiders. Show them how it can be done." She eyes each of the women, then rests her eyes on Tweetie. "No picking up strange women in the woods. In fact, stay out of the woods. I'm not putting cream on your poison-ivy-covered ass." She waves and walks back into the bar as we all say goodbye to her back.

"She's fun," Eloise says.

"Be thankful she was so nice," Jade says as she and Henry walk toward their SUV.

"I guess we'll see you there." Rowan waves, tucking

Kyleigh into his side. "We're going to make out like teenagers while Daddy drives."

Everyone laughs while I cringe, and I walk Eloise to the passenger side.

"Tweetie, do you want shotgun?" Eloise asks him.

"Fuck no, I'm sleeping." He slides into the back seat.

I open the door and lean down to say into her ear, "I hope you can control yourself. I can't be distracted."

She climbs in. "I'll try, but you're so sexy I'm not sure I can." She waves her hand, fanning herself.

I chuckle and shake my head, rounding the back of the SUV. All I can think about is that list in her bag and how much I want to be the one to help her fulfill it too. Hell, even more than the other one. Finding that just made this trip that much harder for my blue balls.

twenty-nine

Eloise

Conor booked us a suite at the hotel, which means I have my own room, and he has his, and they're on opposite sides of the living area. It was a nice gesture, but I'll admit to being a little disappointed. I understand that he's being respectful because we haven't talked about us or where we're going. That needs to change. We need to have a conversation so I can tell him where I'm at.

When I step out of my room, I hear ice cubes dropping into a glass. Conor is at the bar, concentrating on making his drink. I take the opportunity to watch him. He's wearing blue slacks with a white shirt with the faintest light blue stripes running down lengthwise. The dress shirt is tucked into his waistband, secured with a black belt. I'm assume his matching jacket is hanging somewhere. God, he's gorgeous with his chestnut hair styled away from his face, his strong jawline prominent, and his lean, muscular frame evident beneath his clothes.

He glances up and looks back down at his drink, but then

his head pops back up. Without a word, he sets his glass down and walks toward me, his gaze running up and down my body several times.

"I'm sorry, I went a different route." I clasp my hands in front of me and shift my stance, crossing my ankles.

"Don't be. You clearly know your body best." He hasn't looked at my face yet.

When he took me to the boutique, I decided to buy the dress he picked out. It was a shorter dress that hit above my knee. But I ended up returning to the store and exchanging it for the one I'm wearing. It's light blue with spaghetti straps and a ruched overlay that ends just past my kneecaps. There's no slit, but with the clingy fabric, it reads classy and sexy I think.

"You're killing me, Eloise." He takes my joined hands, weaving his fingers through mine and resting my arms at my sides. "You're by my side all night, you hear me?"

I smile. The lust in his eyes brings an ache between my thighs. "I'm your date."

"Yeah, you are." His voice is hoarse, so he clears his throat. "Do you want a drink before we go?" He drops my hands and steps back, turning toward the bar.

"Sure." I follow him to the bar, admiring how his ass is snug in his slacks.

"Champagne, wine, or I'm making a vodka tonic if you prefer."

"I'll have a vodka tonic too." I place my clutch on the bar top and watch him pour the drink, squeeze the lime, and plop it in the glass.

Neither of us says a word, but the energy between us feels as taut as a tightrope.

"Thank you for agreeing to be my date." He hands me my drink, raising his for a cheers.

I clink my glass to his. "Thank you for asking."

We both take a sip, then rest the glasses on the bar top.

"I have something to tell you, and I hope you're not mad," he says. "I wasn't going to say anything, but it's all I can think of, and I feel guilty for it."

My stomach clenches. "Now you're scaring me."

He sips his drink. "When I was packing the truck, your tote turned upside down."

I wave him off. "Oh, there's nothing breakable in there. I'm sure it's fine." I touch his upper arm, but he's still tense.

He concentrates on my hand on his bicep, then lifts his gaze to me. "A list fell out."

My smile dies a swift death, plummeting with my stomach to the floor. "Oh."

He nods. "Yeah."

"Excuse me while I drown myself in my drink." I pick up my vodka tonic, ready to down it and then consume the entire bar until I blackout and forget this moment.

Conor lays his hand over the top of my glass and pulls it away from me. "I'm sorry. I wasn't trying to snoop or anything."

"Now you really have to show me your list." My cheeks feel as if they're on fire.

He chuckles. "Done. I'll show it to you tonight. Although it's not nearly as intriguing as this new list of yours."

I push him in the shoulder and leave the bar, going to stare out the window at Lake Michigan. "I have no idea how I haven't died of mortification in the past month."

He comes up next to me, so close his shoulder brushes my bare one. "I have to know though, have you really never come from oral?"

A strangled cry rushes up my throat. "Do these windows open?" I press my hands onto the glass.

His knuckles run along my arm until his hand is in mine. "Come here." He guides me over to the couch. "Sit down."

"Do I have to?" I groan.

He sits facing me, his knees hitting mine. "Don't be embarrassed."

"You'd be cool if I read your sex bucket list? If you never came while a girl gave you a blow job?"

He tries to hide his laugh but loses the battle. "The fact that you haven't come from oral sex isn't something to be ashamed of. It's not your fault. It's the weak-ass partners you've been choosing."

"Let me guess, you're up for the challenge?" I arch an eyebrow.

"You have no idea how badly I want to rip that dress off you, pin you to the bed, and make you scream my name because of what I'm doing with my tongue."

A rush of adrenaline bolts through my veins with the thought of him being rough with me, taking what he wants.

"And stop blushing because that's only getting me more turned on." He stands abruptly from the couch. "Fuck, finding that list is killing me."

"Am I supposed to apologize for that?"

He swipes his drink off the bar and turns around. "Fuck no. But if you thought I was all over you to complete your other list, you have no idea how badly I want to lock these doors and help you put a checkmark next to each item on your sex list."

"Well, I don't think there's a washing machine here, so..."

His eyes widen. "I didn't see that one." He takes another swig of his drink before dropping the empty glass onto the bar top.

"I have to have sex on a washing machine."

"Fuck me." He grabs a bottle of vodka.

I wiggle, using the armrest of the couch to help me get up with this tight dress on. "Why are you so frazzled?"

He side-eyes me while he pours himself another drink. "You know why."

"I think we need to talk." I take the bottle from his hand and set it on the bar. "I want you to know that I'm ready to move on, move forward."

He shakes his head. "No, you're not."

"I'm sorry?" My head tilts.

"You're not ready. It's only been a month since you were supposed to be married."

A knock sounds on the door, but we both stand in place, our eyes locked.

"So that's it? You're telling me I'm not ready, so that's how it is? You've made the decision, and that's that." I yank my clutch off the bar top and walk past him to the door.

"It's just the chemistry between us that's making you think that," he says to my back.

"Guess you know best." I open the door to find Tweetie there. He's dressed in a maroon suit that's clearly been tailor-fit especially for him.

"Can I have a drink?" He moves to step inside, but I put my hand on his chest, pushing him back.

"We're going to be late."

Tweetie peers over my head at Conor. "Feels a little chilly in here."

Whatever look Conor gives him from behind me, I don't know, but Tweetie doesn't push it and stands in the hallway with me, waiting for Conor to join us. Conor walks out still putting one arm into his suit jacket, allowing the door to shut behind him. The three of us walk toward the elevator, me leading the way to be as far from Conor as I can before I cause a scene and go off on him.

He thinks he gets to make the decision whether I'm ready or not? What bullshit.

I press the down button, and we step into the elevator a few seconds later when it arrives.

"Mommy and daddy, can you please stop fighting?" Tweetie stares us both down from the corner of the elevator.

I don't say anything. Neither does Conor.

The elevator arrives at the lobby, and Tweetie gets out, beelining it over to the rest of our group, surely telling them all Conor and I seem to be in a fight.

"Can we talk?" Conor whispers as we step out of the elevator.

"You already made the decision. What's to talk about?" I smack on a smile and walk up to the group, gushing over how gorgeous Jade and Kyleigh look.

Conor shakes hands with the other guys, but he's quiet otherwise, and I feel his eyes on me.

Well, they can stay there because I'm not going to be with another man who wants to dictate my feelings and my decisions for me.

thirty

Conor

WE ARRIVE AT THE VENUE WHERE OUR AGENT, Jagger, is holding the gathering tonight.

Eloise looks stunning. The dress she chose hugs all her natural curves, and I wouldn't be surprised if I end up in a fight by the end of the night. Especially since she won't allow me to stand next to her for longer than a minute before she finds some excuse to leave my side.

She's a hot single woman in a room full of horny hockey players. Sure, some are married or in committed relationships, but the majority aren't, and I've caught more than one of them watching her.

I'm in a huddle just off the bar with Henry, Tweetie, and Rowan.

"So, what'd you do?" Tweetie asks.

Henry and Rowan look between us, seeming confused. They were probably too enamored with their own women to notice the cold shoulder Eloise is giving me.

The last thing I'm going to do is tell them about the sex list.

"Nothing," I say.

The three of them raise their eyebrows and share a look with one another.

"Let us more experienced guys help you out." Rowan nods to Henry.

"Christ, it's been, like, a year for you, Magic," Tweetie says.

"Longer than you." Rowan is baiting Tweetie to try to pry out more information about Tedi and whatever happened that turned Tweetie into the man he is now.

Tweetie ignores his comment. "I'm going to get a drink."

"Okay, what's going on with you two?" Henry steps closer, our circle growing smaller.

"We're getting closer," I admit.

"Isn't that the point? The whole reason you stopped her wedding?" Rowan sips his drink.

"Yeah, but it's only been, like, a month. She just had her final conversation with Tristan." I bring my drink to my lips.

"So what, she walked into your room wearing lingerie and fuck-me heels, and you denied her? I don't get why you're fighting it." Henry looks over his shoulder to make sure no one is paying us any attention.

How much self-control does he think I have?

"I'm not getting into the whole thing, but there wasn't lingerie or fuck-me heels. We didn't even kiss, but the gist is I told her she wasn't ready."

They both rear their heads back, look at one another, and burst out laughing. Assholes.

"I'm doing her a favor." I bring my drink to my lips, the ice knocking together since it's almost empty. I finish it and set it on a nearby table. I cannot get drunk tonight. All my inhibitions will dissolve, and I'll wake up in Eloise's bed. If she'd even let me in, that is.

"Keep going. This is hilarious." Rowan's face is red from laughing at my expense.

"Fuck you guys." I pivot to walk away, but Henry grabs my elbow.

"Sorry, sorry. But your mistake was telling her that she isn't ready. What were you thinking?"

I shove my hands in my pockets and shrug. "Because there's no way she is."

"And why do you think you're the one to make that decision?" Rowan asks.

"I'm saving her."

"Saving her?" Henry's head rocks back, laughing so loudly we're garnering attention.

What a dick.

"My power crew." Jagger comes over and slaps my back. "Why don't you have a drink?" He doesn't wait for me to answer before he's shaking hands with Rowan. "This is the year, right?"

"Wasn't last year our year?" Henry jokes.

"I thought with Pinkie coming on the roster it was." Jagger thumbs at me and smiles and winks.

He did negotiate a great deal for me to come to Chicago last year. It was exactly what I needed. I can understand why he left behind agenting for actors and actresses. I'm not sure if he was as good at working with movie stars as he is at working with professional athletes.

"It's your year. I feel it in my gut. You played together for a while last year, now you're all best friends. You can thank me at your parade." He sips some of the dark liquor in his glass, his wedding ring glistening under the chandeliers.

We talk about the start of the season, and he congratulates Henry on his engagement, then proceeds to give Rowan shit for not proposing yet, and finally he turns to me. "So, your lady friend is garnering a lot of talk tonight."

Fuck, I knew it.

"Why hasn't she been by your side tonight?" he asks.

"He fucked up." Rowan gives me a smug smile.

Jagger turns to me, laugher bubbling up out of him. "What did you do?"

"I'm not getting into it. And she's not my lady."

He glances around the immediate area, then leans in. "I would keep that information to yourself."

"She is my fucking date though."

He laughs. "I love athletes and their alpha protective competitive side. It's like a trifecta only you assholes are born with."

"I don't think you're that different," I grumble.

"That's why I understand you so well. We're one and the same." He claps me on the shoulder. "Now, go find your lady and clear this shit up before someone steals her away from you."

Rowan and Henry don't say anything.

Before I can respond, Quinn, Jagger's wife, comes by. We all take turns hugging and kissing her on the cheek, saying our hellos. Jagger is quick to put his arm around her, his hand resting on her hip in a territorial and protective way. He catches me looking at his hand, and when I meet his eyes, he's smiling at me, nodding for me to go.

"Hey, Quinn, you're a romance writer, right?" Henry asks. "Is it true that hockey romance is a big thing?"

Quinn laughs and nods but pats Jagger's chest. "It's true. There's a big market for sports romance these days, especially hockey. But I write about arrogant wealthy playboys and the women who bring them to their knees."

Her and Jagger's eyes lock, and it's obvious how much they love one another. The admiration in his gaze is something I see in Henry and Rowan all the time.

She rises to her tiptoes, and he lowers his head to kiss her. "I'm going to call the kids."

"I'll meet you on the balcony in a second," he says.

She puts her hand on my bicep. "I met Eloise. She's sweet. Don't mess it up."

All three assholes laugh.

"Too late," Rowan says.

She draws back and waits for me to explain. When I don't say anything, she hooks her arm in mine. "Escort me over to the balcony."

"Hey, remember how you got that big salary. She's mine," Jagger calls out behind us.

Quinn pats my hand. "Don't worry about him. He's mostly bark, very little bite."

I open the door to the balcony for her, and we walk to the railing overlooking the city. The sun has begun its descent, leaving us with pinks, oranges, and yellows in the sky.

I tell Quinn the short version of my whirlwind story with Eloise, and she listens, not interrupting at all.

"I just don't want to be..." I stop myself because I haven't felt this for any woman in my entire life, and I do not want to fuck this up. This thing between Eloise and me, it's something I can't explain. Something I'm scared of losing.

"You really like her." Quinn faces the skyline. "Feelings are tricky little bastards. They can take over pretty quickly, and most of the time, it feels like they come out of nowhere. You met this person you weren't expecting to, and it sends your life spiraling in a different direction." She turns to me, resting her arm on the balcony. "It sounds like she wasn't happy with her fiancé, and my assumption is that she feels something strong for you. That you're giving her something he didn't, and she wants to explore that some more."

"But it's only been—"

"Time is relative, Conor. I've known people who fall in

love in a month. I've known couples where it takes longer. Sometimes people are enemies at first who find themselves falling for each other." She shrugs. "There's a reason why there's not one true definition of love."

Love? Who mentioned love?

She laughs and places her hand on my arm. "Don't look so scared. All I'm saying is that it's not for you to decide when and if she's ready. Only she can make that decision. And it's your job to trust that she's making the right decision for her."

My shoulders sag as I nod. I fucked up.

"You athletes crack me up. I think because you're embarking on something you don't have control over, you think it has to be hard, and you somehow have to be the one to take charge because that's what you do in your sport. Think about it. You're too slow, you practice to get faster. You're not stopping the pucks enough, you see a coach to help you. You need more stamina, you work on your cardio and diet. You guys know how to navigate your career, but no one knows how to navigate love because it takes blind trust."

I chuckle. "I can see why you write romance."

She laughs and shakes her head, eyeing something or someone over my shoulder. "I think it's my years of experience more than my writing skills. Plus, I'm married to a complicated man who took years to figure out what he lost before he came to his senses."

"When I found you again, I didn't give up though, did I?" Jagger comes around us and kisses his wife. "All done fixing my player?"

Quinn smiles at me. "He didn't need much help, but I think he's sorted."

"Good. We can't have the best goalie in the league fucked in the head over a girl."

Quinn lightly smacks his stomach.

"You have ten minutes before I'm starting my speech, so

go." Jagger points. "You've taken enough of my wife's time." He steps between us, giving me his back.

I peek my head around his arm. "Thanks, Quinn."

She winks. "Anytime."

I leave them on the balcony, enter the ballroom, and scan the room until I find Eloise with a glass of wine in her hand. Talking to Rigby fucking Calloway.

thirty-one

Eloise

"They say I'm going to win the Hart Award this year. It's like the most valuable player award. I almost got it last year, but I've been working my ass off this summer to make sure I get it next."

Rigby, I think he said his name was, has barely let me get a word in since he introduced himself.

"You said your name is Eloise, right?"

"Yeah." I sip my wine.

"Family name, I presume?"

"Yes, my gr—"

"My name is a family name too. Technically, I'm a third, but that sounds so pretentious, you know? My grandpa wasn't happy, said I should be proud to be a third. I'm not sure if I told you, but I'm from the South. Where did you say you're from?"

"Chica—"

"Chicago. Do you like it there? I play in Nashville. I'm not sure I could handle the weather in the Windy City." He sips his drink.

"I should go." I thumb toward the room, not motioning to anything specific, but it hits a hard chest.

I turn to look over my shoulder, and Conor wraps his arm around my waist, tucking me into his side.

"Rigby," he says, extending his free arm for a handshake.

"Nilsen." Rigby shakes Conor's hand, but his gaze veers to where Conor's fingers wrap around my hip.

Oh god, does Conor really think I'd go for this guy?

"I see you met Eloise," Conor says, voice neutral.

I drain the rest of my wine. "I need a refill." I slide out of Conor's arms.

"I'll get you one. Come on." Conor takes my empty glass. "Have a great year, Rigby."

"I'm sure you'll see me. Well, you'll see my cellys after my pucks get by you."

Conor huffs, stops, and circles to face him. I place my hand in his free one. Conor stares Rigby down for a second, then gives him a cocky smile. "Can't wait."

He doesn't let Rigby bait him, which I'm glad about. The last thing I want is another fight breaking out to defend my honor.

"Come on. Let's get you a drink." Conor tugs me forward.

Once we're a good distance from Rigby, I pull him into the corner of the room, not interested in another drink. "What are you doing?"

He looks behind him, grabs my hand, and walks us out the doors of the ballroom.

"Conor..."

He doesn't stop until we're at the end of the hall. Whirling me around, his hands fall to my hips to stop me. "I'm an idiot. I was being stupid."

"Okay."

Conor cocks his head to the side. "No objection?"

I shake my head. "Nope."

He chuckles softly. "I guess I deserve that." He doesn't say anything for a moment. "Listen, after I spied on you at the restaurant, Jade forced me to go to her house."

My forehead wrinkles. "Why?"

"Because she thought I wouldn't be able to give you space. And she was probably right. I would've tried to check something off your list, or take you drinking, or turn you on by smoking a cigarette."

I roll my eyes. "Okay, the smoking thing can end anytime now."

He gives me one of his wicked smiles that makes my body go all tingly.

"She also mentioned that if I push too hard, too fast, I'll be your rebound. *Just* your rebound."

It all connects now. Why he's been so hands off and distant and why I feel as if I've been the one trying to drag us over the line with him kicking and screaming the whole time.

He takes my hands and squeezes. "I really hope this doesn't scare you off, but I've never felt this way before." He releases one of my hands and places his palm over his heart. "This chemistry. This desire. And it's not just sexual before you say that. It's more. So much more that I can't explain. So, I don't want to be your rebound guy. I want to be your guy, period."

I slide my hands out of his and step closer to him, the scent of his cologne drawing me in. "That's why you've been pushing me away?"

His hands slide down my sides, anchoring to my hips. "I shouldn't have told you that you weren't ready. I've been schooled by more than one person that it was a stupid thing to say. But I just don't want to move too fast and have you regret this."

I wrap my arms around his neck, eliminating the remaining distance between us. "You know, I was there that night too." I twirl my fingers around the strands at the back of his head, my fingers running down the back of his head and neck. "You weren't the only one who felt something."

"But—"

"There isn't a but, Conor. I want this. I can't explain the feeling either, but I know I'm ready, and you're not the rebound guy. You're the guy who opened my eyes to the possibility of finally having the kind of relationship I want with a man who will make me happy and encourage me and do crazy things like—"

"Have sex on a washing machine?"

I laugh. "Yeah. And donate blood with me. And do random acts of kindness. There's something here, Conor, and I understand that the timing isn't great, but I want to explore this."

His hands squeeze my hips. My breath catches, but he pauses, his lips hovering over mine, his eyes searching for permission I've already given him. My mouth tingles with anticipation, waiting to feel him, to taste him for the first time.

He closes the gap, brushing his lips along mine, feather light and tentative. It's barely a kiss, but a spark races through me, and my heart pounds so loudly he can probably hear it. Then he pulls back, hesitation still glimmering in his eyes.

"Are you sure?" he murmurs, his voice unsteady, so different from his usual cocky self. His gaze flicks to my mouth and back to my eyes, as if he's still worried.

"If you ask me one more time, I'm going to find some other guy to fulfill my list with me." I raise my eyebrows.

A low laugh slips from his lips. I tilt my chin up, his warm breath fanning my face, and I watch the hesitation in his gaze melt away until there is only desire. It steals my breath.

He kisses me again, deeper this time. His hand slides to the small of my back, anchoring me to him, and his erection presses into my stomach, making the space between my thighs hum with pleasure. His mouth moves against mine with hunger and unrestrained energy from having to wait this long to kiss me.

I swallow his moan. I've never felt more desired than he's making me feel in this moment. With only one kiss, I'm dizzy and desperate for him. I can't imagine how it will feel once I have him naked and under my fingertips.

His grip becomes firmer, as if he can't bear for there to be any space between us. Our kiss is messy, raw, and full of emotion, building with a relentless intensity I've never experienced before. He closes the kiss, and I gasp against his mouth.

"Fuck, Eloise," he whispers, his teeth grazing my bottom lip and sending a shiver down my spine.

My fingers tangle in his hair, not wanting this moment to end.

"Hey, you two!" Tweetie shouts down the hall. "Oh, sorry."

I'm not sure what sign Conor gives him behind my back, but his lips capture mine again in a quick kiss. "Sorry, we gotta go."

He takes my hand and leads me down the hallway but turns the opposite way of the ballroom at the end of the hall.

"It's that way." I point.

Conor maneuvers me so my back is pressed against the wall between the elevators, and he presses the button. "If you think I'm not taking you directly up to the room, you're crazy. Get your list ready because we're crossing some shit off tonight, and the first one is gonna be you coming all over my fucking face."

My body warms as if my blood is lava, but I have no time to recover before the elevator dings, and we're inside, my back to the wall, his hands clasping mine over my head, and his mouth devouring my neck.

"I wore this dress for nothing." My breath is desperate and near panting.

He draws back, his fingers running over my spine. "Are you kidding me? I've been imagining taking it off you since the moment you walked out of that room earlier. You have no idea the amount of restraint I've had."

The elevator dings, and the doors are barely open before Conor has us through them. He rushes down the hall, dragging me along with him. Not that I'm complaining.

He pulls the keycard out of his pocket and glances at me. "Ready to have your world rocked?"

I take the keycard from his grip, scan it over the lock, and push open the door with my back. "For the record, I'm going to rock your world."

He chuckles, gripping my waist and pulling me into him. "You've been rocking my world for weeks, so I have no doubt."

He kisses me again, and it's messy, but at the same time, it's everything. Everything I've wanted for so long, and now I'm finally getting it.

thirty-two

Eloise

Conor kisses me, walking us backward through the sitting area to his bedroom. His cologne still lingers in the room, and there's something intimate about being in his space, even if it is just his hotel room.

He swivels me around, keeping his hands on my hips to steady me, then his fingertips inch up my side, finding my zipper. As he slides it down, freeing the snug fit from my body, his lips fall to my shoulder. "You have no idea how much I wanted this moment the minute you stepped out of your room earlier. The thought of being the lucky bastard to shed this from your skin had me hard the whole night."

"We barely stayed at the party long enough." I wrap my arm around him, my fingers weaving through his hair, not wanting him to pull his lips from my skin.

Conor's mouth drifts up to the nape of my neck, his calloused fingers grazing up my bare arm, lowering the spaghetti strap from my shoulder. I slip my arm out, helping his quest.

"You should be down there for Jagger's speech." Even I can hear the complete lack of give-a-shit in my voice.

"I'm right where I should be." He does the same with the strap on the other side and goose bumps follow his touch. "I should have made you do a striptease for me. Wasn't that on your list?"

I moan, unable to answer the question he already knows the answer to because he's pushing the fabric over my breasts and down my waist, past my hips before it puddles at my ankles.

"Fuck, Eloise."

I whimper when his hands and mouth leave my skin.

I feel him step back, and I start to turn to find out why he's stopping, but his hands grip my hips so I stay in place. "Stay right there for a second. Your ass in this thong... Jesus. Are you trying to give me a heart attack?"

How long have I yearned to hear a man devour my body with his words? For him to tell me how hot I get him, how he can barely control himself, and the restraint is killing him? I've never had a man talk to me like this.

"Can I turn around now?" I'm not asking because I'm embarrassed for him to see my body, because I'm not. He's made it more than clear that he likes what he sees. But I want to see him now.

His hands leave my hips, and I circle around. If hearing his words of desire wasn't already a major turn-on, watching his gaze rake over my body while I stand there wearing only a strapless bra, panties, and heels makes my core clench with need.

He steps back, resting his ass on the desk and biting the pad of his thumb. "Take off the bra."

I reach around and unhook my bra, holding the cups with my other hand to keep it in place. "I think you need to take something off now."

His flirty smile creases his cheeks, and he sheds his jacket, tossing it on the chair in the corner. I tilt my head and raise my eyebrows.

"Not enough, huh?" He unbuttons his shirt, his eyes never leaving mine. "I get it. You've wanted to see me for a long time too."

I pretend to hate his cocky demeanor when, in reality, I love it.

He pulls his shirt from his pants and strips it off his chest. I've seen Conor without his shirt, but knowing that tonight I'll be able to run my fingers down the peaks and valleys of his chest and abs, sprinkle kisses along his bare skin—it steals my breath.

"Your turn." He lifts his chin at me.

I release my bra, and it falls to the floor.

Conor groans. "Perfect. I knew it." He's whispering more to himself than me, I think.

My body heats with what I'm sure is a blush over every inch of bared flesh. I nod toward his lower half, and his hands manipulate the belt, sliding it out of the loops, tossing it to join his shirt on the chair.

"Pants too."

He toes out of his shoes. "So eager to see my cock." There's that cocky grin again.

I don't respond, and he doesn't wait for an answer before he strips off his pants and throws them toward the chair, but he misses, and they fall to the floor.

His erection presses obscenely against his black boxer briefs, and I find that I can't turn away. My gaze is too greedy.

After shedding his socks, he pushes off the desk and closes the gap between us. "How have I been able to control myself until right now?"

His fingers hook into the sides of my thong, and he lowers to his knees in front of me, staring up at me. He leans into the apex of my thighs and breathes in my scent while his finger runs along the damp silk fabric, and he hums with appreciation.

"Conor." I'm nearly breathless now that the time has come.

"I know." Inch by inch, he lowers my thong down my legs, his gaze not chasing the fabric, but remaining on the most intimate part of me. "Finally."

His vision draws away to get the flimsy fabric over my heels. I step out of them, and he throws them over with his pile of clothes. Then his palm lands on my calf, and his other hand slips off my heel. He does the same with the other one.

His palms slide up the outsides of my legs, and he blows a breath of air on my core before he places a sweet kiss on the top of my mound and stands.

"Get on the bed," he whispers as if someone might overhear us.

I step back until I feel the edge of the mattress against the backs of my thighs. My ass falls to the soft mattress, and again, Conor goes to his knees, his hands wrapping around my legs to grip my ass, pulling my pussy to his face.

"I need to taste you." His finger runs down the length of my opening, and he slides his finger into his mouth, moaning at the taste of me.

I'm not sure what sound slips out of me, but Conor's wicked grin says he's enjoying my reaction.

"It's time we cross something off your list, don't you think?"

"What if I don't..." I voice my worry because I don't want Conor to think that if I can't come, it means I didn't enjoy it. No matter what, I know I'm going to love Conor's mouth on me. But I'm usually just too in my head to relax enough to climax.

"Then I'll do it again. And you'll tell me what works and

what doesn't." I open my mouth, but he shakes his head. "I'll sit here on my knees and have a twelve-course meal if I have to, but I'm not leaving this room until you come on my tongue, Eloise."

I nod, tension still present in my muscles from the pressure of feeling like I have to come. How many times did I lie on the bed with Tristan and wish I could orgasm? How many times did I pretend I did? I don't want that to be my first experience with Conor.

He inches forward, his tongue following the same path his finger just did. His fingers flex on my ass, and he tugs me closer, his mouth ravenous as though his last thread of restraint has broken, and he can no longer take his time.

Conor groans in approval against my heated flesh as his mouth devours me. Slowly, the tension in my legs fades away until I'm no longer having to suppress the urge to close them. After a minute or two, it becomes impossible not to greedily grind against his tongue. My core heats, and I clench the bedspread, trying not to fall back onto the mattress, because watching Conor take small peeks up at me, gauging my enjoyment, is a show in and of itself.

The strokes of his tongue become more urgent, more consuming, and suddenly I'm not thinking about whether or not I can finish, but about how long I can keep Conor between my legs. The tip of his finger plays with my entrance while his tongue circles my clit.

"Oh, god," I pant, my hands threading through his dark strands.

He doesn't try to look at me, but he thrusts his finger inside me and sucks my clit simultaneously as I writhe under him. He doesn't relent, continuing his rhythm and pushing another finger inside me. I buck and tighten my hand in his hair, but Conor doesn't even seem to notice.

He's feasting on me like a man possessed, like a man who

can't get enough, and seeing him enjoy this as much as I am shoves me to the edge of the precipice. I've never felt this kind of anticipation before. I see now how people become addicted to this feeling, this adrenaline from what's coming.

He slows his pace a bit and curls his fingers, reaching a spot inside me that no one has before, and my hips rock upward of their own volition.

"Conor!" It's a plea for more and a warning that the feeling is almost too intense for me to handle all in one.

He removes his mouth from me, watching. "Fuck, Eloise. I'm going to be addicted to your taste from here on out. I hope you're enjoying this because I'm going to have a hard time not having my face between your legs every time we're together."

I whimper, and he doesn't wait for me to say anything, swirling his tongue around my clit and continuing a slow in and out motion with his fingers.

"I can't hold on." I arch my back, unable to stay still. "Oh shit."

My fists clench the bedspread, and I press my ass to the bed, trying to stay in place. I don't want this to end.

He peeks up to watch me, feeling me hitting the edge. Seeing his gorgeous caramel eyes staring into mine with so much desire and approval undoes me. Every muscle in my body clenches, and I come on a scream, bucking against him.

My eyes slide shut from the euphoria filling every cell of my body. The bedspread slides out of my grip, and my back falls to the mattress as I pant, trying to catch my breath.

Conor slowly withdraws his fingers, gives me one last long lick, and rises to his feet. "I feel like fucking Superman right now."

I peek one eye open and giggle. "Don't get too cocky. We'll have to see if you can do it a second time or whether it was beginner's luck."

The hard ridge of his dick presses against his boxer briefs. "I told you, Eloise, twelve-course meal."

He palms his dick over his boxers, and I slowly sit up and get up on my knees, placing my hand over his. "Let me repay the favor."

Taking control, he switches our hands so mine is on the bottom, and he tightens his palm over the back of my hand as I rub his dick. "We don't have time for that. You squeezed my fingers so tight, I need to feel your pussy clenching around my dick."

I have a feeling I'll be reliving this night for the rest of my life.

thirty-three

Conor

Her hand is on my dick. Sure, there's a piece of fabric over it, but fuck, it feels so damn good, as though I've waited for-goddamn-ever for this moment. I remove my hand from the top of hers, allowing her to use her magic touch on me like I did her, but her mouth won't be on my cock tonight because I need to be inside her. To feel her warmth, her pussy walls contracting, to watch us come together after the unbearable build-up since that night stargazing.

"I love seeing your hands on me."

She peeks up through her thick eyelashes and squeezes me with just the right amount of pressure to drive me wild.

"How about my mouth?" She leans down and pulls the waistband of my boxer briefs over my erection to rest under my balls.

"If I see you suck me off, I'm gonna lose all control, and I've waited too long to sink inside of you for that not to happen. It's bad enough you're staring at it like it's the eighth wonder of the world."

Her soft hand wraps around me, fisting my cock. It twitches in her palm. "Just one lick." She lowers her mouth and runs her tongue up my shaft.

I curse and thread my fingers through her blond strands, tightening my hold when she encases the head of my cock in her mouth. "Fuck. You did this on purpose, knowing I wouldn't be able to stop you."

Looking up at me through her eyelashes, her blue eyes are filled with mischief. Keeping her hand on the base of my cock, she pumps me while simultaneously sucking me down. I can't strip my eyes off her, and I grow even harder watching her deliver my pleasure.

I'm so enthralled with the sexy image before me that I don't immediately stop her. Not until my balls draw up, and I have no choice before I come down her throat.

I groan. "I need to be inside you." I give her hair a light tug, and her mouth pops off me so I can cradle her cheek in my palm and run my thumb over her swollen lips. "Lie down."

She wastes no time, falling down onto the mattress, her blond hair splayed across the pillow.

"Open your legs."

Again, she does as I ask, widening her legs and giving me a perfect view.

I grip my dick, my eyes raking over her naked body. I can't believe she wants me. Out of all the bastards in this world, how do I get to be the lucky one?

After I dig in my bag for a condom, I crawl up the mattress.

"Presumptuous having those with you, aren't you?" She tilts her head.

"Well, if you weren't willing, I figured I'd find someone who was."

She giggles, and I love that she gets my humor.

"Maybe I should go find Rigby." She shifts to get out of bed.

Like hell she is.

"I've heard he's got the smallest dick in the league." I tear open the package and roll the condom down my length.

Her eyes are transfixed by my fingers. "I knew you boys compare dick sizes in the shower."

"You should be thankful. I'm the biggest by inches."

She laughs again and crooks her finger at me.

I happily oblige. Without putting my weight on her, I use my knees to spread her further, making room for me between her thighs. I stare down at her and run my finger from her temple down her chin. "You make me crazy. In the best way."

Her fingertips graze down my chest and back up before wrapping around my neck and urging me toward her. I've never been with a woman like this. I've never taken my time because I didn't want it to end. Eloise has unearthed a side of me I didn't even know existed. As much as I love it, it scares me—what if I suck at this whole serious boyfriend thing?

"Hey." Her voice pulls me from my thoughts.

"Hey." I smile down at her and rest my elbows on either side of her head, keeping my body above hers.

"You okay?"

God, how pathetic am I? I'm almost balls deep inside her, and she's feeling like she has to ask me if I'm okay.

"Yeah." I dip my hips, lining up my cock with her opening and use my hips to rub my tip through her wetness. "So wet for me."

She nods, her eyes filled with a hunger I can't wait to abate. Bending my head down, I lick the seam of her lips, teasing her a bit before capturing her mouth. I circle my hips, my hard cock running through her swollen folds. She feels so damn good.

With my restraint all used up, I slide in an inch, then slide back out, doing it over and over, allowing her to get used to my size. Once I'm fully inside her, she arches her back and lets out a strangled cry.

"I know... I know." I momentarily let my face fall into the crook of her neck, then I shift my hips, pulling out and thrusting back in.

Her fingers press into my shoulder blades, and her legs come up to my hips as I pull back so I can watch her. I run my hand up the outside of her silky, smooth thigh and slide back into her warm, wet pussy.

When I wedge my hand between our bodies and find her clit, her head pushes back into the pillow the minute my thumb makes contact. Bending down, I lick up the column of her neck, up and over her chin until my lips are on hers.

She's making so many noises, I know she's getting closer, so I keep up the pace of my hips, my body sliding over hers. Her nipples run along my muscular chest every time my cock slides in and out of her, and it makes me want to dip my head and bite her nipple.

But she whispers, "Kiss me," her hand wrapping around the back of my head and pulling me down to her.

Our kiss is wild and messy, and sweat beads along our skin the longer we go at it. Pressure builds in my balls, and I want to come so badly, but at the same time, I never want this to end. I thrust my tongue into her mouth and hammer in and out of her faster and then faster again, until the only sounds that fill the bedroom are the slapping sound of skin meeting skin and our heavy breaths.

She writhes underneath me. I know she's close, so I strip my lips off hers, burrowing my head into the crook of her neck.

"I'm never going to get enough of you, Eloise. Never. Plan on fucking all night, because I'm far from done with you."

Her body tenses under mine, and I kiss my way back to

her lips. My kiss doesn't linger, though, because I selfishly want to hear her scream.

As soon as her pussy clenches around my cock, and she cries out, "Oh, god," it's over for me too. I thrust once more, my hand slipping off her clit as I empty myself inside the condom.

When I have nothing more to give, I slide off her, my back to the mattress as I work to catch my breath. "There's my conditioning for the day."

She turns to her side, resting her head in her palm. "That's disappointing. Here I thought I'd get a lot more from sleeping with the infamous Conor Nilsen."

I give her a quick kiss and hop off the bed. "Don't worry. I've still got more to give."

Once I'm in the bathroom, I dispose of the condom and wash my hands quickly, eager to get back to bed with Eloise, knowing my words about never getting enough of her were true.

thirty-four

Conor

I'M NOT SURE HOW WE GOT INTO THIS POSITION, BUT I'm not complaining.

Eloise is straddling my lap, all sexy in my button-down shirt from earlier tonight. My hands splay on the outsides of her thighs, and damn, her skin is so soft.

"More?" she asks, offering me a bite of the piece of pizza she's eating.

I suggested room service, but she said she was dying for pizza.

I open my mouth, and she holds it out, watching me take a bite. Then she takes a bite. I can't take my eyes off of her, the smile on her face, her infectious energy. It's as if someone transported me somewhere I never knew existed, let alone knew I wanted to spend all my time there.

"I like this," I admit.

She continues eating her pizza, mumbling, "What?" around a mouthful of food, covering her mouth with her hand while she chews.

"Being here... with you." I'm still hesitant to confess all the feelings running through me because I'm afraid to scare her off.

She kisses me briefly and sits back up.

I'm wearing only a pair of shorts, and my dick is very aware of the lack of fabric between us, but I've already had her twice. Since we left the dinner before the actual meal, our stomachs were growling after we finished our second round. My dick twitches just thinking about how she rode me, and I finally got to enjoy her tits in my hands and mouth.

"I like it too." She drops the crust in the box and grabs the waters I took out of the mini fridge when the pizza arrived. "I've never had this before."

My fingers dip under my shirt, running along her hips. "What?"

I throw the question her way, curious and anxious to hear her response.

"It's just... easy. Being with you takes no effort."

It's the best thing I've ever heard. "That's exactly it, but I'm sure you had something like this with Tristan. At least in the beginning." I hate that my insecurities are making themselves known, and I'm sure she can probably see right through me.

She places her water bottle on the table after she's done taking a drink. "I never felt comfortable like this. Like I could just be myself without fear of judgment." She shrugs. "The world he was born into isn't easy. I'm pretty sure you're judged from the moment you come out of the womb. I saw it in my dad. It would come out in little ways. If my dad picked me up from my mom's, he'd drop little comments like how my mom couldn't braid my hair properly, or that the dress I was wearing wouldn't do, so he'd stop and buy me one on the way to wherever we were going. I once overhead my grandma telling someone at their country club I was deciding between

Stanford and Yale." She laughs. "I was never getting into an Ivy League school."

"Lots of pressure to conform, to not detour from the norm." I understand a little of what she's saying.

"Exactly." She pauses. "From the time we got together, I constantly second-guessed what I wore, my makeup, and would go over the conversations I had with his family and friends in my head for days afterward."

Now that I can't imagine.

"But with you..." She shakes her head and looks at me as though she can hardly believe it. "It's like I've known you forever. You take the good and the bad that comes with me."

I fiddle with the bottom button of my shirt, watching my fingers. "I battled with whether I could really be feeling what I thought I was when we first met because of the instant connection I felt with you. I was worried it was lust, or like you worried that maybe it was just because you were something I couldn't have. But I think you just nailed it. It's the familiarity. The instant I sat down next to you in that VIP lounge, I didn't want to be anywhere else."

"So, you wouldn't have helped some other random girl get her friend to her hotel room?" She raises her eyebrows, and I undo a button on the shirt.

"I was desperate to stay with you, but didn't know what the hell I expected. Then we talked and..."

"You figured out I wasn't the happiest?"

I nod, shame sweeping in. "I'm really sorry." I undo another button, and she doesn't stop me, so I continue on. Will this thirst for her ever be quenched?

"For what?"

I look into her eyes. "For stopping your wedding. I was an asshole for doing that. And then the fight..."

She brings her hands to my face and stares into my eyes. "It's in the past."

"But still, your family..."

"You met my mom, she was relieved. She never wanted me with Tristan anyway. And the only people who care is everyone on my dad's side. My mom's side has never liked my dad's side and vice versa." She kisses me quickly and pulls away too soon. "What you did is kind of romantic in a way."

"That's what my drunken self thought when the idea came to me, then the chipmunks spurred me on, but still, I had this whole vision of me running through the doors, and it would be like it is in the movies...you'd turn to me and run down the aisle into my arms. The fight and you running off after wasn't part of my vision."

She giggles and kisses me again, but I place my hand on the back of her head to keep her there. I slip my tongue into her mouth, and she grinds her heat on my hardening dick. Fuck, she's everything I didn't know I needed.

Minutes later, she closes the kiss. "How about a bath?"

"You all slippery and wet? I'm game." I grip the tails of my shirt, inching up and holding each side tightly. "But first you need to be naked." I tug and pull, the shirt bursting open and buttons flying all over the room, pinging off the tables and floor.

"Show-off." She shakes her head with a coy smile.

"I always wanted to do that." I wrap her arms around my neck. "Hold on tight." Standing, I hold her to my chest, her nipples poking my pecs.

"Oh, I like this." She kisses my cheek first, then her mouth finds my earlobe, and she nibbles.

"If I make it through this bath without my cock inside you, I should get a goddamn prize."

She giggles, her laughter like music to my fucking ears. "I love it when you talk like that."

"How?"

"Like you can't get enough of me. Like every time you see me, you want me."

I walk us into the bathroom, place her on the counter, and start the water in the bath. "I do."

Once the water is warm, I add the stopper and go back over to Eloise while we wait for the water to fill the tub. Fifteen minutes later, we're both in the tub, her back to my chest, my arms wrapped around her.

"Can I ask you something?" She leans her head on my shoulder and turns her head to face mine. She looks unsure.

"Anything." I want her to know she can always ask or talk to me about anything.

"When I mentioned the pressure to be someone you aren't, you sounded like maybe you understood what I was talking about." She circles her head and grabs my hands, moving our joined fingers through the water.

I kiss her temple and gather my thoughts. "In a different way than you were referring to, but similar in a sense. There have been times in my life that I felt I had to be a certain type of person because I was an athlete. Or people thought certain things about me, and I was always trying to prove them wrong. Like the sign, the Nest, outside the condo and the women who hang around. They're in love with someone I'm not."

"What do you think they expect?"

"Most just want to say they slept with me. The sex could be shitty, and they'd still brag to their friends that I was the best lay they've ever had. It's not me they want. It's my reputation, my profession."

Her fingers tighten in mine. "I'm sorry."

"Don't be. Most guys would love to be in my position. And I can't say there wasn't a time when I took advantage of it, but I'm not that guy anymore. Don't ever tell Kyleigh this, but I think seeing her and Rowan together finally helped make that click for me."

"They are happy." She leans her body into mine and wraps our arms around her.

"Sickeningly so."

She giggles.

"I never really thought I'd be able to have a relationship while I was playing. The schedule is grueling, the time away from home isn't ideal, but they make it look so fucking easy. Henry struggled with it too, and I hate to say this because I love the guy, but I don't want to end up like Tweetie."

"A playboy?"

My head moves side to side. "Yeah, that for sure. But there's more. He's covering something up and dealing with it in a shitty way. He's going to have to retire soon and what will he be retiring to? To sit around and talk about the good ol' days in the league? Maybe he'll get a coaching job, but..." It's so hard to explain when she doesn't know Tweetie that well. I don't want to be trashing him—he's a great guy. Fuck, he let me live with him when I first got to town and had nowhere to go. That's, like, best friend shit.

"But what?"

I sigh. "Will that be satisfying? Hockey has been my entire life for as long as I can remember. The goals changed over the years, but it always had to do with hockey—get on the top travel team, get a scholarship at a top college, get into the league, get the best agent, get the endorsements, win the Cup. When it's all over, I don't want to walk away from the game to an empty house. I want to walk into the arms of the woman I love and have her whisper to me that we're going to start the next chapter of our lives. Maybe we'll have a few kids at our feet too."

She sighs and kisses my jaw. "I like that vision."

"Me too."

I don't say that I hope it's her. That when I picture it, I see her with open arms and our kids hugging our legs. I don't want to scare her, but fuck, I'm not sure I can slow down this train. I'm in deep when it comes to her and barreling headfirst into love.

thirty-five

Eloise

CONOR AND I COME DOWN THE NEXT MORNING AND are the last to arrive in the lobby. Kyleigh and Jade are seated in two chairs by the windows and chatting, and they each give me a knowing smile as we walk toward the group holding hands.

"Our boy did good?" Tweetie waggles his eyebrows at me.

I could tell him that Conor's the best I've ever had in more than just a sexual way, but I keep my thoughts to myself.

"Shut the fuck up," Conor says.

"You missed a great fucking meal, but—"

"Don't finish that sentence," Henry interrupts. He raises his eyebrows at Conor. "My car is ready to go."

Tweetie pats Conor's chest. "Leave our boy alone. He was getting laid."

Conor shakes his head, and I catch him looking at me from the corner of his eye. I squeeze his hand to tell him he doesn't have to worry about me being put off by Tweetie.

Last night, I could tell he was worried about me judging

Tweetie when he was talking about not wanting to end up like him, but who am I to judge anyone? I just hope if Conor's suspicions are right, and Tweetie is trying push away his feelings over something that happened in the past, that he can eventually heal.

"I'll go out to valet." Conor tugs me toward him and presses his lips to mine. "Be right back."

"Don't worry, I'll take care of her." Tweetie wraps his arm around my shoulders. "You were the belle of the ball last night."

"Oh?" I'm not sure how to answer that statement.

"Get away from her, Tweetie. Come over to the girls' corner." Kyleigh waves me over.

He releases me. "We have two hours for our girl talk in the car." He smiles at me.

I chuckle, walking over to Jade and Kyleigh, and sit on the couch across from them.

"So?" Jade asks.

Kyleigh raises her hand. "For the record, he's my brother."

Jade and I laugh, and I set my hand on Kyleigh's knee. "I won't give any details."

Details about how her brother rocked my world last night and gave me orgasms I thought were only of the fictional variety.

"Thanks. But you're together?" Kyleigh gives me a hopeful look. I nod, and they smile wide. "Now we have to plan some girl things." Kyleigh claps her hands together lightly.

"If only Tweetie could settle down," Jade says, and we all turn to look at him.

He's chatting up some woman at the complimentary coffee bar. She's laughing at whatever he's saying. I'm not going to mention anything that Conor told me, although I'm sure these two know more of the story than me.

"If we wait for him…" Kyleigh doesn't finish her sentence and shakes her head because her phone dings, and she pulls it out. She types for a moment then tucks it away, facing me again. "Well, I have some other good news."

"What?" I lean in a little closer, excited to hear whatever she's going to say.

"Yeah, what?" Jade asks, sounding like she doesn't like being kept in the dark.

"I'm working with this client to design her wedding dress, and her soon-to-be husband is taking her on a European honeymoon. She's super stressed about what to buy for it and doesn't want to pack too much but also wants to make sure she has enough. Anyway, because she loved the dress I picked out for her body shape…" She flutters her eyelashes.

Jade and I laugh, shaking our heads.

"She asked if I was a stylist too. I told her that I only do wedding dresses, but that I have a friend who does that kind of thing."

Jade's forehead crinkles. "Who?"

Kyleigh points her manicured nail at me.

I rear back. "No."

She nods. "Yes, you."

I shake my head vehemently. "I don't have any experience styling anyone."

"You have your first two clients sitting right here in front of you." Kyleigh waves her finger between her and Jade.

"She's right. You know how many compliments I got on the dress you picked out last night?" Jade nods. "And on my Instagram, more and more people keep saying it's the perfect color and style for me."

"Me too. Not the Instagram thing because I don't put Rowan on anything business-related, after…" She glances at Jade, and Jade's lips press into a thin line. I'm clearly missing something. "But on Rowan's picture, every person made a comment about the dress."

"You had so much success when you were doing that blog thing, remember?" Jade asks, taking me back to before Tristan, back when I was so excited to make content.

"That wasn't anything big." I shoo her away, unwilling to take the compliment.

"Just give it a try. She's super sweet. It's her second marriage. You'll love her. I promise." Kyleigh pulls out her phone. "Let me tell her you said yes so I can forward your information?"

I glance at Jade and bite my lip. "I don't know."

"Do it, Eloise. There has to be something on that list of yours about a career."

There is. I wanted to be working in a field I love, not just doing a job. Which was inspired by Jade and her photography at the time.

I suck in a fortifying breath and nod. "Okay, I'll do this one."

"Yay!" Kyleigh shouts and sinks back in the chair when everyone glances over.

"Baby, you okay over there?" Rowan asks.

"I could use a coffee refill." She smiles sweetly, and her thumbs move over the screen on her phone. "Done. Oh, I'm so excited for you."

"You're going to do great." Jade pats my knee.

"We're ready, let's go," Henry calls to us. "And go to the bathroom because we're not stopping on the way."

Jade scoffs. "Stop being so bossy."

"Yeah, Daddy, save it for the bedroom." Tweetie gets a glare from an elderly lady with a cane walking across the lobby.

We all file out of the hotel, and Conor is waiting at the passenger door with the door wide open for me. "Hey, gorgeous, need a ride?"

I play along. "Depends on where you're taking me."

"Stop your weird flirting shit and get in the car." Tweetie climbs into the back seat.

"I wish we were alone." Conor wraps his arm around my waist and pulls me into him.

"We will be tonight, in the tent. I've never had sex in a tent." I kiss his jaw. "Will you keep me warm?"

His hand slips down my waist to my ass, grabbing it. "It will be a first for us both. Fuck, I just had you a half hour ago, and I already want you."

Tweetie's head pops out between the driver and passenger seat. "There are children in the back seat. Jeez."

I kiss Conor's jaw one more time. "The sooner we get there, the sooner we're in a tent."

He waits for me to get into the SUV, then shuts the door and rounds the front of the truck.

"Picture time." Tweetie holds his phone out to me. "Selfie."

Conor takes Tweetie's phone, and we squeeze all three of our faces into the frame. Conor hands it back to Tweetie and puts on his seat belt before we pull away.

"Do you mind if I tag you, Eloise?" Tweetie asks.

I think about it for a moment. If he tags me, there's a chance Tristan or someone in his life will see it and comment, or at the very least, I'll be the center of gossip. But who cares? I'm living my life without caring what other people think anymore. If the pictures from the bachelor party and the honeymoon are any indication, Tristan has already moved on, so why can't I?

"Yeah, please don't show me with two Chicago Falcons," I joke.

Conor's hand lands on my knee. "Only one of us matters."

"That's rude," Tweetie says. "Done."

Conor squeezes my knee, and his hand remains there for almost the entire ride. It's the best two-hour ride of my life.

We caravan to the camping location, and Henry takes charge of the reservations and getting us our passes, then directs us to our site. We follow him over the hills on the dirt roads until I know I could never find my way out of here.

Henry pulls their SUV into the site and Conor parks behind him. We all file out of the vehicles and stare at the empty space that only has a firepit and a picnic table. I'm not sure what I thought it would look like, but it appears I'm the only one surprised by the lack of amenities.

"I have to go to the bathroom. Anyone else?" Jade asks.

"I'll go," I say, and we walk along the road we came in on. "Where is it?"

She points at a small white building at the top of a hill.

"That's the nearest bathroom? What about showers? Where do I change?"

Jade laughs and swings her arm through mine. "Oh, this is going to be fun."

She's laughing, but seriously, I just started dating a guy last night, and he's going to want to have a lot of sex, but I'm going to have to shower in a little white house with multiple people? This situation is not ideal.

thirty-six

Conor

AFTER WE ARRIVED AT THE CAMPGROUND, WE HAD time to set up our tents, then go to the store and grab some items none of us thought to bring before it got dark. Henry started the fire because he runs shit like a dad, and we're all his kids. I guess that role is hard to put on pause just because your kid isn't around. Not that any of us have a clue what we're doing.

But it's Eloise I'm most concerned about. She's been acting weird ever since we arrived. Jade keeps poking fun at her about their trip to the bathrooms. She definitely seems out of her element.

Before we join everyone by the fire, I grab Eloise by the wrist and pull her to the back end of the SUV, giving us as much privacy as possible.

I lean my back against the truck, anchoring her to me with my arms. "Talk to me."

She bites her lip.

"I'm going to pull those teeth from your lip."

She shakes her head.

"Are you betting I won't?"

She stops biting her lip, and her forehead hits my shoulder. "I'm not sure this is for me."

I chuckle and tuck her in my arms. "What did you expect when you wrote it on the list?"

Her shoulders lift. "Romantic stuff. Stars and bonfires."

"You're about to get those things."

She draws back, and her expression reads more embarrassment than dislike. "I swear I'm not some snob, but…" She lays her hand on my chest. "We can't have sex tonight."

Oh, it all makes sense now. "You got your period?"

"No." She covers her mouth from laughing. "I have an IUD, so I haven't had one for two years."

"Really?" I'm sure I look fucking excited because although it doesn't bother me to sleep with a woman while she's on her period, some women don't want to.

"You thinking about how you don't need condoms anymore?" she asks, raising her eyebrows.

"Actually no. I've never done it without one."

She pats my chest. "Well, until we both get tested, we need to use them."

"But after?"

She nods. "Sure."

My dick twitches, but I force myself to focus on the topic at hand. "So, if not your period, then what?"

She inhales and looks off into the darkness around us. "I feel dirty."

"I like dirty." I grin at her.

She pushes my chest. "I'm being serious."

"So am I."

"But—"

"But nothing. Just enjoy yourself. If we get into the tent, and you don't want to have sex, no big deal. I'm a big boy."

"Really?"

"I do know how to masturbate. I've become quite the expert at it since we met." I wink at her.

She tilts her head. "Conor."

I pull her toward me so there's no space and kiss the top of her head. "I'm serious. There's no pressure on that kind of stuff at all. But there's a bonfire happening and look up."

She tips her head up, and so do I. The dark sky sparkles with stars. It's so much better than that time at the lakeshore.

"Oh, it's beautiful," she says, but I tilt my head down to look at her.

"Yeah, it is."

She lowers her head, catching my eyes. "Smooth."

"I thought so." I chuckle, kissing her cheek. "But in all seriousness, nothing is as beautiful as you." I slide my hand down to hers, capturing it. "Now let's go have fun with our friends."

"Thanks for talking me down."

I stop her right before we walk by Henry's truck and into view of where they're all laughing and carrying on around the fire. Pushing her back against his truck, I keep our hands entwined behind her back. "It's my job."

She smiles. "But—"

"I want the job. I want to be the one to calm your fears, to empower you, to be the one you seek out to find refuge."

She sighs, and her eyes lock with mine. "Where did you come from?"

"Chicago."

Her forehead falls to my chest again, and I lay my hands on her cheeks, lifting her head so she looks at me.

"Do we have a deal?"

She nods.

"Good."

I lead us to the bonfire where everyone else has a drink in

their hands and is shooting the shit. We sit in the two unoccupied chairs, leaving me next to Tweetie and Eloise.

"Sorry, Rowan, but it's the one thing that comes with you that I hate." Kyleigh turns off the screen on her phone and puts it in the drink holder on her chair.

"Me too, but most of all I hate that you have to deal with it." Rowan frowns.

"What am I missing?" I hand Eloise a seltzer from the cooler beside me and grab a beer for myself.

"A picture that Rowan put up with him and Kyleigh yesterday got swarmed by the puck bunnies." Tweetie cringes.

"It's all passive aggressive bullshit. That he must be a great boyfriend because I've put on some pounds since we started dating." Kyleigh gulps down a good amount of her seltzer.

The reason I almost didn't move into the Nest was because the puck bunnies linger and hang around there, but I'm done being in hiding and not living my life. They don't have access to me beyond the gate.

"One person congratulated me on my pregnancy." Jade rolls her eyes.

"Are you serious?" Eloise looks as though she can't believe someone would do that.

If she only knew.

"It's evil, I tell you." Jade glances at Henry. "You're worth it, don't get me wrong, but I can't say I won't be happy when you retire, and I don't have to deal with those women."

"Just tell me when it gets too much. You know where I stand on the issue," Henry says.

I believe that if Jade wanted him to, Henry would retire tomorrow. He has everything he's ever wanted now. Sure, he'd miss the game, we all will when the time comes, but I think Henry will ease into retirement easier than the rest of us.

I grab Eloise's hand because the thought of her having to go through what they are scares the crap out of me. At this point, everything is going so well between us. I don't want anything to mess it up.

"Do you ever say anything back?" Eloise asks.

"No," Kyleigh and Jade answer at the same time.

"It's not worth it. They come back harder and more vicious." Kyleigh gets up from her chair, but leans over Rowan, pinching his cheeks. "You're just lucky you're so damn adorable."

He grabs her and swings her into his lap. I inwardly roll my eyes, but I understand it now because I'd love for Eloise to be in my lap right now.

"Conor better watch himself." Kyleigh takes a pull from Rowan's beer, pointing the top of the bottle at me. "I have a feeling he might not hold back when it comes to you, Eloise."

"I can handle myself," she says, looking at me.

"Come here," I mumble and tug her arm lightly.

Eloise obliges and stands. I pat my lap, and she happily sits down, wrapping her arm around my neck. I just want her close to me during this shitty conversation about the hazards of my job.

"Oh, looky here. Am I the only one who sees empty seats around?" Kyleigh says, ribbing me because I'm always on her for sitting on my friend's lap.

I flip her off behind Eloise's back.

We all sit and talk bullshit about everything but hockey. Tweetie tells us a funny story about when he was with the Florida Fury at a team building event, and Kane and Jana Burrows were secretly a couple. Jade and Henry tell a story about college, and we all share stupid shit we did as kids.

Eloise lays her head on my shoulder, and I kiss her forehead. "Let's go to bed."

"Okay."

She climbs off my lap, and I stand. "See you guys tomorrow, we're going to bed."

We say our good nights to everyone.

"Can you walk me up to the bathroom quick?" Eloise asks.

"You can go in the woods," I say, but she shakes her head.

After grabbing our flashlight, we trek up the short hill to the white building.

"Okay, stay here." She pushes open the door, tiptoeing in. The automatic light turns on, meaning no one else is in there.

I hear the stall door shut and the shuffling of clothes.

"Pretend you don't hear me. This isn't how I imagined this going," she calls.

"Just so you're aware, I do know you pee." I chuckle.

"Knowing and hearing are two different things."

I shake my head at her concern.

A minute later, I hear the toilet flush, and the stall door opens. Then she screams, and I push through the door. Eloise is jumping from one leg to the other.

"Rat!" she shouts, jumping into my arms. I catch her but drop the flashlight on the floor. "Kill it!"

"Okay, first of all, calm down. I'm sure it's just a mouse or something."

"I don't care what it is." She buries her head in my neck. "I told you. I'm not meant for this."

I smooth my hand over her back. "Relax, I got you."

I bend down to get the flashlight, and she clings harder, her fingers digging into my back. We walk out of the bathroom, and I carry her down the hill, the flashlight guiding the way.

"Sorry," she says. "It scared the crap out of me."

"I know." I can't deny it, I would have flipped out too.

Once we're a safe distance away, she has me set her down. We round the two SUVs and see that everyone has gone to bed, except Tweetie. He picks his head up from where he's looking at his phone.

"Oh, hey, guys." He pockets his phone quickly, and there's a look on his face I'm not sure I've ever seen.

"Everything okay?" I ask.

"Yeah, always." He smiles, but it's forced.

I walk Eloise to our tent, unzip it, and wait for her to get in. I scan the flashlight around to make sure there're no critters or anything inside.

"Do you mind?" I nod back toward the fire.

She shakes her head. "Just zip me in." She crawls over to me and presses her lips to mine. "He's your friend. Go make sure he's okay."

"Thanks. I won't be long."

I zip her up and walk back over to the bonfire. Tweetie has his phone out again, as if he's reading something.

"Who is the text from?" I ask.

He shuts the screen off and places it in the cupholder. "No one."

I sit in the chair next to him. If he doesn't want to tell me, I can at least sit here for a while because something is bothering him. We're both silent for a minute, and he surprises me when he speaks.

"I'm sure you've heard the stories back in Florida," he says, his voice low and quiet. "Tedi Douglas?"

I lean back in the chair and get comfortable, knowing the time has finally come. Tweetie is about to let me in. I have no idea why he's chosen now, but I'm not going to question the why. I'll be here for my friend and listen.

thirty-seven

Conor

"Tedi Douglas?"

The name sounds familiar, but I'm guessing probably only because of the guys mentioning her and Tweetie before.

"I've heard some rumors." I go the honest rather than clueless route. He deserves that. Since Tweetie deflects feelings with humor, I need him to know that he can trust me with his feelings. That I won't judge him for missing someone who meant a lot to him at one point in this life.

"When I was in Florida, I met her through our center Aiden Drake's now wife. She worked with her. They handled social media and stuff."

I walk over to the cooler and grab a water.

"I was a lot younger then and assumed she only wanted me because I played hockey. She was all over me from the start, quick to sleep with me. I figured we'd have a short fling, and it would fizzle out. But that not what happened."

I take a seat and continue listening, wondering who the text was from and what it said.

He's quiet for a beat as if he's reliving some memory. "Then I got traded to Nashville, and I was pissed."

"I get it."

When you play for a winning team like Tweetie did with the Fury, it's gotta suck being the one who gets let go. It's the nature of our job, but I've seen a lot of guys get fucked in the head over it.

"Yeah, well, you got to come to a winning team, fucker." He laughs, although it's not his usual hearty one, and tips back his beer.

"You wanted me here, remember?"

He nods. "Fuck yeah, and we're going to win the Cup this year. I feel it in my bones."

Tweetie said the same thing last year. After this conversation, I think maybe he's got something to prove.

"I know." I agree, and I hope like hell we do. We thought we had it last year, and we came up short. "Let's get back to why you're staring into the flames like you're looking into your soul though."

His gaze lifts to me. "You like her, right?"

"Eloise?" I try to decipher his wandering thoughts.

He nods.

"Yeah."

"Like, you think she could be it for you?" He lowers his voice as if afraid she might overhear us.

"Definitely." It's weird to admit it after such a short time together, but I wasn't lying when I told Eloise I've never felt this way for anyone. I've never wanted to do so much for a woman who wasn't a part of my family.

"Keep her out of this world as much as you can." He shakes his head. "I shouldn't have tagged her in that picture earlier. I wasn't thinking, sorry."

"Are there shitty comments?" I dig my phone out of my pocket.

"No. And some people probably think she's mine anyway, but it's only a matter of time. I'm just saying that this life we've chosen has the potential to ruin what you two have."

I'm guessing this is his way of telling me the outside world had something to do with why he and Tedi didn't last.

I open my mouth to ask, but he continues, "It's a curse, right? We get to do what we love. We're the lucky assholes who get to play hockey for a living, but it comes with a price. Everything does, I suppose." He leans his forearms on his legs and looks at me.

I understand where's he coming from. I had my own incident two years ago, and it put up my defenses, but thankfully, that's behind me now.

"Is that what happened with you and Tedi?" I finally ask the question point blank.

He blows out a breath. "It was a clusterfuck of bullshit I don't wanna get into tonight." He nods toward the tent. "Go be with your girl."

I sit and stare at the fire for a second. "You know you can talk to me about anything, right?"

"You're a good guy, Pinkie, but I'm not going to sit by the fire and pour my heart out." He stands, grabbing the stick and moving the embers and wood around.

"I'm your friend." I pour my bottle of water over the fire, the embers sizzling.

He moves the embers around some more, and I grab the jug of water, dousing it further.

"I know, but I'm not like you guys. I don't want to get all up in my feelings, let alone talk about them."

"But maybe—"

"Go get laid, Pinkie." He cuts me off quickly.

"If you change your—"

"I won't." He snatches the jug of water out of my hand. "Go." He nods toward my tent.

I stand for a second before patting his shoulder, which hopefully conveys that I'm here for him if he needs me. Then I head to the tent, unzip it, and toe out of my boots before stepping inside.

Eloise has a flashlight in the crook of her neck, holding her book above her head.

"Hey," she says quietly, putting her bookmark in place and setting the book and flashlight down next to the air mattress. Since the flashlight is still on, I can see the cami tank she's wearing that outlines her tits perfectly when she sits up. She's bathed in shadows, but it only makes the swell of her breasts more obvious. "Is he okay?"

I take off my socks and strip off my shirt. "I'm not sure. I think it might take some time for him to open up to me," I whisper since his tent is right next to ours.

Inching up to my knees, I unbuckle my shorts and drag them down my legs. I'm about to crawl into the sleeping bag when I catch Eloise ogling me. My hand cradles her cheek, and I kiss her.

"I love your eyes on me," I murmur against her parted lips.

"I feel the same." She presses her lips to mine, and I take the opportunity to slip my tongue into her hot, waiting mouth.

Her tongue strokes mine, and I slide us down on the air mattress, keeping our kiss going. Her fingers run along my back. I can't get enough of her hands on me.

I pull back. "We don't have to. We can just make out."

She smirks, and I wait for her to tell me what's going on in that beautiful brain of hers. "I didn't want to, but then you had to go and take off your shirt."

"You're saying I'm too hot for you to keep your hands off of?"

"Oh shut up, and kiss me." She pulls my head down to hers.

I don't waste any time, moving my thigh between her legs, kissing her with every ounce of passion I feel for her. The night wind softly presses against the tent, and she shifts closer, pushing the sleeping bag off our lower halves.

"You have this power over me," she murmurs, her voice barely above a whisper.

I chuckle softly, my gaze dropping to her lips before returning to her eyes. "Me? There wasn't a second today that I wasn't thinking about you in this exact position." My fingers inch up and slip under the hem of her cami, and her back arches. "These pajamas are a tease." I palm her tit, running my thumb over her nipple as she moans. "How quiet can you be while I make you come?"

I give her a kiss before lowering myself and lifting her cami, revealing her glorious tits in the dim light of the tent. When I suck a nipple into my mouth, she lets out a soft moan, her hands running through my hair on the back of my head.

"You're always playing a game."

I peek up, resting my chin on her stomach. "It's more fun that way. It's why you like me so much."

She giggles. "I guess you're right about that."

I twirl her hard nipple with my tongue, suck her tit into my mouth, then move to her other side to do the same. She sucks in a breath when my mouth pops off her other tit, and I again move up her body, situating my hips between her open thighs.

I stare down at her shadowed figure. "You're so beautiful."

I brush a stray strand of her blonde hair from her face and run my finger from her temple to her cheek. Our eyes lock, and the air in the tent shifts, heavy with unspoken emotions. With her warm body underneath me and the intimacy of the small space, suddenly my heart beats harder.

"You're mouth-watering hot," she whispers.

I grind my hardness against her core, and her fingers tighten in my hair. "Now who's propping up my ego?"

When I dry hump her, she spreads her legs wider, allowing me better access. "You know it's not the way you look."

"It's my charming personality?" I circle my hips, and she sucks in a breath.

"Swoony. You're swoony, Conor Nilsen."

"Fuck, you're turning me on, Lulu." I use the name because it's a deflection. I want to be the man she falls for, the man she deserves, but I don't want her to think I'm perfect or that I'm not going to fuck this up sometimes. Mostly, I don't want to hurt her.

"I lied when I said I don't like you calling me that." Her hands glide down my back, gripping my ass and pushing me against her.

"I know you secretly love it." I drop a kiss to her lips, the heat between us growing thicker with every grind of my hips.

When our lips meet again, the world outside the tent disappears. All those worries lay just outside the door, leaving us in the cocoon of this moment. I deepen the kiss, cradling her jaw.

"I love these lips," I murmur against her mouth.

She pulls back just enough to look into my eyes. "Don't stop," she whispers, her voice barely audible but full of certainty.

My lips find hers again, this time with more urgency. When we have no choice but to come up for breath, I run my lips along her jaw to her ear. "I can't wait to get inside of you."

She pushes against my chest, and I roll to the side and flop down on my back. She tears off her cami, tossing it to the side by her book, and I waste no opportunity, molding my hands to her tits.

"I love this position." I raise my hips off the air mattress.

Without a word, she leans to the side and flicks off the

flashlight, and we're plunged into darkness. I hear her moving around, and when my eyes adjust to the darkness, I see that she's shed her pajama bottoms. I help her free my dick from my boxer briefs and it juts up almost obscenely. Her ass is on my thighs while she palms my dick.

"In the side pocket of my duffle. Put it on me. I want to watch you."

Bending over, it takes Eloise a moment to find the pocket of my duffle in the dark, but I hear the crinkle of the package, then she straightens up. I watch her dark silhouette tear the foil open, get the condom out, and place it over the tip of my dick. It twitches when she makes contact, and my mouth waters from watching her roll the condom down my length.

"Now get up on your knees, line me up, and sink down on me."

She does as I ask, and I cup her cheek, running my thumb over her bottom lip as she guides me into her wet heat and slowly lowers herself on me. I wait for her to get accustomed before my hands move to her hips, my fingers digging into her flesh.

"You want control?" I ask.

She anchors her hands on my pecs, lifting her ass, and my length slides out of her before she sinks back down.

"Shit, baby, have at it. Ride me."

She does, and it's a fucking turn-on, watching her come on a whisper before she collapses against me.

Definitely jerk-off material for away games on nights when she won't be in my bed.

thirty-eight

Eloise

We arrive back at the condo after camping, and I have to admit, the whole roughing it thing grew on me. Conor tosses the pile of mail we grabbed from the box on the breakfast bar.

"That's a lot of mail." It looks as though he probably hasn't checked it in at least a week.

"I always forget to grab it." He chuckles.

"I'm going to shower," I say, walking toward my bedroom.

I'm not even at my bedroom door before he wraps his arms around my waist and pulls me to his chest. "We're showering together. I've had to have silent sex all weekend, and I want to hear you this time."

I giggle, and my feet lift off the floor as he carries me through the bedroom door. "Do you ever get enough?" I'm joking because I'm certainly not complaining.

"Your room or mine?" He ignores my question, walking us farther into my room.

"Well, you clearly made the decision."

"Shower in yours, sleep in mine," he says, setting my feet on the floor and immediately lifting the hem of my T-shirt.

"Why sleep in yours? Don't want to sleep under a flowered comforter?"

His hands continue their exploration, my T-shirt traveling north until I have no choice but to lift my arms. He sheds it from me and, without missing a beat, unhooks my bra. "Bring the comforter if you want, but I've been wanting you in my bed since the night we met."

He reaches around and unbuttons my shorts.

"Shouldn't you be heating up the water?" I ask.

He lowers the zipper, pushing the fabric off my hips. I step out of my shorts, and he slinks his hand past the elastic waistband of my panties, his finger sliding from my clit to my opening and back again.

"Stay wet for me." Then he's gone, disappearing into the bathroom. When he emerges, he's already naked. "Your shower smells like you. It got me hard."

His wicked smile is so damn sexy. This man has me smiling like a fool.

"I'm pretty sure you were already hard." I close the distance, and Conor hooks me around the waist and pulls me into him.

"I'm always hard around you." He kisses the nape of my neck. "Let me get you nice and clean... before I dirty you back up again."

He takes me by the hand, opening the shower door. The water is nice and warm, and steam rises around us.

"Oh, this feels nice." I hum in approval. "Not that I'm complaining about the conditions of the campground. I love my shower shoes and having to press a button over and over again to get the water to stay on."

He nudges me under the stream of the water. "So, camping is a one-and-done, huh?"

I tip my head under the water, and the scent of campfire smoke fills the steamy air surrounding us. "Well, I will say that I liked the tent sex more than I thought I would. If you can figure out a way to get a bathroom like this next to our campsite, I'm game."

He chuckles, his hard length pushing against my stomach as he leans forward and runs his hands down my hair. "I'd build it for you. Turn around."

I circle around, giving him my back, and I hear the squirt of the shampoo bottle. His fingers work it into a lather in my hair, my scalp needy for more of his massage. "Your fingers are magical."

"I know. You're a lucky girl," he says in a low voice.

"That I am."

This is what I've always wanted. Sure, Conor knows his way around a woman's body and could probably get me off by just looking at me the right way, but it's this connection I feel with him that I've always wanted to experience. This ease of being with him and how we can joke around. That instead of taking showers separately, he initiated us having one together because he wants to spend more time with me. That all means more to me than anything he could ever buy me.

He pats my ass when he's done lathering me up.

I giggle like the schoolgirl he makes me feel like, and I tilt my head back to get rid of the shampoo. He steps closer and runs his hands down my hair.

"Something is poking me." I wedge my hand between us and grip his length. "Oh, what's this?'

"If you keep touching him, you're going to find out."

I slide my palm up and down his shaft. "I'll play that game. How long before you're thrusting into my hand?"

He steps away, and my hand slides off him. "You're a dirty girl. I'm trying to be a good boy here." I hear him grab something off the shelf. "This next?"

I look over my shoulder and see that he's holding my conditioner. "Definitely after this weekend."

He squirts it into his palm, and I step out from the stream of water, allowing him space to run it through my strands with his fingers.

"Now." I grip his shoulders and turn him toward the water. "Your turn while my conditioner sets in."

I grab the shampoo, and the same smell of campfire smoke seeps out when the water hits his hair.

"Is my sister being nice to you?" he asks.

"A lot nicer than I hear you were to Rowan when they got together."

He straightens his neck to look at me. "It's hard. She's my baby sister, and hockey players aren't always as good to their girlfriends as Rowan is."

I poke him in the stomach. "And you? What kind of hockey player are you?"

I'm not worried. Conor is pretty straightforward with how he feels for me. And he's always touching me. But at the same time, he's not taking pictures of us and posting them online like Rowan and Henry. I know it's early for us, and most of his social media is his endorsements and him working out with the guys, so I try not to read into it too much.

"I'm a one-woman hockey player if that's what you're asking."

I urge him to tip his head back, and the shampoo runs out of his hair under the water. "I wasn't." My voice comes out a little more defensive than I intended.

He stands straight, taking me by the shoulders so we switch places, and again I'm under the stream of the water. "You were though, no?"

"The season is about to start. Things will be different." I've tried not to give it too much thought, how things might shift between us once a good portion of his day is dedicated to his career.

Conor takes my loofah and pumps some body wash onto it. "This is the part I've been looking forward to." He watches as he runs the soap-filled loofah along my skin. "It's not going to be easy, but I'll do everything I can to reassure you that when I'm away, you're still top of mind."

"Then you won't win the Cup." The last thing I want is to be a distraction to him getting where he wants with his career. He's worked too hard for too many years.

"Let me worry about that. You just be naked or in sexy lingerie when I get home." He keeps me under the cascade of water.

Once I'm rinsed off, I take the loofah and wash him, giving his dick some extra attention. I don't mention the season or what's in front of us because I don't want to spend energy worrying and being anxious about problems that may or may not present themselves. I want to take life as it comes and enjoy our path that I hope leads to love. At least for tonight, we're going to keep it fun.

We finish showering, and I'm surprised he never tried to make a move. Not even a kiss.

He opens the shower door and grabs a plush towel from under the cabinet and wraps it around me. "I think I deserve a reward."

"Let me guess, you want a blow job for not even feeling me up?"

He chuckles. "No." He pulls another towel out and dries himself before wrapping it around his waist. "I'm hijacking your pillow. You can find it in your new bed." He shoots me a mischievous smile and walks out of the room. "But if you'd rather give me a blow job, no complaints."

I watch him pick up my pillow off the bed and walk out of my bedroom.

"Hurry because I want sushi and then you." He spins around. "Actually, maybe sushi *on* you?"

I don't answer or give him a reaction, just a smile, and he winks before disappearing from the room.

Going back into the bathroom, I get my hair wrap and twist my dripping hair up into it. Then I dry myself off and grab my lotion.

With Tristan, this is one of those times I would have just gotten dressed and waited for him to tell me what he wanted to do, but Conor isn't Tristan. So, I take the lotion bottle and pad to his bedroom. He still has his towel on, and he's looking at his phone.

I lean my shoulder on the doorframe and wiggle the body lotion in the air. "You forgot the next step. You have to lotion me."

He tosses the phone on his bed and grabs the bottle it from me. "Welcome to the Nilsen massage parlor, where we guarantee a happy ending with every massage."

Jeez. This man has me wrapped around his finger.

thirty-nine

Conor

"How did you talk me into this?" Eloise asks, lying flat on her back as I use my chopsticks to pluck a piece of sushi off her nipple.

"A new idea you don't have to put on your bucket list." I slide the California roll into my mouth.

"Maybe that's what I should do with my life. I can be a sushi model."

I lean over to make sure she sees my expression that conveys my thoughts on anyone else seeing her like this.

"They don't lie there naked," she says. "They wear bikinis and stuff."

My expression doesn't change. "I would really like it if you didn't go into that field of work."

A salmon roll slips off her stomach from her laughter. "That was a sweet way of asking."

I pick up the piece of sushi. "I'm sweet like that. World's best boyfriend." I point at myself before raising the chopsticks to my mouth.

"Boyfriend?"

After I swallow, I bend down and kiss her lips. "Boyfriend. Is that okay?"

The label slipped out, but I want it. I want to be her boyfriend and for her to be my girlfriend. I want us to be a couple. My ego will be bruised if she says no, but I'll just keep at it until she agrees.

"That's a little presumptuous." She shrugs, and another piece of sushi slips off her, but I catch it before it lands.

I hold up the piece of sushi in my chopsticks. "Well, if you don't want a boyfriend with ninja-like reflexes, then I suppose I'll have to find someone who wants me." I'm pretty sure she's joking, but there are times she has a killer poker face, and I can't read her.

"I was just clarifying."

"So, you're my girlfriend?" I raise my eyebrows.

"As long as you take that last piece of sushi off me so I can sit up."

"Deal." I bend over and suck the piece of a tuna roll into my mouth before chewing and swallowing. "Now do you want to eat off me?" I move to shrug off my shorts.

"No, that's okay. I'm full." She ate before I asked her if I could eat the remaining pieces off of her. "I feel like I should shower again."

"Be thankful I didn't pour soy sauce in your belly button." I shove all the empty containers in the takeout bag and walk into the kitchen to throw them away.

"That's never happening," she calls after me.

I grab the pile of mail off the counter and walk back into the room, tossing it on the bed.

"Speaking of me not being a sushi model, your sister's been referring me out."

"Excuse me?" My forehead wrinkles as I climb into bed with her.

She's put my Falcons T-shirt back on, and seeing my name and number covering her body makes me want to pound my fists to my chest.

"To be a stylist for someone."

She's sitting up, sorting through the mail, and I place my hand under my shirt, running my fingertips in a circle. "You have great style. I got schooled about that after you picked your own dress for Jagger's event."

"You've brought that up a lot. Does it bother you?" She lies down and cuddles into my arms.

"Not in the slightest. But explain to me what a stylist does."

I run my hand down her arm, and she rests her chin on my chest. "Helps someone with their wardrobe and style choices. I guess essentially, I'm helping them dress for their body type and helping them present themselves to the world the way they want to be seen. Kyleigh has a client who is going on a European honeymoon, and she wants me to pick out the clothes she'll bring. She's supposed to message me sometime soon."

"Do you think you'll enjoy it?"

We haven't gotten to the point where I have any idea how much money Eloise has from her trust fund, and I only want to know if she wants to tell me. It's her business, and even though I want us to be long term, that money is hers and hers alone. If she wants to live off it and never earn a penny doing anything else, that's her choice. It has no bearing on why I'm with her.

"I think so. I love dressing myself and putting looks together, going out and having the thrill of finding the perfect complement to whatever outfit I have in my head. But I want to do some research to make sure I'm picking looks for a client and not just items I gravitate toward personally. Everyone has their own style, items they're comfortable in. I can't think of anything worse than someone wearing something they hate because I told them to. I've done it enough over the years."

I kiss the top of her head and hold her tighter. "Just that thinking tells me you're going to do awesome at it."

She presses her lips to my chest. "Thank you."

"For what?" I love having her in my arms, all warm and soft. Why did I ever think I didn't want this?

"For encouraging me. Telling me you think I'd be good at it. Boosting my ego, I suppose."

"Hey." I put my finger under her chin and tip my head to look her in the eyes, so she knows how serious I am. "I believe it, I'm not just saying it. I know you'll be good at anything you decide to do. I'm not boosting your ego. I'm just by your side."

She scoots up and presses her lips to mine. "You make me wish I met you five years ago."

"Five years ago, I might have fucked this up, but I understand what you're saying." Five years ago, I wasn't in any frame of mind to make a relationship work. Sure, maybe this feeling I've had since the first night I met Eloise would've been there, or maybe it would have been different, I don't know. But I do know I would hate being in Tweetie's position where he found her and fucked it up, then pretended for years not to care.

"Too cool for monogamy back then?" She rolls out of my arms, but I grab her back, spooning her from behind.

"Where do you think you're going?"

"Ice cream. You want some?" She grinds her ass into my dick.

"I have a cone for you to lick if you want."

She frees herself from my grip and scurries off to the kitchen. With her leaving, I sit up to go through the mail, which turns out is mostly just junk. I flip and flip, until I see a hard cardboard envelope with printed handwriting addressed to me.

"No on the ice cream?" Eloise calls, and I hear the freezer open, the cabinet open, a bowl leave the cupboard, and a spoon leave the silverware drawer.

"If I can lick it off you." I place the envelope to the side of me, continuing to sort through the junk and bills, separating the two.

"You've done enough eating off my body tonight."

"Not even close. Bring the chocolate sauce and whipped cream. You'll be my dessert." God, how many flyers can people send?

"That's very cliché of you, Conor Nilsen."

I toss the junk in my wastebasket and set the mail I need to go through later on my dresser, but that cardboard envelope slips out and falls to the floor.

"Hey, you still need to show me your list," I hear her say.

I open the envelope, curious to see what this is. "Sure, but I have to add to eat a sundae off my gorgeous girlfriend."

"Ha. Ha. You've seen both of mine. It's time I see yours."

I pull out the contents of the envelope, and the first thing I see is a note in girly script with curls on every letter.

HERE'S YOUR CHANCE TO SCORE. MISS ME?

My heart races as I remove the Post-it Note to see a picture of a topless woman with my number painted above her tits. What the fuck?

"Okay, I'll smear it, and you can lick it off." Eloise's voice is closer now.

I scramble to open my underwear drawer and tuck the envelope and picture under my boxer briefs. Then I slam the drawer shut and pretend to look through the stack of mail, working to calm the anxiety racing through my body.

"Hello?" Eloise says.

I turn around and smack on a fake-ass smile for the first time ever with her.

"You look pale. Are you feeling okay?" She can tell something is off, I see it in her face.

"Yeah, I think maybe I just had too much sushi. I'll be right back." I walk over to her and kiss her cheek, then continue to my bathroom.

Once the door is shut, I sit on the toilet and put my head in my hands.

How the hell did she find me again?

forty

Eloise

IN TWO DAYS, PRESEASON TRAINING CAMP STARTS for the boys, so we all decided to head to Peeper's downstairs because we'll have less time together from now until the end of the season.

Conor has been touchy, practically never allowing me out of his sight. I can feel his anxiety over the upcoming change to his schedule. Yes, he's been accessible up until now, but he has to go back to his job, which keeps him away from home a lot.

"Come here." Conor grabs my hand and guides me onto his lap.

I sit and wrap my arms around his neck. His arms tighten around me. We're going to have to have a conversation about this, but not right now. Not when we're having fun with friends. But he can't be worried about how I'm handling everything while he's supposed to be blocking shots on goal.

He kisses my neck. "I would rather be upstairs, driving into you," he whispers, and my face heats.

No one is looking at us. Kyleigh and Rowan are playing darts against Jade and Henry, and we're to play the winner.

"It's unfair that Jade and Henry are a team," Tweetie says. "I think we should put our names in a hat and draw to make it fair."

"Why don't you just practice more?" Henry asks, sitting on a stool with Jade's back to his chest.

"I can't time warp back to ten years old and have Jade's dad teach me." Tweetie shakes his head.

"I want to know why I never received lessons from Reed," I say.

Reed is Jade's stepdad and was Henry's Big Brother when he was younger. He obviously taught them to play before I met Jade during freshman year in high school.

"He tried. Remember that New Year's Eve party?" Jade raises her eyebrows.

"Oh right. I guess I just suck at it." I shrug.

"Don't worry, you're good at a lot of other things." Conor kisses my neck again.

"Cool it with the sexual innuendos." Kyleigh throws her dart, and it doesn't land on the board.

"Oh, come on, I've been watching you pet Rowan for an entire year." Conor pats my ass.

"And you've had something to say every damn time." Rowan kisses Kyleigh when she comes back from the board without much success.

Jade and Henry are going to win, which surprises none of us.

"Get ready, love birds, you're our next victims." Henry tips the top of his beer bottle at us.

Conor pats my hip. "Let me go to the restroom before we're up."

I stand, and he presses his lips to mine quickly before he leaves the backroom.

His teammate Alvin, which I'm not sure is his real name, sidles up next to me and sits. "You sure changed our boy," he says, leaning back in his chair with his legs stretched out.

The two guys who are usually with him sit on either side of us.

"Excuse me?"

"In a good way," the one on my left says.

"Of course," the one next to him says.

"It takes a special woman to tame a playboy like Pinkie." Alvin raises his hands in front of me. "It's a compliment."

I sip my drink, telling myself I don't really care what Conor did before me, it's how he treats me now that matters, but I can't deny that a small piece of me wonders if I'm good enough. Tristan sure treated me as though I was disposable.

"Alvin and the Chipmunks, get the fuck away from her." Tweetie slaps the back of Alvin's head. "What are these dumbass rookies saying to you?"

"Nothing." I stand to compose myself because Tweetie must have seen the expression on my face in order to make him ask what we were talking about. "I'm going to the bathroom."

I walk across the room, hearing Tweetie tell them they're idiots and to mind their own fucking business.

Jade grabs my hand before I can leave. "Are you okay?"

I nod and open the door, sliding out. I just want to see Conor, feel his arms around me. Then my body will relax, remembering who we are together and that he's not the guy those rookies seem to think he is.

I head down the small hallway toward the bathrooms and stop in my tracks. Conor's standing in front of a brunette, the same brunette I found with her friends, writing the sign outside the security gate. She runs her fingers down his chest. He steps back but leans in, saying something to her. She pushes off whatever he said with a flirty smile and wraps her arms around his neck.

I clear my throat.

Conor turns his head, his face going pale just as it did the other night when I know he was hiding something when I came back into the bedroom with my bowl of ice cream.

He lifts her arms off him and steps back, saying something I can't hear before he walks toward me, grabs my hand, and leads me down a different hallway, pushing open the back door.

"It's not what you think," he's quick to say.

"Okay then, tell me what it is."

He releases my hand, walking along the loading dock. "She's just a fan, and I was telling her I wasn't interested. She just couldn't seem to understand it."

There's something on his face that I can't read. As if he's worried I won't believe him.

I decide to trust him until he proves to me different. I saw him step back from her touch after all. "Okay."

He stops his pacing and turns to me. "That's it?"

"I can't say my stomach didn't drop when I first saw you two, but I believe you."

Rushing over to me, relief washes over his face as he cradles my cheeks, pressing his lips to mine. He distracts me with a soul-searing kiss, the firmness of his lips, the gentle way his tongue sweeps into my mouth all conveying that I'm the one he wants and no one else. By the time he closes the kiss, I gasp for a breath.

"Let's go upstairs," he murmurs along my lips.

"No, we're hanging with friends tonight. You can wait a few hours."

His hands run over my body, grabbing my ass and pulling me into him. "One more kiss then?"

"Sure."

This time our kiss has an urgency and desperation the other one didn't. As good as it feels, a piece of me thinks there's something more to that girl based on his reaction to me not being upset about seeing them together.

"Oh, god, get out!" Ruby shouts from behind us. "This isn't your bedroom, it's my bar. Go."

Conor laughs and slides his hand in mine. "Sorry, Rubes, just needed a little alone time with my girl."

Ruby tosses a dish towel over her shoulder. "And you got it. Now get in the backroom. The girls are out tonight and desperate to get in there." She eyes me.

I offer her a smile that probably conveys Conor's already had one run-in with a very handsy one. "Sorry, Ruby."

She shoos us away, and Conor guides me through the bar toward the backroom. As we make our way through the crowd, the brunette passes by and shoulder-checks me. My mouth drops open, but she continues walking, giving me a look and a smirk over her shoulder.

Man, the girls weren't joking when they said it's hard to date a professional hockey player.

forty-one

Conor

HAVING TO RENT ANOTHER CAR, I WONDER IF I should buy my own. I can probably rent a parking space or even park it at my dad's.

Sure, we could have taken an Uber, but there's something about driving a woman somewhere as a surprise, which is hard to do with a ride share. I could have used a car and driver, but I don't want anyone else with us tonight—for reasons that will be obvious to Eloise soon.

I drive us to an outlook over Lake Michigan in the north suburbs of Chicago and park the car.

"What are we doing here?" Eloise looks around the empty area that has a view of the skyline to our right. "Are you going to murder me?"

I laugh and unbuckle my seat belt. "Care to join me in the back seat?"

"What?" she asks but blindly follows me by opening her car door and stepping into the back seat.

"We're crossing an item off your list." I change the music

on my phone to play through the speakers of the car. It's a playlist I put together last night.

Her head cocks to the side. "Which item?"

"We're going to make out like teenagers." I scoot closer to her and wrap my arm around her shoulders.

"Okay." She wiggles in her seat. "Should we have rules?"

My eyebrows draw down. "Rules?"

"You know, like we only go to first base, or are we thinking anything but sex? What are the limitations?"

I chuckle at her excitement and insistence that we plan out how we're going to make out. "I was going to let it go wherever we want it to."

"Did you bring a condom?" She raises her eyebrows, and I shake my head. "That's a shame."

I look around the back seat. "I'm not thinking we could have sex back here. You do realize your boyfriend isn't exactly teenage-sized."

She places her hand on my chest and inches closer to me. "I'm very aware how big my boyfriend is." Her hand ventures down, cupping the bulge in my jeans.

Damn, I should have worn joggers. "You keep doing that, and I'll be speeding home."

She doesn't remove her hand but squeezes my length. "You're the one who brought up how big you are."

I throw my head back against the seat with a sigh, knowing I'm going to miss being able to do this kind of thing on a whim. "I can't believe I'm starting back already."

The other night when I saw Lila at Peeper's after she sent me that picture in the mail, all I could think was she's going to ruin this for me. She's going to destroy what I have with Eloise because why would anyone want to deal with the kind of shit she might throw my way? Tweetie's words were running through my head.

Lila cornered me coming out of the bathroom, and I tried

to make it clear, for the millionth time, that I wasn't interested. I reminded her about the restraining order back in Florida. That I'd get another one here if I had to. When Eloise saw us, my heart sank, and I thought for sure she'd bolt or think I was playing her, but she trusted me when I told her Lila was just a fan. And she is. A very obsessed fan. But I'm going to take care of it and make sure what happened in Florida doesn't happen in Chicago. Lila is not going to ruin this for me.

"Can I ask you something?" Eloise whispers.

I turn my head and look at her. "Always. Anything."

"You seem really worried about the season starting. You keep warning me about how hard it's going to be. How you won't be home a lot. Are you scared about something specific?"

Fuck, have I been that transparent? How many relationships of my teammates have I seen crash and burn during the season? Too many to count. The distance and time away almost always causes a problem.

I shoot her a smile that probably doesn't ease the question in her eyes. "I think I'm trying to prepare you, but in all honesty, I am scared."

She inches away. "You think I'll do what I did to Tristan?"

"What?" I frown, unsure what she's talking about. What does this have to do with Tristan?

Eloise fidgets with her fingers in her lap, her eyes downcast. "I had problems with Tristan, then I met you and ran away from my wedding. You think the same kind of thing will happen with us. I'll grow tired of being alone, or—"

"No." I place my finger under her chin, lifting her face to look into my eyes. "This has nothing to do with Tristan. That was completely different. I've just seen a lot of relationships, especially newer ones like ours, not make it. And I really don't want that to be us. It has nothing to do with you and everything to do with my job. I can't control the outside influences that will invade our bubble. Offseason is easy. But in season is an entirely different story. The travel is hard enough, but then when we're in public, everyone wants to chime in on how they think I played or what we're doing wrong when we lose."

She nods but doesn't say anything for a beat. "I'll have Kyleigh and Jade, and I need to really get this stylist thing off the ground, and you tend to be a distraction." She looks at me through her eyelashes.

"A distraction?" My eyebrows raise up near my hairline.

"A good one, but there's not a lot I can get done sitting on your lap all day." Her joking smile turns me on.

I close the gap between us, and her back is pressed to the door as my lips seek hers.

She stops me with a hand on my chest. "We'll take it one day at a time. I have no doubt we can do this. And maybe we go to a sex shop and get some toys for phone sex?" She waggles her eyebrows.

"Fuck, you really are perfect." I press my lips against hers. As always, being with her relieves some of my worry because we're so good together, how can we not make it?

The kiss is soft at first, tentative, giving her a chance to pull away if she wants to discuss anything further. But she leans into me, her free hand curling around the back of my neck, bringing me closer.

The space between us feels impossibly small, the air of the car charged with the heat radiating off each of us. Her fingers tangle in my hair, and my hand grips her waist, keeping her against me. The leather of the car seat creaks as I tilt my body into her, not wanting an inch between us.

When we have to take a breath, I rest my forehead against hers, both of our breathing labored. The windows are steamed up around us.

"I really wish we had a bed right now." My voice is rough with yearning.

She smiles, her hand resting against my cheek. "Kiss me again."

And then my lips are on hers, and I dive my tongue deeper this time, more insistent, as though this thing between us might slip through our fingers if we don't hold on tightly enough.

Outside, the world is carrying on, but in this car, nothing else exists—just us. I wish I could put a protective bubble around us and not let anyone or anything penetrate our happiness.

forty-two

Eloise

As soon as I get inside the Uber, I pull out my phone to text Conor.

> I'm sorry I missed you before you went to the rink. Good luck tonight.

> How did the appointment go?

I love that he's more concerned about me than the fact I missed seeing him off before his first game of the season. I feel like a shitty girlfriend.

> It went great! I'll fill you in later. I can't wait to see you play.

> Yeah, there's something I forgot to warn you about.

Shit, what is this about?

> My dad is going to be there tonight. He sits with Kyleigh, which means he sits with you too.

My stomach gets queasy, but before I have time to respond, he sends another text.

> I'm sorry. I should have planned a dinner or something. Guess I just don't like to share you. But Kyleigh will be there, and he's a great guy. You'll be fine. Still, I'm sorry.

He sounds so worried.

> I can't wait to meet him.

I'm not sure whether I feel nauseated from not eating enough at lunch or from the fact that meeting parents isn't easy. But I have to remind myself that meeting Conor's dad likely won't be like meeting Tristan's parents, where I felt as though I was under a microscope.

> Don't worry about me. I'm good. See you there.

> I can't wait to show off for you.

I chuckle softy, and the Uber pulls to the curb.

> If I'm going to see all your moves, I gotta get ready.

> You've seen my best moves… hang around after the game, Kyleigh will bring you to see me.

> Okay… see you in a bit. Good luck!

I pocket my phone and climb out of the car outside the apartment building. I enter the security gate code and jog up the stairs. Kyleigh's already coming down the stairs decked out in Rowan's jersey, a pair of jeans, and cute boots.

"Oh, look at you." I press the code to unlock the door to the condo. "Give me, like, ten."

"No worries. How was it?" She follows me inside the apartment.

"Great." I take off my light fall jacket and hang it on the coat hook, toeing out of my shoes. "She's as wonderful as you said."

I toss my purse on the breakfast counter and notice a box there with a note on top.

"Oh, and here I thought my brother didn't have any game. I should've expected this." Kyleigh comes up next to me.

"What is it?"

She shrugs, but I can tell from her smile she knows exactly what's inside.

I take off the note and read it.

FROM ME TO YOU.
I'D BE HONORED IF YOU WORE IT.

I place the note facedown next to the box.

"Yeah, I don't want to know what kinky shit he wrote." Kyleigh leans her hip on the counter, waiting for me to open the package.

I do, and inside, tucked under some tissue paper, is a Chicago Falcons jersey with the number forty-nine and NILSEN on the back. Kyleigh smiles, watching me hold it up.

"I never thought I'd be a hockey girlfriend." Back when I went to Henry's high school games with Jade, I never aspired to date one of the players—in good part because of the shit she dealt with from other girls. Though I ended up having to deal with the same thing at the country club with Tristan. Everyone wanted to marry a Somerset.

"You'll come to find out that it's pretty awesome. Now go put on that jersey and let's go. You want to be there for warm-ups."

I glance at Kyleigh, and she shakes her head, laughing and shooing me with her hand.

Within fifteen minutes, I've refreshed my hair and makeup, changed, and put on Conor's jersey. Kyleigh calls the Uber, and on our ride, I fill her in on how my meeting went with her client. We're planning to have one more shopping day before the job is complete. And the best part is that she's referred two of her friends to me. I've done some research on how to make being a personal stylist a successful venture, and the possibilities in front of me are exciting.

"So, you like it?" Kyleigh asks.

"I love it. I cannot thank you enough for thinking of it and suggesting it in the first place. I'm not sure I ever would've thought of styling as an option for me."

"I'm happy for you. It's great to be your own boss. Let me tell you." She turns to me and opens her mouth to say something, then turns away.

"What?" My head tilts.

"Have you met my parents yet? Because I'm pretty sure my dad is going to be there tonight." She cringes.

"Conor messaged me about a half hour ago to let me know." I laugh.

She shakes her head. "I swear men, but you have nothing to worry about. My dad loves everyone. He's not going to grill you with questions or anything."

"I can't wait to meet him." And I find that it's the truth. I want to meet the man who played a role in making Conor the amazing man he is.

We talk about the game and what to expect. She tells me about her parents and their divorce, which I know a little about from Conor.

We arrive at the arena, and Jade and Bodhi are already in their seats when we make it to our row.

"Eloise! Kyleigh!" Bodhi runs over to us and hugs our legs. "First game!"

"Did we miss warm-ups?" Kyleigh asks Bodhi, and he takes her by the hand over to the plexiglass.

"His jersey, huh?" Jade asks, plucking at the sleeve. She's wearing Henry's jersey and even has his number on her cheek.

"He left it for me. It would be rude not to wear it." I sit with her.

I only see the opposing team on the ice. I hope we didn't miss warm-ups. Kyleigh seemed like she really wanted to be here for them.

"You wouldn't want to upset him before his game." She playfully rolls her eyes, and I knock her with my elbow.

"Yeah, it was the polite thing to do."

Once our laughter dies down, she turns to me. "You're happy?"

"Very."

She plucks the jersey again. "And you understand the statement you're making by wearing this and sitting with us?"

"I do."

"If Tristan or your grandparents see—"

"I understand, Jade. But he's my boyfriend, and if people have a problem with that, then it's their problem, not mine."

A smile rises on her face, and she opens her arms, swarming me in a hug and shimmying us side to side. "I love that we're hockey girlfriends together."

I do love this world Jade's been living in since she got back together with Henry. It's one where they all have each other's backs.

A knock on the plexiglass draws our attention, and we both turn. Conor stands on the other side and eyes me. Already, the lust in his eyes spurs my lady parts into a frenzy. His gaze roams up and down my body, causing heat to radiate through me. He winks and skates off toward the net.

I watch him for a bit, and holy shit, now I get why he's so good in bed.

My mouth drops open. "Is he doing the splits?"

Jade and Kyleigh laugh, and Kyleigh pats me on the shoulder. "That's why we don't miss warm-ups. Although I'll be watching Rowan." She concentrates on another area where Rowan and Tweetie are together.

But I can't strip my eyes off Conor. The hip thrusts or flexors or whatever the stretch is makes my pussy purr for him. My body heats, and my mouth waters watching how smooth he is on the ice. I glance around the area to see who else might be ogling my man, but I remind myself that I'm the one who knows what he looks like under those pads.

His ass might look great as he gyrates against the ice, but I've had that bare ass in my hands. My fingertips have dug into his flesh and spurred him to thrust harder into me. I might be his girl, but still, I get why puck bunnies want the players. They're doing a Magic Mike show before the game.

"You must be Eloise," a deep voice says, drawing my attention away from Conor.

I turn and come face-to-face with what I assume Conor will look like in his older years. And here I've been ogling his son thinking about how he fucks me until I'm boneless. I hope I wasn't obvious.

He extends his hand to me. "Troy Nilsen."

I slide my hand in his. "Eloise Corbin. It's a pleasure to meet you."

"You, too. Are you a hockey fan?" He comes along side of me, watching his son with the countenance of a proud father.

"Honestly? Not really. I don't understand the ins and outs of the game."

Troy chuckles. "Well, at least you picked the guy on the team with only one task—to stop the puck from going in the net. And I'm happy to explain whatever you want." He looks at me and winks. Just like his son, I bet he was pretty damn smooth in his day.

"Smile!" Kyleigh gets in front of us, holding up her phone, and snaps a picture.

She moves over to Bodhi and takes a picture with him eating a plate of nachos, then one of her and Jade. I sit down next to Troy, and Conor winks and waves on his way back to the locker room.

Before the game starts, Troy goes to get a drink. As we wait for the festivities to begin, I pull up my social media, wondering if I should take a picture of myself here at the game and make us social media official. Tell the world that I'm with Conor Nilsen and currently sitting in the front row and wearing his jersey. But when I enter the app, I go into my notifications to see that Kyleigh has a personal account and has tagged Jade and myself and her dad in the pictures she took with the caption, "Starting the season with a bang."

I scroll through the comments, pausing when I come across one in particular.

<3Nilsen49

Oh cute, the blonde thinks he's hers. Joke's on her I guess.

My heart lodges in my throat. This is what I was warned about, and I can handle it. It's just some random stranger. When I go to her account, I find it filled with videos of Conor, but the one that catches my eye is the one she just posted of him doing his warm-ups earlier tonight.

Whoever this girl is, she's in this arena too.

forty-three

Conor

We win the game three to zero and file off the ice, heading into the locker room.

"What the hell did I tell you?" Tweetie says when we sit down to take off our equipment.

"What?" I take off my pads and undress because I want to hit the showers and get out to greet Eloise as fast as I can.

"You had her wear your fucking jersey. I bet word is all over the puck bunny scene that you're seeing someone."

I thought about not giving it to her, but knew I'd see Kyleigh wearing Rowan's and Jade all cozy in Henry's jersey. The selfish part of me wanted Eloise to wear mine. I want everyone to know she's mine. But I get Tweetie's point too.

"If she's going to be part of my life, I can't hide her in a closet," I say, knowing it's the truth. I hope that the women will back off now, knowing I'm taken. A lot of them have respected Rowan and Henry's relationships. Usually, they just move on to the single players.

"It's too early, man." He shakes his head, untying his laces.

I'm really hoping Lila will see Eloise in my jersey and find some other player to become obsessed with. But I'm sick of not doing things in my life because of fear. I can't control someone's reaction to me living my life.

"I hope for your sake, they're kind." He tears off his jersey and pads.

"I'll handle it."

And I will. I'm handling Lila already. I told her to go back to Florida and leave me the hell alone. Hopefully, she'll listen. If she doesn't, I'll have to file another restraining order. I haven't seen her since, so that's a good sign. And I know Eloise is strong enough to deal with this world and all the shit that goes with fame. I just don't want her to have to.

I head to the showers, leaving Tweetie and his pessimistic view behind. Not all relationships are the same.

I shower, dress back in my suit, and head toward the room that holds the family members to grab Eloise and go celebrate our win. On the way, my phone vibrates, and I figure it's probably my mom congratulating me, so I pull it out to respond. It's from a number I don't recognize that isn't in my contacts.

Anonymous: Great game. Loved your warm-ups. I'm a little worried about your taste in women though.

My bag slips off my shoulder and lands with a thud on the floor.

Fuck. It has to be Lila. She was here? At the game? I don't want to message back like I did in Florida—it only made it worse—so I delete the text, shut off my screen, and continue to my destination.

Eloise is with my dad, laughing at something he said, and it makes all the bullshit go away. My dad has a genuine smile when he turns to me and winks, silently telling me he likes her. Of course he would, I had no doubt. Sure, Mom will be a tougher audience, but after her antics last year, she'll probably welcome Eloise with open arms regardless of how she really feels.

I shake hands with my dad, giving him a hug as he pats me on the back and says, "Great start to the season."

"Definitely. Thanks for coming, Dad."

I shift my attention to Eloise, and she curls into my arms, kissing my jaw. "What do they call it when you blocked all the goals?"

My dad chuckles.

"A shutout."

Her arms tighten around my stomach. "Congratulations on your shutout then."

I kiss the top of her head. "Don't expect to see them often."

"You must be his lucky charm," my dad says to Eloise.

She tips her head, beaming up at me.

I bend down and kiss her again. "We have a theory about it."

Her forehead creases. "What?"

Tweetie comes into the room. "Man, I'm gonna have to get a girl. First Landry, then Hensley, and now Nilsen. All of you have the games of your fucking life the first time your girl comes to watch you play." He shakes his head.

"That's the theory," I say to Eloise. "I think it's more that we want to impress you guys, so we go all out."

"You don't have to impress me," she says, still not letting me go. Not that I want her to.

Kyleigh and Rowan come over and my dad turns to talk to them, congratulating Rowan on a great game. It's crazy that Rowan, Henry, and Tweetie all scored our goals, which means our foursome is flying high.

"I do have to impress you." I kiss her again, wishing we had some privacy so I could show her just how much I missed her today. It was the first day since we became a couple that we didn't see one another for the majority of the day, and while she seems okay, I'm not a fan.

"Are you hungry?" she asks. "The girls talked about going to eat."

"I'd like to pick up food and go home honestly."

"Okay," she says without argument.

We say goodbye to everyone, especially to my dad who declined the invitation to grab a meal with everyone too.

On our way out of the arena, Eloise's phone dings. She pulls it out, and her footsteps stop.

My hand tightens around the strap of my bag. "What is it?"

Fucking hell, if Tristan is calling her because he was watching the game and saw her and wants to give her grief, I'm gonna be pissed. The camera operators always shoot to the family members at some point.

"It's my grandma. My dad's mom. She wants to have dinner." She turns her phone screen to me, and there's a text message with a picture of her in my jersey, pounding on the plexiglass.

"How do you feel about that?" I put my arm around her shoulders.

"I think she wants to lecture me, but it's probably something I need to deal with. I've avoided it long enough."

I don't have any suggestions or ways to help her through this besides being there with her. "Can I come with you?"

Her eyebrows raise toward her hairline. "You would?"

I hate that a piece of her still doubts how far I'm willing to go to make sure she's supported and happy, but I hope she'll realize in time that I'll always be there for her. The longer I stand next to her, supporting her, the more those doubts will disappear.

"I want to. If you want me there."

A soft smile creases her lips, and I lower my head, kissing her.

"Just tell me the day and time."

"You're the best." She kisses me one more time before we walk out of the arena.

"I know."

We get into the Uber I ordered, and on the ride back to the condo, she's on her phone. The longer she looks at it, the more her smile dims.

"What's going on over there?" I place my hand on her thigh.

She looks at me. "Nothing."

"What is it?" I ask again.

"It's just... Kyleigh posted a picture."

My stomach drops as though I had the worst game of my career. "And?"

"And you have a real admirer because she doesn't like me for sure."

I don't need to read the comments she's talking about to have an idea of what they say. "Block her. Block them all, Eloise."

My tone is probably a little too authoritative, but I don't want her reading comments where other women are nitpicking her looks. She's perfection personified.

She places her hand on my leg. "I can handle myself, bossy." Eloise turns the screen of her phone off and slides across the seat. She brings her mouth to my ear as her hand slides up my thigh. "Tonight, I'm going to congratulate you on your shutout with my mouth." Her feather-light touch makes my dick twitch in my dress pants.

I hold her hand between my legs, staring into the rearview mirror and happy to see our driver's attention is on the traffic in front of us.

She sucks on my earlobe and breathes into my ear. "You like that, don't you? My hand on your big cock."

Fuck, I look out the window at where we are, wanting out of this Uber. Thankfully, we're about one block away from the condo, but there's so much traffic for a Saturday night it will take us longer to drive there than walk.

"Hey, man, we'll get out here. Thanks." I take her hand off my dick and open the door.

We walk quickly down the block, through the security gate, and the moment we're inside my condo with the door closed, she pushes me against the wall and falls to her knees in front of me.

"Fuck," I say, watching her undo my belt. She unbuckles and unzips me, letting my slacks fall to my ankles. "I want you to strip so I can see your tits, but at the same time, I want you to wear my jersey while you suck my cock."

She looks up at me through her long dark eyelashes and tugs my boxers down until they join my pants. My cock strains toward her mouth, and her hand curls around the base of my shaft.

She leans forward and draws the tip of my dick between her lips. I watch as her mouth wraps around the head, then she slides her smooth tongue over me, stroking my length as she bobs up and down on my cock. It's all I can do not to grab her hair and push myself deeper down her throat.

Eloise slides me out of her mouth, but her hand doesn't release me, and she continues to stroke me.

I roll my hips in time with her rhythm. "Please." I'm practically begging, but I don't care.

Smiling, she takes me into her warm, wet mouth again. Her tongue is slick and soft against my rock-hard erection. She moans around my girth, a sound that is so incredibly arousing I almost come right there. Then she takes me in deeper, and my hand winds through her hair. Eloise tightens her hand around me as she tugs me farther into her mouth, setting a pace that puts me on edge.

"I'm not sure how much longer I can last." I drive my hips forward then back before doing it again.

I can barely handle the sight of my beautiful girlfriend kneeling before me with her delicate hand wrapped around my cock. I want my cum on every inch of her. In her mouth, on her face, over her tits, in her pussy.

I groan loudly as I watch her take me so deep that she gags. My balls draw up tight.

Shifting her position on the floor, she leans and places one hand around the back of my thigh as her other hand continues pumping my shaft in time with her mouth.

My fingers tighten in her hair as my cock goes rock hard. "I'm gonna come."

Her eyes never leave mine, gazing up at me and overflowing with lust. What I wouldn't give to have a picture of this on my phone to masturbate to during the upcoming away games.

She continues sucking me until, with one final thrust, my dick twitches, and I pour into her mouth. I pant, trying to catch my breath.

With her hand still on my shaft, she twirls her tongue, cleaning me off until my dick is soft against her tongue.

"Congratulations on your shutout." She gives me a coy, self-satisfied grin.

I rest my hands under her arms and nudge her to stand. "If you can promise one of these each time, maybe I'll have more shutouts this season." I smack her ass. "Now strip down except for my jersey."

She squeals, and I capture her mouth. I'll never have enough of her.

forty-four

Eloise

We're on our way to dinner with my grandparents, and the nerves are starting to get to me. I know how they can be when they're not happy with me, and I don't want any of that directed toward Conor.

I could have told him not to come, but I want his support. Besides, if they have a problem with him, that's their problem. What they should be concerned about is whether I'm happy or not.

"My mom is worried," I say to Conor, who seems kind of distracted tonight. He's been on his phone more than usual when we're together.

"How come?" He slides his phone back in his pocket.

"My grandparents can be persuasive, and I've always cowed to their wants. I told my mom that if they give me a hard time, then we'll leave."

He places his hand over mine. "You lead the way, and I follow."

"Thanks again for coming."

"I want to be here." He squeezes my hand, and our eyes lock for a moment before I look out the window. "Hey, I forgot to mention, you know that day we were going to volunteer at the animal shelter? Can we push it by an hour?"

I shrug. "Sure."

"SportsVerse wants to interview me." He says it so casually, as if it's not a big deal.

"What? Why aren't you jumping up and down?" I sink back into my seat. "Or is it not a big deal? Have they interviewed you before?"

He chuckles as we pull up along the curb at the restaurant.

We climb out of the car, but I tug on Conor's hand because I don't want to go in there until we finish our conversation. "So, is this, like, a new thing?"

"I've been interviewed plenty, but it's my first time being spotlighted. I'll be on the cover. Which reminds me, we have to talk about how much you feel comfortable with me saying about our relationship."

I wind my arms around his neck, pressing myself against him. "I'm so happy for you. I wish we could be celebrating instead of going to dinner with my grandparents." I pretend pout.

"We don't have to celebrate." He kisses me. "Now, stop delaying and let's go."

My shoulders sag, and I sulk, allowing him to lead me inside the restaurant.

"We will be celebrating when we get home," I say.

He doesn't argue, but there's still a quietness about him tonight that concerns me. Maybe he's nervous about this meeting too.

We walk up to the hostess.

"Corbin, party of four," I say.

She smiles, but her eyes are more on Conor than me. "Yes,

your party is already here." She steps away, and Conor waits for me to go first.

I spot my grandparents at a table for four right in the middle of the window that looks out onto the street. It's probably the best table in the restaurant, which doesn't surprise me.

"Here you go." The hostess stops and holds out her arm toward the table.

My grandparents lift their gazes from their menus. There are no smiles over seeing their granddaughter or standing up to shake hands with her boyfriend.

My grandfather puts out his hand at the two empty seats. "Please sit."

Conor holds his hand out to my grandfather. "Good evening, sir. Conor Nilsen."

My grandfather stares at his hand for a moment and doesn't shake it. "Yes, I remember you."

We're off to a great start. Wonderful.

I place my hand on the back of the chair, but Conor beats me to it, sliding it out for me. I sit, and he pushes me into the table before he takes his own seat. I pick up the menu, and Conor glances around the table, probably waiting to see if anyone is going to say anything, but when no one does, he picks up his own menu.

His hand slips under the table and rests on my leg. Since I'm wearing a dress, his rough palm is against my skin, and his touch works to ease my nerves a bit.

The waitress comes over, and my grandfather orders a bottle of wine for us to share without asking whether anyone actually wants wine.

"Excuse me," Conor grabs the waitress's attention before she leaves. "May I have a sparkling water?" She nods, and he turns to my grandparents. "I'm in season, and I have a game tomorrow."

They both nod but say nothing else.

This is going to be the most awkward dinner ever.

"I'm assuming since you insisted on your boyfriend coming—" my grandmother glares in Conor's direction "—you're okay with us being frank."

"May I interject for a second?" Conor asks.

My hand squeezes his on my thigh to tell him to just let my grandmother get her rant over with. But my grandparents relax in their chairs. My grandfather holds his hand out to tell Conor he has the floor.

"I want to apologize. Barging into the wedding, drunk on top of it, isn't something I would normally do."

My grandmother's back straightens, and she rests her elbows on the armrests, clasping her hands in front of her. "Then why did you decide to ruin everyone's day?"

"Grandmother," I say, but Conor squeezes my knee.

"I met Eloise, and there was an instant connection—"

My grandmother waves. "Connection? Instant? You blew her entire life up so you could sleep with her." Her eyes are so cold and mean that it's hard to remember why I cared about impressing this woman.

Conor exhales a breath.

I lean in across the table. "That's not it at all. And he didn't blow up my life. I could have just as easily told Conor to go away and still married Tristan."

The waitress brings over the bottle of wine, and I'm thankful for the reprieve. She opens the bottle, pours my grandfather a small amount to sip, and once he says it's good enough, she pours some for everyone.

"I'm happy. Conor makes me happy," I say as they sip their wine.

My grandmother swallows and looks at Conor. "I'm sure you do very well, young man. Some of my friends have told me about your salary and things. Some of them are even enamored that you wanted our Eloise. But you do not have the connections or the wealth for our lineage."

I wrap my shaking hand around my wineglass.

"It's not to say that we don't admire all the hard work it took you to get where you are." My grandfather places his wineglass on the table. "But, son, you don't come from our world. You could very well get hurt tomorrow, and then you're done, because you've probably spent your money on frivolous things."

Conor picks up his sparkling water, sipping and swallowing before placing it back down on the table. He removes his hand from my leg and both of his hands grip the armrests, as if he's calming himself before he responds.

"Here's a little about me. My dad is a defensive attorney in the city and a partner in his practice. My mother is a wedding dress designer who has her own business and does well. At least according to our standards, probably pennies to you. I worked my ass off my entire life to get to where I am in the league. I'm the lucky one who earned his spot with blood, sweat, and a lot of injuries. It taught me how to be resilient, and I'm grateful and proud of what I've accomplished. I've fallen for your granddaughter. I'm happy to show you my bank accounts and portfolio because I actually don't spend my money on frivolous things. I could get injured tomorrow, and financially I'd be okay not to work another day in my life—"

I put my hand over Conor's to stop him from talking and look across the table at my grandparents. "I'm sorry that you were embarrassed that I didn't marry a man who wasn't going to make me happy in the long run and who treated me with disinterest at best and disrespect at worst. Why would you rather have me marry Tristan, who clearly never loved me? Who always put me second to everything else in his life, rather than Conor who has picked me up from the lowest point in my life and helped me figure out who I am?" I dig my finger into my chest.

"So, you're going to marry him?" my grandmother asks, not addressing anything else I said. The disgust in her tone says it all, I suppose.

I'm not going to get anywhere here.

"No." I shake my head.

"You aren't?" Conor's head whips in my direction. "Ever?"

I place my hand on his cheek and shake my head. "I meant I'm done here." I turn back to my grandparents, down the red wine, and slide out my chair. "If you can't accept Conor, you can't accept me, not that you ever really did accept me. You have a status to live up to, and I don't fit in the mold you keep trying to shove me into. So, go tell your friends that you've disowned me or tell them nothing at all. I really don't care." I stand.

When Conor doesn't, I put my hand under his bicep, nudging him up.

He stands next to me, and I hook my arm through his. "But know that it will be you who's missing out because when our kids ask me about my grandparents, you'll just be fictional people that they'll never know. You'll be like reading a history book. Just facts about who you were. But that's all that matters to you, right? Figures and facts. Never any heart."

"Eloise, sit down." My grandmother is seething. "You're causing a scene."

"You want to see a scene, Grandmother?" I put my hands on Conor's shoulders and turn him to me, then smack my lips to his, sliding my hand to the back of his neck to make sure he doesn't pull away.

But of course he doesn't. He actually licks the seam of my lips and slides his tongue into my mouth, earning a gasp from my grandmother.

"Have a great life." I take Conor's hand and walk away.

Conor stops us and digs his wallet out of his back pocket. He throws a bunch of hundred-dollar bills on the table. "Dinner's on me."

His fingers entwine with mine, and he escorts me out of the restaurant. Once we're outside, I grip his shoulders and kiss him so hard I wouldn't be surprised if his lips were bruised.

"It's over." I sink into his arms, and he holds me tightly.

I'm disappointed that things didn't go differently, but I think I knew they wouldn't. Still, I'm happy I said my piece and no longer have to worry about living up to their unattainable standards.

"Our kids?" Conor finally says.

I smack him in the stomach and look up at him. "No kids?"

He runs his palm down my cheek. "Definitely kids."

"Take me home?"

He places a light kiss on my lips and flags down a cab so we can return to the happy bubble we've created together.

forty-five

Conor

My phone vibrates with another fucking text from an anonymous number. I've blocked every damn number Lila's been sending them from, but they keep coming. This is why I changed my number back in Florida.

All her messages go on and on about how we're so good together. How we're meant to be. The ones where she bashed Eloise pissed me off the most, saying that Eloise doesn't know what I need.

We're at our first out-of-town game, but thankfully we fly back tonight, so although Eloise will be asleep when I get home, I can still cuddle up to her.

I toss my phone in my bag and head out onto the ice for practice before going back to the hotel to nap before our game tonight. Tweetie, Rowan, and Henry are all messing around, doing tricks with their puck handling rather than practicing their shots.

"About time," Tweetie says.

"Did any of you have to pose for pictures with that new social media hype person the league sent to us?" Rowan asks.

Rather than joining the conversation, Tweetie skates away.

"I heard every team was assigned a person." Henry shoots his puck into the empty net.

"I'm not sure ours is going to do much for us. He didn't even have me in my jersey, and he acted like I was getting a headshot." Rowan shakes his head. "I look like the mail room manager for some big corporation."

The two of them laugh, but Henry stops, watching me cross the ice to the net. "What's going on?"

Rowan skates around the net, stopping at the side of it as I throw my water bottle on top and get ready to put on my helmet.

"Whoa, wait." Tweetie skates to Rowan's side. "I'm not shooting pucks at you when it looks like you might just slap them back at us with double the force."

I toss my helmet on the net. "It's all fucked up. I'm gonna lose her."

I finally let them see the hell I've been living in since Lila found me again. The only people who knew about Lila in Florida were Kane and Jana Burrows, the coach and team owner, because they deserved to know.

"What are you talking about?" Rowan asks.

I glance around to make sure Coach isn't out here yet. "Let's just pretend to do stretches. I don't need to lose my job and my girl in the same week."

They all drop to their hands and knees and stretch. They really are the best friends and teammates a guy can ask for.

"Back in Florida, there was this woman I slept with. She got... attached."

"Fuck, I hate that," Tweetie says, but I'm pretty sure he has no idea the level I'm talking about.

"She got it in her head that we were more than we were.

We had one night after a crazy game we won. I slept with her. I'm not denying that. And I stupidly gave her my number."

Rowan nods. "That's why when you called to tell me you were getting traded—"

"It was from a different number. I changed my number because she texted me day and night. Then she started leaving shit outside my place and sending packages to the arena. I eventually had to file a restraining order against her in Florida."

"Shit, man, you're making me scared to have a one-night stand now." Tweetie, unable to stay in one spot for long, gets up and skates in front of us, pretending to practice his stick work.

"Well, the worst part is that she found me here. She sent me a nude picture in the mail, and she's messaging from anonymous numbers over and over and over again. Now she's leaving bitchy comments on Eloise's social media posts."

Henry blows out a breath. "Shit, man, that sucks. You gotta go back to the police and file a report."

"He's right," Rowan chimes in.

"I don't want Eloise involved in this. She shouldn't have to deal with this kinda shit." I don't want her anywhere near Lila or this situation.

"You have to involve her." Henry glances at Rowan, and he nods.

"Trust me, you want to be truthful with Eloise. You have to trust that she'll understand and be able to handle it," Rowan says.

"Which I'm sure she will," Henry adds.

"Fuck that. Handle it yourself and keep it clear of Eloise." Tweetie skates to a stop. "It's way too early for her to get mixed up in you having a stalker. You'll scare her off."

I'm on Tweetie's side this time. Sure, Eloise and I are great, and every day I find out more stuff that I love about her, but to throw this at her in the first week of the season? She'd run, and I wouldn't blame her.

"Don't listen to him." Henry nods toward Tweetie. "He's the single one."

"The single one who learned his lesson. The single one who is single because of this fucking job." Tweetie raises his voice. It's the first time I've ever heard him so adamant and angry.

I know what Tweetie told me at the campfire, but I don't think the others do, so I'm sure they're thrown by his outburst.

"Relationships crumble under lies." Henry continues because that's his role in our friendship—he's the rational one.

"His survived after my sister lied." I point at Rowan, and they both shake their heads.

"The Nilsen Liars." Tweetie laughs and skates to the net, circles it, and taps in the puck.

"Fuck off. She was going to tell me who she was," Rowan sticks up for my sister, but we all know she could have handled it better.

"You're gonna be the one to ruin it," Henry says. "If you keep this from her and handle it on your own, she's going to find out eventually. She'll know something is amiss, then she'll grow suspicious, and it won't end how you want it to. Trust me." Henry gets up on his skates and practices his stick work.

"Think about it," Rowan says. "I know you're a fixer, but this time, you can't just be Prince Charming on your white horse." Rowan pats my shoulder and joins the other three.

"Now put on your helmet. We have to beat Buffalo tonight." Tweetie passes the puck to Henry.

I put my helmet on and do a few exercises before telling them I'm ready for them to shoot at me.

After the practice, we head back into the locker room.

I understand where Henry and Rowan are coming from,

but I'm going with Tweetie on this one. He's had a relation-ship fail because of this bullshit, and he's right, I need to keep this as far from Eloise as I can. So, I hammer a message to the last anonymous text I received.

> Meet me eleven tomorrow at Beans.

The three dots appear immediately. It's as if she sits by her phone and waits to hear from me even though I haven't responded once.

> I knew you'd come around.

Then I send a message to Eloise.

> I miss you.

> I miss you too, but I'll be naked in your bed when you get home. Feel free to wake me up. ;)

> Send me a picture of you right now.

She sends it to me, and I think she's at a department store based on the mannequins behind her. Her blonde hair is pulled into a ponytail I'd love to have wrapped around my fist right now, and her smile is wide and happy.

Fuck Henry and Rowan. She's been through enough shit. She doesn't need my drama.

forty-six

Eloise

A KNOCK SOUNDS ON THE DOOR OF THE CONDO, AND I wipe my hands on the dish towel, padding across the floor to answer.

Kyleigh has two to-go cups of coffee from Beans in hand, one of my favorite cafés. "I got you one."

I take it from her. "Thank you so much." I sip, hoping the caffeine hits my veins and magically makes me a better baker.

"Oh, cake." She walks in and sidles up to the breakfast bar.

"I'm making Conor a cake. Or trying to." I go back to trying to measure out the ingredients for the frosting. He may only eat a small slice since he's in season, I'm not sure, but it's the thought that counts, right?

"I thought this was already off your list." She cups her coffee with both hands, watching me.

"Yeah, but since the last one never rose, I figured I'd try again. Especially to celebrate his big interview today. He said this is his first solo article and cover." I can't help the huge smile on my face.

"I know, I just saw him. I'm so proud of him. He's waited a long time to be recognized in the league like this. Rowan always says how much more attention Conor deserves. Hopefully this will be the start of it."

"Did you say you saw him?" I ask, not letting my eyes leave where I'm trying to carefully measure the ingredients.

He texted earlier and said the interview went great, and that he was heading to the gym to get in a workout.

"Yeah, he was at Beans. The two of them were tucked into a corner, deep in conversation, so I bought the coffees and snuck out before he spotted me. I didn't want him to think I was spying on him, although he'd spy on me." She laughs, but I'm still confused because he should be at the gym. "She's a little younger than I assumed she'd be, but maybe I'm just getting older, and everyone looks young now."

"Younger? How so?" My mind is now far from how much to measure out for the frosting recipe and more on if I put Conor's dick in the mixer, would it chop it up or just spin it around.

She shrugs. "Just younger than me. She did have the cutest brunette bob though. Makes me want to cut my hair short."

"Did you say bob?"

"Eloise, do you need Q-tips? You're not hearing anything I'm saying." Kyleigh brings her cup to her mouth while I think about the girl from Peeper's. She had a bob and was a brunette. Could it be a coincidence? I'm not sure.

"You know what, I forgot that I need some vanilla and completely forgot to pick it up." I wipe my hands on the dish towel and go over to the coat hook to grab my jacket and purse.

"Oh, I have some vanilla at our place." She slides off the stool.

Of course she does.

"I need fresh vanilla beans. I'm supposed to scrape it out."

I hate lying to her, but I don't want to seem like her brother's psycho girlfriend either. I could be wrong, and the interviewer just has the same style as the girl who keeps popping up around Conor. And maybe I misunderstood Conor's text earlier.

"Well, I'm happy to go with." She walks to the front door, and I open it.

"It's okay. I'll be quick. Thanks for the coffee." I run back and grab it, following her out the door.

She ascends a few steps and looks at me again. "Are you sure you're okay? You seem off."

I shake my head. "I'm just mad at myself. I really wanted the cake to be iced and ready for Conor when he got home. Sorry to rush you out."

"Oh, don't worry about me. Call me later."

"I will." I've already turned around and am heading down the stairs, still putting one arm in my coat sleeve.

Outside the security gate, there's a new sign for the Nest, and I tear it down, tossing it in the trash can on my way down the street toward Beans. Ten minutes later, I peek in through the window of the coffee shop, but I can't see anything, so I'm left with no choice but to go inside.

I slide in behind a tall guy who looks over his shoulder at me a few times. I peek up and wave. "Just surprising someone. Sorry."

I slide behind a column, and the people doctoring their coffees at the counter all watch me. I peer around the corner, and sure enough, Conor's at a table with her. Unless the woman he told me was just a fan also works for SportsVerse, he lied to me.

My veins heat with anger. I take a moment to collect myself, but trying to rationalize it in my head is impossible because I keep circling back to the fact that he lied to me. If this were months ago, and it were Tristan I caught, I'd probably rush out of here without making myself known. But not anymore.

"Fuck this," I mumble and round the column, heading over to the table.

She sees me first and reaches forward, placing her hand on his wrist. A veil of red lowers over my eyes, and I come to a stop beside the table.

"Hi, Conor." I cross my arms, glaring at her hand on his wrist.

He follows my vision and retracts his arm, making her hand fall to the table. "Eloise, what are you doing here?"

He's seriously going to ask me that? "I was just seeing how your interview was going." I eye the woman.

"Interview? Sweetie, I told you to just tell her the truth," the brunette says.

Conor stands, blocking me from her view and clasping my elbow. "Let's go home and talk."

I wrench my arm from his grip. "I don't need to talk. Who is she?" I ask through clenched teeth.

"I'm his girlfriend and was before you slid in during our breakup."

"What?" Conor whips his head around. "We were never a couple."

I step around him so I can get another look at this woman.

"Oh stop lying, Pinkie, we were together back in Florida," she coos.

Conor closes his eyes. "She's lying."

I find it weird she uses his hockey nickname, but whatever. "You were supposed to be at the gym right now."

He runs a hand through his hair and down the back of his head, pulling at his neck. "I just..." He looks around the coffee shop, and I'm sure there are a lot of eyes on us, maybe even some phones out at this point. "Can we please just go home so I can explain this all?"

I watch as the girl places her hand on his back. My hands clench into fists to stop myself from ripping her arms from her body. "You finish up here and meet me afterward. I'll give you fifteen minutes before I pack up my stuff and leave."

"I'm coming with you." He puts his hand on the small of my back.

I step to the side so it falls away. He sighs.

"Pinkie!" the brunette says as we walk away.

Conor stops and turns around. "You've fucked with my life long enough, and I swear to God." He leans closer to her. "If I lose her because of you, I'm going to make your life just as miserable as you've made mine. We were never a couple. You were never my girlfriend."

She swallows, and her eyes fill with tears, making me actually feel bad for her. Unlike when I first got here, I don't think he has anything going on with her. But at the same time, I want answers. I want to know why he would lie to me.

Thankfully, she doesn't follow. Conor walks in line with me, but he doesn't try to hold my hand or touch me. He keeps his hands in his pockets until we get to the security gate of the Nest. He punches in the code, and once we're in the condo, he sees the cake and his shoulders sink.

"Talk," I say, waiting for him to tell me who exactly the brunette is.

forty-seven

Conor

I'm going to lose her if I don't start talking, but I don't know where to start.

"Oh my god, Conor... just tell me." When I still don't say anything, she cocks her hip out. "Should I call you Pinkie? Would that help to get your lips moving?"

"Why were you baking a cake?" I ask.

She crosses her arms again. "It was for you, but now I think it's going to be for me to wallow in after the big fight we're about to get into."

My chin hits my chest. "I don't deserve the cake."

"No, I don't think you do. And if you don't start talking soon, I'm going to leave."

"I slept with her," I finally confess.

She gasps. "When?"

My eyes fly up because I am a fucking idiot. That was a shit way to start this conversation. "Over a year ago. Back in Florida."

Her shoulders fall, and she rounds the couch, sitting down. "Continue."

I walk into the family room and sit in the chair adjacent to her. "I gave her my phone number to hook up again, but I was never interested in dating her. I saw her at the bar we used to hang out at after the games, called Carmelo's. I had a good game one night, got a little drunk, and went home with her. After that, she acted as if we were in a relationship. She'd message me day and night, and when I stopped responding and blocked her, she sent me gifts at the arena. She found out where I lived, and she left stuff there for me. I found her on my porch after a game at two in the morning. I tried to be nice, but she just didn't seem to get the point. I eventually changed my number and moved. In the end, I had to file a restraining order against her, and she was banned from the games." I scratch the back of my head.

Eloise doesn't say anything but crosses her legs, waiting for me to continue.

"She got into the parking lot once and broke into my car, was waiting for me naked in the back seat. I called the cops, and she was arrested. It stopped after that, and I ended up getting traded and put it all behind me."

"So, let's fast forward to you lying and telling me she was just a fan when I caught you with her the first time. And then you telling me you were at the gym today when you were having coffee with her." She waves for me to speak.

I'm so mad that Lila put me in this position. My life was on track. Eloise and I were doing so well, then bam! Sure, I fucked up by not filling Eloise in, but if Lila would've just backed off, it wouldn't be an issue.

"The first time she reached out when I was here was when she sent a picture in the mail."

She sighs, and her head falls back against the couch. "When we got back from camping?"

I nod.

"That's when you started acting all weird. Where is it?" She crosses her arms.

Fuck. I stare at the floor, feeling like the world's biggest douchebag. "In my dresser drawer."

She stands and rounds the couch. I get up and follow her to my bedroom.

"Get it," she says, gesturing toward the dresser.

"I totally forgot it was in here." I open my underwear drawer and dig to the bottom, pulling it out. "I was going to throw it out, but I forgot. I haven't looked at it at all. I swear."

I hand the picture to her, and she glances at it before ripping it in half. "Do you have any idea how stupid all this makes me feel?"

Tears well in her eyes, and she charges out of my bedroom... *our* bedroom for the most part, because since camping, she's slept in my bed every night.

"I didn't want to scare you," I say, chasing her.

"Scare me? So, you lied to me?" She whips around and runs her fingers under her eyes, wiping the tears there. "You lied."

My stomach bottoms out. I feel as though I'm going to be sick. "I'm sorry, I didn't want you to find out about her and leave me. I thought I could get rid of her, and then it wouldn't matter. But she refused to listen. Even today at Beans, she kept telling me how good we were together, no matter how many times I told her that I was with you. That you were the one I had fallen for." I step closer, but Eloise puts up her hand to stop me.

"You chose to lie to me. Why do people think I'm incapable of dealing with shit? I don't need to be handled with kid gloves. I'm a grown woman!" Her voice raises.

"I know you can. That's not it. It's me. It's all on me because you don't deserve to have some woman harassing you because she believes she's dating your boyfriend. A woman who is putting shitty things on your social media—"

Her head rears back. "Wait, how do you know about that?"

I swallow the lump in my throat. "You mentioned that one comment, so I've been checking your socials to see if she was continuing to send them. I've caught a few before you deleted them off your posts."

She throws her arms up in the air. "What else, Conor? What else have you been handling behind the scenes to make sure I stay in some bubble?" Jesus, she's animated when she's angry.

"Nothing." I shake my head.

"And that was her at Peeper's when you told me she was just a fan."

My shoulders sag. "I thought I could handle it." I step closer. "Please. I'm so sorry. I was stupid for not telling you."

She puts up her hand again. "I need to be alone." She walks by me into my bedroom, purposely keeping a distance so our bodies don't touch. She comes back out with her pillow. "I'm sleeping in the other room tonight. Don't bother me."

Her door slams shut, and my head falls forward. I'm such an idiot. I fucked up this entire thing.

forty-eight

Eloise

T HE FRONT DOOR SHUTS, AND I HOLD THE PILLOW that still smells like Conor up to my nose.

Five minutes later, my phone rings, and a knock sounds on the condo door. I glance at my phone screen and see that it's Jade. I slide my thumb across it to answer and pad across the condo to the front door.

"I'm fine," I say as I open the door and answer the phone at the same time.

Kyleigh walks in. "I have her. Get here as soon as you can," she says loudly enough for Jade to hear her.

"We'll be there in ten," Jade says before she hangs up.

I walk into the kitchen and put my phone on the counter. "I take it he told you."

"He's up at my place. I told him he's an idiot." She moves to the counter and grabs the measuring spoons and cups, reading over the recipe that's still sitting there.

"What are you doing?" I say, climbing up on a breakfast stool.

"I'm making the frosting and finishing your cake." She looks at me over her shoulder. "So *we* can eat it."

"It probably sucks." I sound like a whiner.

"I'm sure it's great. Now let's finish this. I assume you don't want to tell the story twice, so we'll save the talk about my shithead brother and finish this thing so it's ready with three forks when Jade gets here." Kyleigh smiles at me, and when I join her on the other side of the counter, she opens her arms and hugs me. "He's a good guy. But sometimes good guys do some really stupid shit." She squeezes me tightly. "I told him I'm going to knee him in the nuts if you're not my sister-in-law one day because you can't put up with his idiotic behavior."

I laugh. "Thanks. I know he's a good guy, but I'm so sick of men acting like I'm some delicate flower."

She nods. "I gotcha."

Fifteen minutes later, there's another knock on the door. Kyleigh opens it, sticking her head out into the stairway while Jade walks in.

"You're the only one who can talk sense into him," Kyleigh shouts up the stairs.

"Thanks for the confidence, babe," Rowan shouts back.

Jade drops her purse on the floor and sheds her coat, tossing it on the back of the chair before she wraps me up in a hug. "Men are assholes. I told Henry he better make sure I don't follow him up there and punch Conor in the gut."

I smile at both my oldest best friend and my newest best friend. "Thanks, girls. I really appreciate the girl power."

"Cake?" Jade's eyes bug out of her head.

"It was supposed to be for Conor, so I say we smash it in his bed." Kyleigh gets an evil look in her eye.

"You're very destructive," I say.

"Hey, I have a lifetime of noogies to pay him back for." She scoops up another heap of frosting and spreads it on the two-layer cake. "I'm kidding anyway. We're going to eat it of course."

"You made a cake. Cross it off your list." Jade pats me on the back.

When she says list, all I can think of is Conor bringing home those cake supplies so I could cross it off my list. God, I already miss him, but I'm so mad at him.

Once the caked is iced, Kyleigh digs three forks out of the drawer and hands them out to us. "Now tell us what happened and who this girl is."

We circle the cake on the stools, and I tell them the entire story Conor told me about Florida and how she's tracked him down here.

Afterward, Jade runs her hand down my upper arm. "I get it. I do. And you definitely need to have a conversation, but..." She looks at Kyleigh.

"What?"

"You're his first," Kyleigh says, raising her fork. "Which is no excuse. I'm not making excuses for him lying to you and not trusting you with the information, but he's new to this whole girlfriend thing."

"I'm really shocked at how well he's been doing," Jade says more to Kyleigh than me.

"The jersey thing floored me." Kyleigh pierces the cake with her fork and takes another bite.

"Just the whole way he's been with you. You didn't see him before." Jade takes another bite. "Honestly, this is a good cake, Eloise."

I shrug, but it's edible, so that's an improvement at least. "What do you mean I didn't see him before?"

They look at one another again, and I groan.

"He wasn't looking for a girlfriend. It's not like he had a rotating door of women, but he gave no one a chance. Then one night under the stars with you, and bam, he's ready to buy a ring." Kyleigh smiles. "He has good taste though. You're marriage material. The others, I'm not so sure."

"My problem is that he broke my trust. I felt his anxiety with the season starting. He was so worried what his schedule would do to us, and I took that as a lack of trust on my part."

Jade shakes her head. "That's not it. I think they feel the distance more than us sometimes. Not to say we don't miss them, but we're living our lives while they're at away games in a hotel or on a plane or a bus. We all have careers, I have Bodhi, a house that's being renovated. But to them, we're just sitting here twiddling our thumbs waiting for them to return."

We all laugh.

"Jade's right. You know how many times Rowan calls me while he's away? Sometimes if he struggles napping, he expects me to talk to him until he has to get on the bus to go to the rink. As though I don't have things to do." Kyleigh shakes her head.

"I think it's because they miss us so much more than we miss them." Jade cringes. "Which sounds horrible, but it's different when you're the one away from the comforts of your everyday life. Can we really complain though? They're faithful men who aren't into going to the clubs and hooking up with random women. They're there to play a game, and once it's over, they want to get home to us." Jade digs her fork in again.

She has a point.

My mind goes back to when Conor returned home last night. The way he cuddled up to me and kissed my neck, whispering how much he'd missed me. And it felt so good to have him back, but I did get more done setting up my new business while he was gone.

"I just need him to understand that we're in this together. Side by side. Not him in front of me pushing a lawnmower, mowing down any obstacles."

They nod and continue eating the cake.

Eventually, we talk about Bodhi and how he's loving second grade, and Kyleigh talks about a client who's driving her nuts.

I appreciate them coming here to make sure I'm okay, but I have to clear this up with Conor. I wonder what he's talking about upstairs with the boys and what their take is on all of this.

forty-nine

Conor

"You're an idiot," Rowan says. "Why would you ever listen to him?"

I put my head in my hands and groan.

Rowan picks up his phone and dials Tweetie. "Get your ass down here. You fucked it all up for Conor." He hangs up before Tweetie can say anything.

"I wanted to protect her."

Rowan shakes his head. "How mad is she?"

I stare at the Monopoly board game on the coffee table. "Is this the shit you do with my sister? You play Monopoly?"

Tweetie knocks on the door, and Rowan stands, patting me on the shoulder. "I know you're in the 'sex all the time where she brushes up against you, and your dick goes hard' stage, but that does end. You'll be playing Monopoly by next year."

"I don't think we'll ever be playing Monopoly." I lean back in the chair and slip off my shoes, crossing my ankles.

Tweetie walks in, looks at me, and lowers his head. "I take it some shit went down and now you're my wingman again?"

"God, I hope not. I'm praying this is just a fight, and she's going to forgive me."

He sits on the couch and picks up the dice. "And she's going to forgive you up here?"

Rowan swipes the dice out of his hand. "It's Kyleigh's turn."

Tweetie looks around. "Do you see Kyleigh anywhere?"

"If Conor could handle his shit, I'd have convinced her to buy Boardwalk by now."

Tweetie stares at the game, then at Rowan. "Tell me this is some kinky version of Monopoly."

I shake my head. "Apparently after a year of couplehood, this is what you do instead of having sex."

"Another reason why I'm not in a relationship. I always sucked at Monopoly." Tweetie taps his finger on the armchair. "I guess I'm here to say I'm sorry, but why else am I here?"

"We're here to talk to Conor. The girls are downstairs. Well, Kyleigh is, and Jade and Henry are on their way." Rowan pushes the coffee table toward the wall as if Tweetie can't be trusted.

"Did someone call a Code Red? I don't get the urgency. You're in a fight. Since when do we have to assemble for one of you guys having a fight?" Tweetie reaches for the television remote, but Rowan snatches that away too.

"Let me guess, you play Monopoly while watching one of her reality TV shows? Let me spoil it for you, they're in love and then the cameras turn off, and they break up," Tweetie says.

Rowan rolls his eyes. "I like reality TV, thank you."

"I'm sure you like Monopoly too." Tweetie raises his eyebrows at me.

Another knock sounds on the door. It has to be Henry,

which means Jade is at my place downstairs. Rowan answers the door, and Henry walks in while Rowan screams something to Kyleigh below.

"Why would you ever listen to Tweetie?" Henry smacks the back of Tweetie's head when he passes and sits in the chair next to me. "Monopoly?"

"According to Rowan, you play Monopoly when you get bored with sex," I say. "You probably only have a couple months left before you'll be having game nights."

"That's not what I said, jackass." Rowan comes over with four beers, handing one to each of us. "Where's Bodhi?"

"He's at Reed and Victoria's."

"So, who won your Monopoly game?" Tweetie asks, and the three of us laugh.

Rowan takes a long pull of his beer. "I hate you assholes."

"I'm still confused as to why we're all here," Tweetie says.

"To talk to Conor and figure out a way to get Eloise to forgive him." Henry opens his beer and downs a swig.

I give Tweetie a quick rundown of everything that happened.

"I told Jade this could be done over FaceTime," Henry says. "I guess since we're a little short of a year, we haven't hit the Monopoly stage yet, and I had other plans tonight."

"I'm not sure Eloise is going to forgive me. She thinks I don't think she can handle things. That I'm trying to take charge of her life. I just didn't want her to have to deal with my problem."

Henry pats me on the back. "Like I told you, it's both of your problem."

"Yeah, I see that now," I grumble.

"Hindsight is twenty-twenty," Tweetie says, and we all stare at him.

"Apparently not for you, asshole," Rowan says, clearly still upset about the Monopoly jokes.

"Just because I haven't acted doesn't mean I don't know what went wrong." Tweetie sits up, putting his beer at his feet and resting his forearms on his knees. "I know you probably think I can't offer any good advice because you guys have never seen me in a relationship, but I'm gonna tell you something, Pinkie. If you want her, you shouldn't be up here wallowing. You should be on your knees, begging and pleading for her to give you a second chance."

"She said she wants space."

"'She said she wants space.'" He mimics me, and I scrunch my eyebrows, not appreciating him mocking me. "Fuck, man, how quick did you get your ass up here after she said she needed space?"

I shrug. "I don't know, like five minutes."

He blows out a breath and looks at each of us. "I know you shitheads want to know what happened between Tedi and me, but it doesn't matter, our time has passed. Regardless, I still have one huge regret from the end of that relationship."

We all share a look since we've all been waiting for any information about the breakup that seems to have broken Tweetie.

"I didn't fight. I sat back and convinced myself that she needed space. That things would turn out okay. That was the wrong fucking decision. So if you really have this instant connection like you keep bragging to everyone about, you should be on your knees, fighting to keep it alive."

Rowan raises his eyebrows, and Henry nods.

"There you all go." Tweetie takes a pull from his beer and points at each one of us. "Anyone else have a problem? Psychologist Tweetie is in."

We all shake our heads and chuckle. Henry flicks his beer bottle cap at Tweetie, and he catches it.

"Why are you still here?" Tweetie asks me. "Go fix it because your personal problems cannot ruin our season."

I stand and hand Henry my beer, then pat Tweetie on the back. "Thanks, man."

He shrugs his shoulder to get my hand off him. "Just don't let me find you playing Monopoly with her in a few months."

"Fuck you all," Rowan says.

I rush to the door, and when I swing it open, I find Jade and Kyleigh there. They're each carrying a plate with cake.

"I'd knee you in the nuts if you weren't my brother, and I didn't want to be an aunt one day."

"And I won't do it because I want Kyleigh to be an aunt but do something like that again, and I can't make any promises," Jade says.

I ignore their threats. "Why are you eating my cake?"

"*Your* cake?" Kyleigh laughs and walks in. "This isn't your cake anymore."

Jade follows my sister inside and stops at my side. "She's hurt, Conor. Fix it."

"I will."

She nods, and I walk out to the stairs, jog down, and press the code to unlock my condo, but when I open the door, it's dark inside except for the light under her bedroom door.

Here goes nothing.

fifty

Eloise

I HEAR HIM BEFORE HE KNOCKS ON MY BEDROOM
door.

"I need to talk to you, Eloise. Please."

When I open the door, he looks so depressed that my heart
pinches. But I swallow down those people-pleasing habits of
mine, leave the door open, and walk back over to the bed.

"If you still want to sleep in your own bed tonight, I
understand, but I just want to talk to you. I'm so sorry, Eloise.
I was being stupid trying to fix this without involving you. I
should've showed you the picture and explained the situation
the minute I opened that envelope. I should've told you what
happened in Florida. And I definitely shouldn't have lied to
you today." He slides out my makeup chair and sits.

I'm on the bed, sitting against the headboard and holding
the pillow to my chest. I was just about to take off my makeup,
so my hair is thrown into a bun, and I'm in my shorts and
cami pajamas.

He opens his mouth but closes it before speaking again.

"Over the years in the league, I've seen a lot of relationships destroyed by the drama that can come from being a pro hockey player. So many times, a guy would come into the locker room and say I found her, she's the one. And then either the demands of the season demolish it, or the guy makes a bad decision on the road during a weak moment. Shit, I've seen a player sleep with another player's wife. I didn't want to chance the outside world ruining things for us, so I tried to keep it a secret. I was wrong."

"Yes, you were." I squeeze the pillow a little tighter.

He nods. "I know. And I'll never do it again."

I shift to the edge of the bed, wanting to be closer to him when I tell him why I was so angry. "Conor, being with Tristan was like being in the dark all the time. Sometimes I'd show up to a party and hear stories from people about something he'd done three days before that he'd never shared with me. One time at a party, a girl introduced herself to me, and when I said I was Tristan's fiancée, she said she didn't even know he was dating, anyone let alone engaged." My fingers twist in the pillowcase from reliving the embarrassment of that moment. "He just lived his life without any concern for me, only what he wanted. That's not the kind of relationship I want. And I don't want to be the girlfriend you 'take care of.'" I put "take care of" in air quotes.

He nods, and I see how upset he is. I want to crawl into his lap and hug him so tightly, but I need to convey to him what I want from this relationship and how important it is to me.

"I want to be a strong presence at your side. You're going to go through a lot of ups and downs in your career. It's not an easy road for anyone. We're going to run into difficulties, and I need to trust that you'll include me in your decisions. I want you to lean on me just as much as I lean on you." I get up from the bed, pad over to the dresser, and take out the check I wrote earlier. "Jade told me how much the rent is.

This is my half for the time I've lived here." I hold it out to him.

He accepts the check but blows out a breath. "Eloise…"

"No, Conor."

"Are you moving out?" His voice cracks.

My heart aches at the fear in his eyes. "No. But I asked you a lot about how much I owed you, and you kept brushing me off. I appreciate your kindness, but I want us on equal footing."

I sit on the bed again.

"I understand now, I really do, and I'm sorry." He shifts in the chair, his eyes meeting mine. "Truly."

"I just want us to be partners."

"I respect the hell out of you. I don't see you as a delicate flower, just so you know. It was more about my fear of losing you than thinking you couldn't handle it."

Unable to keep the distance between us any longer, I walk over to him. "I know. Your sister and Jade helped me see that. But from now on, we're a team, okay? And don't be so scared I'm going to run off because of some puck bunnies. I want this to work out just as much as you do. Remember, you weren't the only one that night under the stars. I was there. I felt it too."

He nods, wrapping his arms around my waist and nuzzling his head into my stomach. I run my fingers through his soft hair and he clings to me tighter.

"Are you going to sleep in here tonight?"

"I should. To teach you a lesson." I laugh, but I'd probably sneak into his bed in the middle of the night. "But I think it would pain me just as much as it would you."

He releases me, stands, and picks me up bride style.

"Conor," I say, and he lowers me toward the bed.

"The pillow goes in my bed."

I pick it up, and he walks us through the door, past the

kitchen, and into his bedroom, where he deposits me on the edge of the mattress.

"I'm sorry," he says again.

I press my finger to his lips. "It's over. Now, we move on." I remove my finger and press my lips to his, thankful the fight is over.

"Well then, let me apologize properly. I hear make-up sex is pretty great." He flips my legs out from under me and my back falls to the mattress. He crawls over me. "Hey, you don't like Monopoly, do you?"

"Um... no. Why?"

"Good answer." Then he strips me of my clothes and shows me just how sorry he is.

Orgasm after orgasm, the fight slips further and further from my mind.

fifty-one

Conor

Fucking meet-and-greets. I hate them more than anything.

It's been two weeks since my blowout with Eloise, and things have returned to normal between us. I ended up changing my phone number, and Eloise has started another social media account for her business and paused her private one for now.

I still hate that her life is being disturbed, but I'm trying to adopt her line of thinking because I wouldn't like it if she was going through something and didn't include me.

"You ready to be admired all day?" Eloise asks me, fixing a piece of my hair.

My hands find her hips as always, before straying down to her ass. "I like it better when you admire me."

"You can thank me later," Tweetie says and pats Eloise on the shoulder. "I like Twix bars."

Eloise looks at me. "What is he talking about?"

"He had surprisingly good advice that night we were in a fight."

"Thanks, Tweetie!" she calls.

Our social media guy, Gill, comes into the room. This guy doesn't seem to have much of a clue. From what I've heard, he's new to hockey. What he's having us do for marketing might work for a corporation, but not a hockey team. But he did set up this meet-and-greet for us, so I guess that's something.

"It's time, guys," he says.

"Give me a kiss good luck."

Eloise presses her lips to mine and pulls away too quickly for my liking. She runs her thumb over my lips to get her lipstick off. "You'll do great. Have fun."

I stand and take her hand. The girls are all here, along with Bodhi. We file out of the conference room, walking down the hallway past the long line of fans here to meet us.

"Damn, this is going to be a while," I say. "You should go."

She squeezes my hand. "Don't worry about me. I'm good."

Once we reach the room, we all part from the women in our lives and sit in a line at the long table. There are piles of markers for each one of us.

"So, who won Monopoly last night?" Tweetie asks Rowan, and Rowan throws one of the marker caps at his head.

It's a running joke that none of us have let go of yet.

Gill clears his throat in the microphone, and we all snicker like boys in grade school. "Hello, everyone. Welcome to the Meet-and-Greet Falcons style. We have some of our top players here ready to sign your stuff, take pictures, and answer any questions you might have. So, let's get this going!" He doesn't turn off the microphone as he tries to unclip the rope draped between the metal poles to let people in. "Shit, I should've practiced that."

"Gill, the mic," Henry says.

Gill doesn't pay attention to him, and all we can hear is the muffle of the mic hitting the velvet rope. Then Gill continues to curse. Tweetie finally gets up, takes the mic and turns it off, then hands it back to Gill before unlocking the rope.

"Thanks." Gill wipes his forehead with the back of his hand as though he just finished running a marathon.

The line goes smoothly, and there are a lot of kids. Our Falcons mascot keeps them entertained and asks Bodhi to help him pass out stickers and tattoos to the people in line.

I try to be engaged with every person who comes by, since I remember what it was like when my dad first took me to a meet-and-greet and how excited I was to have the sole attention of my favorite player.

Tweetie is ahead of me in the line, and one woman is asking him question after question, which holds up the line, so the three us sit and wait. I take a moment to scan the crowd and stop on a long-haired blonde in line. She looks familiar, but before I can get a good look, she tips her head toward her bag, and her hair veils either side of her face.

I have to be seeing things. Lila has short dark hair.

Finally, the woman chatting with Tweetie moves on to me. I sign what she asks me to, smiling and greeting her, but she doesn't seem nearly as interested in the rest of us as she was in Tweetie.

A few more people come through the line. My head is down as I sign something for someone when Tweetie asks for the person's name in front of him, and she says it's Lila.

My head flies up, and I rear back, her eyes locking with mine. "Hello, Pinkie."

Tweetie glances at me as he signs the jersey she's laid out for him. She has more in her hands. He gives me a look like "how do you know her?"

"Why are you here?" I ask, smiling and passing the item

back to the person in front of me. I glance around for Eloise, but she's nowhere in sight.

"I'd like a picture," she says. "And if you could sign the jersey. It's so big, I plan on sleeping in it. And spraying it with your cologne."

Tweetie's eyebrows furrow, and he mouths, "What the fuck?"

Henry elbows me, but I don't let my eyes stray from her. This is what I get for not telling the front office what the fuck has been going on.

Gill walks over. "People are getting disgruntled. You need to keep the line moving," he whispers.

"Oh, could you take our picture?" Lila hands her phone to Gill.

"No picture," I say.

Tweetie's head bobs from me to her.

"I paid like everyone else. I'd like a picture." Her voice is demanding with an undertone that says she's going to make a scene if I don't take the fucking picture.

"Take the picture," Gill says through gritted teeth.

"All of us, right?" Tweetie says, standing from his chair. "Come on, guys. This lady would love a picture with all of us."

Henry and Rowan's chairs squeak along the floor, and I'm the only one still sitting down, glaring at her. Why the hell is she still messing with my life?

Tweetie pats my arm, and I do another scan for Eloise, still not seeing her. I call over Bodhi and the Falcon's mascot.

"Do you know where Eloise is?" I whisper.

Bodhi shakes his head.

"Okay, thanks."

"Picture, Pinkie." Lila waves me over, my three best friends standing around her.

"Come on this side of me," Tweetie says, taking one for the team so he's next to her.

"Pinkie is my favorite. Can I have him here and then Magic on the other side? Sorry, Daddy and Tweetie, you're good and all, but these two are my favorites."

"Understandable." Gill eyes me to get the fuck over to the group because people are griping about it taking so long.

"No offense taken. We're happy to step to the outside." Daddy holds up his hands, an unimpressed look on his face as Magic reluctantly takes the spot on Lila's other side.

I hear laughing and see the girls come back into the room, carrying on with coffees and treats in their hands. I wait for Eloise to look up, but she doesn't, so I walk over to the group and slide between Tweetie and Lila. She puts her hand around my waist and tugs Magic and me closer to her.

"Fucking hell," Rowan murmurs.

"Isn't this fun?" Tweetie says.

"Take the picture, Gill," I say through gritted teeth.

"Oh, it turned off," Gill says and looks at the phone as if it's the dashboard of a space shuttle.

Lila goes over to fix the phone, and finally Kyleigh looks at us. I point at Lila's back and then at Eloise. Kyleigh knocks Eloise's arm and some coffee spills. She gives Kyleigh a funny look, and my sister tells her to look up.

As soon as she does, I point at the blonde sliding back between Rowan and me. Eloise narrows her eyes because I don't think she ever got that good of a look at Lila. Now that Lila is a blonde, it's probably harder to figure out.

"Anytime now, Gill." Tweetie squeezes my shoulder like "hang in there, buddy, almost done."

What feels like a lifetime later, Gill has taken the picture and hands the phone back to Lila.

"You love blondes now, so I dyed my hair. What do you think?" She presses a note into my hand, and I glance down to see an address written on it. "After she goes to bed, come over," she whispers.

Henry overhears and glances at my hand.

I drop the note on the floor.

"Okay, we're behind now. Let's get things moving again," Gill says.

But all I see is Lila walking toward Eloise as she leaves the roped off area.

"Eloise, come here," I call.

Gill opens his mouth to object, and Tweetie tells him to read the damn room. Eloise comes over, eyes wide, and I wrap my arm around her waist until Lila is out of view.

"Just stay in the room, okay?" I ask in the nicest way possible, not wanting Eloise to think I'm trying to run her life.

"I think we might need to take some action," she says.

"You're right. We'll go to the police station and file a report once I'm done here."

She nods and kisses my cheek before she goes back to the girls.

Then I head over to the security guard stationed in the room and ask him to make sure that Lila leaves the building and isn't allowed back in.

When I sit back down in the chair between Tweetie and Henry, I can't concentrate on anything, knowing Lila's not going to go away that easily.

fifty-two

Eloise

After the meet-and-greet, Conor and I drive to the police station while everyone else gets to go hang out at Peeper's Alley.

Jade called her stepdad, Reed, because they have a connection through their old next-door neighbor who is working on renovating Jade and Henry's new house. Her brother-in-law is a police officer, and although he's a detective, he agreed to see us.

We're sitting in the chairs, waiting to be called back, when a tall man with dark hair and olive skin walks out from the back. "Eloise? Conor?"

We both stand.

He puts out his hand. "Cristian Bianco. I heard you're having some problems with a fan?"

Conor nods. "I had a restraining order against her down in Florida, and now she's found me here."

He blows out a breath and waves us forward. "Come on in. We'll go to my desk."

He winds us through rows of desks until he sits in a chair and gestures toward the two empty ones across from him. On his desk are pictures of who I assume are his kids and a beautiful blonde who must be his wife.

"So, do you know her name?" Detective Bianco asks.

Conor gives him all the information he knows, and the detective types it into his computer.

"She gave me this note today during a meet-and-greet." Conor passes over the crumpled piece of paper, and Detective Bianco takes it.

"This can be tricky, which I'm sure you know from what happened in Florida. Why don't you tell me what she's done so far here in Chicago?"

He sits back in his chair, and Conor and I tell him about the texts, the comments, the dying of her hair, and the fact that she thinks she's in a secret relationship with Conor.

Detective Bianco's mouth twists. "There's nothing there I can bring her in for, so my suggestion for the time being is to get a lawyer and see how fast your case can be seen in front of the court. Until then, lay low. This type of behavior generally escalates. The problem is you're a public figure, so she knows where to find you. You might want to consider getting some security personnel."

"Fucking hell. I'm over this." Conor rocks his head back and blows a stream of air toward the ceiling.

I place my hand on his leg. "Do you have any lawyers you can suggest?"

"Talk to Reed. He'll get you situated. In the meantime, be aware of your surroundings and call us if she does anything considered criminal." He looks at Conor. "I know this is frustrating. With my job, I always worry about the safety of my kids and wife. But we'll get this handled. Honestly, it sounds like she needs some medical attention, so hopefully when the judge hears your case for a restraining order, she'll get some help. But I am sorry there's not more I can do right now."

Conor stands and holds out his hand. "Thank you for your time."

Detective Bianco shakes his hand and stands. "Here." He grabs his business card and jots something on the back. "That's my cell phone. Call me, but if you think you're in danger, you need to call 9-1-1 right away."

Conor pockets the card. "Thanks."

"I wish I could do more, but she hasn't outright threatened you, so my hands are tied."

I nod and take Conor's hand. "We understand. Thanks for meeting with us."

"I'll see you out." Detective Bianco steps around the desk. "I have to get home to my kids. Halloween tonight." He smiles as though he really can't wait.

He walks us out to the lobby, and we say one more goodbye before we leave the precinct.

"I'll call Reed," I say. "He'll be able to suggest a good lawyer."

"God, Eloise, I'm so pissed." Conor walks down the block. "I just want her to go away."

He leans his back against a wall, and I step in front of him, taking his head in my hands. "I know. Me too, and it will happen, but this is what she wants. She wants us to be unhappy because she thinks she can slide in and take my place. But we're not going to let her ruin our happiness, okay?" I press my lips to his.

When I pull away, he nods. "Okay."

"Now, let's go have fun with our friends. We're going to beat their asses at darts one of these days." I hold out my hand.

He places his palm in mine, clenching it tightly. "We need to buy you a dart set like mine."

I don't say anything, but having the best of the best darts hasn't helped him win any more games.

I understand why Conor is upset. Lila's really putting a dark cloud over us, but at the same time, my heart hurts for her. She must be mentally unstable to carry on like this. I hope by getting the ball rolling today, someone will step in and give her the help she needs.

fifty-three

Eloise

A HALF HOUR LATER, WE'RE IN THE BACKROOM OF Peeper's Alley with our friends.

"Did you see some of the costumes out there?" Henry asks, coming in with Jade but no Bodhi.

"Where's Bodhi?" I ask.

"He went trick-or-treating, and now Waylon and Owen convinced him to change his mask and go out again. I think it's for them." He shakes his head.

Jade rolls her eyes. "My brothers are using Bodhi to scam candy for them." She sits next to me.

"Reed told us about what happened at the police station." Henry takes the seat next to Jade.

"Yeah, but we'll get it figured out. Hopefully once we can file for a restraining order." I press my hand to Conor's thigh since I can see that he's struggling. I think it's more of a safety concern for him now.

When Conor wanted to get my attention at the meet-and-greet, I saw the fear in his eyes. The way he tracked me and her when she was leaving and came over to make sure he could protect me.

"We have the next game," Conor says.

"Fuck that, I want another shot at Jade and Henry," Tweetie calls.

Conor slides his chair out and leans over, kissing my cheek. "I'll be right back."

I sit back, happy he's calmed down a little. I chat with Jade for a while about Bodhi's time trick-or-treating, and she tells me how much candy he got. How hard Reed was on the older kids coming around with no costumes on and how he has no idea his own teenagers are out there using Bodhi to get candy.

"Eloise, we're up." Conor waves me over to the dartboard.

"Oh, wait. Let me go to the bathroom quick." I sip my drink, then walk out of the private room, weaving through all the people until I reach the bathroom.

Man, it's so much more crowded in here than usual. I wonder if people are crawling from bar to bar since it's Halloween. Little do they know Ruby isn't into big crowds, even if it means more money for her business.

I look for her to say hello, but I can't find her, so I turn down the hallway to the bathroom, thankful there's only a small line. I pull out my phone and check my emails to make the time pass faster.

Then someone says the men's room is empty and the two women in front of me rush over there. I walk inside the women's bathroom, go into a stall, and do my business. After I flush and open the stall door, I notice there's no line now. The other stall is open as well, but against the door stands Lila without the blonde hair, dressed as a witch. How fitting.

The hair on the nape of my neck stands on end, and a chill rushes over my body.

"Funny meeting you here. Or is it?" She whips off her hat and tosses it in the trash can. "God, I hate hats."

I look at the door. The lock is flicked.

She's locked me in the bathroom.

I slyly move my hand to my back pocket where my phone is, but she points at me. "Put it on the counter."

I huff and dig it out of my back pocket and place it on the wet counter. "What are you doing, Lila? They're going to realize I haven't come back and come looking for me."

"You stole him from me. He's mine!" She steps toward me.

"I haven't. You slept with him, but that's all."

"Is that what he told you?" She takes another step forward, and I step back. "He's a liar."

"Was there more between you two than he told me?"

She doesn't answer, and I wonder if she does know the truth but doesn't want to admit it.

"I'm sorry you got hurt, Lila. I've been hurt before too, and I know it's not easy, but I love him too." I try the sympathetic route. "We have something really special, and he's helped me through a really hard time."

"I love him too," she says. "And I loved him first, so you need to step aside."

I hold up my hands as she gets closer to me. "Okay, I will. Is that what you want? Me to just stop seeing him? But Lila, even if I walk away from him, I don't think he's going to come to you."

"Of course you would say that."

Someone tries to open the door, then they pound on it with their fists.

"Stop having sex in this bathroom!" Ruby shouts from the hallway. "God damn it, I hate Halloween. I should've closed the bar." She pounds on the door again. "This isn't a sex club. Get out now."

It's a split-second decision I don't have time to really consider. "Ruby, it's Eloise. Help!"

"You bitch, shut up!"

"Lila, someone is going to break down this door soon. Save yourself and put that hat back on, tip your head down, and leave. I'll tell everyone it was an accident. That you didn't mean to lock it. Or... I'll say I did it."

She stops moving toward me, and I feel as if I might be getting through to her.

"Eloise!" Conor shouts, pounding on the door. "Eloise!"

Ruby must have gone and gotten Conor. The relief I feel is short-lived.

Lila winces but looks at me, and I see it too late. Gold knuckles wrapped around her fingers are hidden by the long sleeves of her costume.

"Once he's done being sad about you, he'll want me back." She punches me across the face, and everything goes black.

fifty-four

Conor

I pound my shoulder into the door.

"Ruby, don't you have an axe here to scare away the people you don't like?" Tweetie shouts, taking turns to hit the door with his shoulder as I search the area for anything to break down the door.

"Here." Kyleigh weaves through the crowd and hands me a fire extinguisher.

I hit the door with it. "Sorry, Rubes, I'll buy you a new door."

"How cold of a person do you think I am? Get the girl out!" she yells.

I continue to use all my force, hitting right where the lock is. After too many hits and my shoulders and arms killing me, the lock finally splinters, and the door flies open.

Lila is standing over a passed-out Eloise sprawled out on the floor. Fear like I've never known grips me. Lila glances over her shoulder, and I grab her free arm, spinning her around into the wall. I crouch beside Eloise and move my hands all over her head, searching for any sign of blood.

"Someone call an ambulance," I shout, running my hand over her freshly bruised cheekbone. "God, baby, wake up. Be okay. Please be okay."

I have no idea what happens behind me, and I don't care. I just need a paramedic to get here.

Her eyes flutter open.

"Eloise?"

"Oh god, what happened?" She touches her cheek.

"Just stay still, baby." I hear sirens outside.

"We're closing. Go find your fun somewhere else!" Ruby screams, and I hear a lot of groans and complaints.

"Eloise." Jade falls to her knees on her other side and sees the bruise, eyeing me when Eloise's eyes drift closed again.

"Where is Lila?" I ask.

"She's at a table with Rowan and Henry watching her. Tweetie went out to lead the paramedics in here."

We wait for what feels like a million years as Eloise just lies there with her eyes closed.

A paramedic rushes in. "Okay, everyone out. What happened?"

Jade does a double-take at him. "Medic Bianco?"

Henry pops his head in. "How do you know the paramedic?"

"Man, sonic ears," Tweetie says from the hallway.

"Who the hell cares?" I shout, then look at the paramedic. "This is my girlfriend. She was hit, and I don't know if she hit her head on the floor too, but she's got a nasty bruise on her cheek."

The paramedic nods. "Okay, give us some room." He bends down where I was.

I pace the small space, biting my fist, then lean against the wall and watch them ask Eloise questions, shine a flashlight in her eyes, and eventually move her onto a stretcher. I follow her out.

The police are here now, asking everyone questions.

"I'll need to ask you some questions," one cop says to me.

"Then visit me at the hospital." I continue walking until I reach the ambulance and watch them put Eloise in the back before I step inside with Medic Bianco.

"So, you're coming too," Medic Bianco says, laughing to himself. "I'm kidding, I'd probably be on the stretcher with my wife. Then she'd knee me in the nuts. Well, maybe not the nuts. She's been begging me for another kid."

"Thanks. Can we concentrate on my girlfriend?"

He puts in an IV, and the ambulance drives away from Peeper's. I sit back and watch Eloise doze in and out, missing her amazing gray eyes every time her eyelids shut.

"These things happen. It wasn't your fault," Medic Bianco says, not knowing how wrong he is.

This is all my fault.

fifty-five

Eloise

I'M TAKEN TO THE HOSPITAL AND GIVEN A BUNCH OF tests to make sure I don't have any damage or internal bleeding. She hit me good.

Besides the contusion on my face, I have a mild concussion. The doctor suspects I fell on something instead of going straight to the floor. But they want to keep me here overnight to make sure nothing develops.

The nurse comes in and glares at Conor. "She needs her sleep,"

"Think of me as a teddy bear to a six-year-old. Would you kick a teddy bear out?"

The tips of the nurse's lips move up, but she's quick to straighten them before he can call her out.

"He's hard not to like," I say as she checks the bedside screen.

She glances at Conor. "No getting in the bed, you got it?"

He holds up his hands. "Deal."

She leaves, and he grabs my hand. "I'm sorry," he says for the millionth time.

Being in that bathroom was scary for a few minutes, and I'm sure that what happened tonight will stay with me for a while.

"What happened to Lila?" I ask.

"She was arrested for assault. She's in jail tonight. They want to know if you want to press charges."

I close my eyes. I have to admit that I feel better knowing she's not on the loose and able to get to us. "I don't think she's okay, Conor. I think it's more than her wanting you. She was convinced that if she got rid of me, she'd have you."

His gaze moves to the bruise which has made my entire cheek swell.

"It will heal," I tell him, seeing the guilt painted over every one of his features.

"Still." His knuckles brush along the skin of my other cheek. "We'll talk about it later. Once I get you home. You need to sleep."

My eyes close. I am exhausted from the day, and I'm just about to drift into dreamland when the mattress dips next to me. Conor's smell lingers around me, and he holds me close.

"What are you doing? She's going to come in here and kick your ass out."

He chuckles and kisses my temple. "Are you okay? Am I bothering you?"

"Never. At least not until we're in our fifties and sleeping in separate beds," I mumble.

"Good, so we're on the same page."

I frown, but it hurts my cheek, so I stop. "I'm sorry?"

"Marriage. Not the whole separate beds things, but you want to marry me too. We can pick a date when we get out of here." He kisses my temple. "Now sleep."

My eyes fly open. "Conor, what are you talking about?"

He chuckles to himself, but when his eyes meet mine, there's no humor in his face. "I love you, Eloise. I've known it for some time now, but I was scared to tell you. Seeing you on that floor... I was so scared, and I couldn't breathe when you wouldn't open your eyes. You're it for me, and I don't want to live one minute without you in my life. I want to marry you and adopt puppies and raise our children together. I want to make a million lists with you and be next to you as we cross them off together. Will you marry me, Eloise Corbin?"

I open my mouth, but no words come out.

"I know I don't have a ring, but I'll rectify that. And if you want me to do a big proposal again in front of our friends and family, I will. I'll surprise you a second time."

I shake my head, tears blurring my vision. "No. It was perfect. I don't want a big production. I want everything you just said. I love you too, Connor Nilsen."

He closes his eyes in relief and kisses my forehead.

"People will think we're crazy," I say.

"They won't when they come to our fiftieth wedding anniversary party." He wipes a tear from my cheek. "Does that mean you're saying yes?"

"Yes."

He does a little holler, and the nurse pushes the curtain aside, peeking her head in. She puts her hands on her hips and glares.

"She said yes to marrying me!"

"Yippee." She fights her smile and shuts the curtain. "You better get that girl a big-ass ring."

"I will." He looks at me. "She'll have the biggest ring."

I shake my head. "I don't need anything huge. I just need you."

He digs into his pocket, and I wonder if he was joking about not having a ring, but he pulls out his phone and holds it in front of us. His thumb moves across the screen until he's in his notes app.

"I get to cross something off my list." He presses his thumb on the line that reads "Ask Eloise to marry me" and smiles at me.

"Conor." My head rolls to his shoulder, and I wish I had my list with me. "I can finally cross off fall in love."

Some people might think we're crazy, but I know that's not the case. Let people say what they want. I wasn't looking to fall in love, but I'm so happy it happened. Sometimes when you know, you know, and it's as simple as that.

epilogue

Eloise

I MADE A FULL RECOVERY, AND WHEN LILA'S SISTER intervened and Lila herself agreed to get help at a mental health hospital, I decided not to press charges. I just want her to get well, both for us and herself.

After the doctor gave me the all-clear, we booked flights to Vegas on Conor's three-day break.

As I stand on the other side of the door in the chapel, waiting for them to open so I can see Conor standing at the end of the aisle, none of the anxiety I experienced the first time I was in this situation lives inside me. The doors open, and I don't have to look up to know Conor's eyes are on me. As my gaze lifts, I see him in his ivory suit, his smile getting wider the closer I get.

My chest doesn't feel tight with stress and trepidation. Instead, it's filled with joy and excitement for our future. I reach the end of the aisle and pass my bouquet to the offi-ciant's wife.

"You look so beautiful," Conor whispers.

"You look handsome too," I whisper back.

He takes my hands and stares into my eyes.

The officiant goes through the classic set of vows and promises. We weren't picky, we really just want to be married. Our hearts know the vows we hold inside them. I don't need Conor to tell me. He'll show me. Every day we'll show one another our commitment to each other. When the officiant reaches the objection part, we both laugh, and the officiant's eyebrows scrunch.

He barely gets to the "you may kiss your bride" part before Conor's hands are on my cheeks and his mouth is on mine.

He announces us, and we walk out of the small ceremony room and right onto the street to flag down a taxi. We have things to do after all.

"We could've gone to city hall at this rate." I climb into the taxi.

"Yeah, but a little vacation to get away is what we needed."

We head back to the hotel and make love for hours before we come up for air and order some food. I don't see us leaving this hotel room until we have to go to the airport, so I'm shocked when Conor gets out of bed to go shower.

"Are we going somewhere?" I ask.

"I have a surprise." He peeks his head in the room. "We have an appointment in thirty minutes."

"Conor, I have to shower too."

"I know, I'm warming the water for you. We're not going anywhere fancy."

"Oh, okay." I wonder what he has planned.

He stops me as I enter the bathroom, kissing me briefly. "My next day off, we'll spend the entire day in bed so you can cross off spend a day in bed with a hottie from the list."

"Oh my god, there are times I wish you'd never seen my list." I open the shower door and step in.

He follows me. "You don't mean that. You love that I saw that list. I think you secretly wanted me to see it."

We wash up fast since we have to get going, although I wouldn't have minded staying in for the night.

After I got out of the hospital, he put his list up on the fridge next to mine, so we both know what the other wants. I feel like we're always trying to surprise one another to check something off.

We take the elevator down to the lobby and head out onto the Strip, the doorman getting us a taxi. Conor gives the cabbie the address, and I cuddle into his arm, lifting my hand and looking at my band and engagement ring.

"It's beautiful."

He kisses the top of my head. "Just like the woman who wears it."

"There you go with your lines again." I pat his stomach.

When the cab driver says we're here, I look out the window to see a tattoo parlor. I tilt my head at him.

"You don't have to, but I'm crossing it off my list," he says.

"Oh, okay."

We get out and go inside. Sure enough, he's made two appointments—one for me and one for him. I haven't even thought about what I would get a tattoo of, though.

Conor walks to the back with one of the guys.

"What are you getting?" I ask.

"You'll see once I'm done." He winks and sits in the chair, talking to the tattoo artist.

"You're Eloise?" A woman approaches me. She's got full sleeves filled with beautiful and intricate designs.

"I am. Can I ask you a question?"

"Sure," she says.

"Can you do a star pattern along the inside of my wrist?"

"Easy peasy." She walks us over to her station, away from Conor.

An hour or so later, I finish up, and he's waiting for me in the waiting area.

"So, what did you get?" I'm excited to see.

He lifts his hand to show me a cursive letter E on his ring finger with a line that wraps around his finger.

"Seriously?"

He chuckles. "We're the long game, you know that."

"Jeez, I love it. I'm going to stare at your finger more than my ring now."

"Well, time for your big reveal." He lifts my hand and gently pulls back the bandage. "Stars. I love it."

"I love you." I walk into him, and he wraps his arms around me.

"I love you too." He kisses the top of my head. "Another item to cross off."

"Thanks for thinking of this."

He takes my hand, guiding us out of the tattoo shop. We get back to our hotel, eat, and retire early since the minute we get back to Chicago, Conor has to get to the rink for his morning skate.

It was the best trip I've ever been on.

Conor

I hate to leave Eloise right after we land in Chicago, but I have no choice if I want to continue playing hockey. We have the Uber drop me off at the rink, and she continues on, meeting Jade and Kyleigh for breakfast somewhere. After today, our marriage will no longer be our little secret.

I kiss her goodbye and walk into the locker room.

I drop my bag and raise my hands. "I have an announcement to make. I'm a married man!" I show off my left hand.

"What the hell?" Rowan comes over to me.

"Beat you to it," I say, then point at Henry. "Beat you too."

"You got married?" Tweetie asks.

"And you didn't invite us?" Henry scowls at me.

"Three-day trip to Vegas," I say.

Coach Buford comes out of his office. "What's going on out here?"

"Pinkie got married," Alvin says.

He lifts his gaze for a moment. "Congratulations," he deadpans. "The rest of you listen up. There's been a development with this whole social media thing the league is pushing. Gill just got the axe, which I think we can all agree is a good thing for him and us."

Everyone laughs. The guy just wasn't meant for that job.

"Since there's no one else waiting in the wings, and the season is already underway, and we're one of the favorites to win the Cup, they're sending in the boss. This Tedi Douglas is going to use us as an example to show others what's possible, so get ready to put those hockey smiles on display, boys." He walks back to his office without another word.

The three of us all look over at Tweetie, who doesn't seem as surprised as the rest of us.

"Fuck off and go play Monopoly." He stalks toward the bathroom.

Things are about to become very rocky around here.

The End

also by piper rayne

The Nest

Mr. Heartbreaker

Mr. Broody

Mr. Swoony

Mr. C (Title to be revealed)

Chicago Grizzlies

On the Defense (Free Prequel)

Something like Hate

Something like Lust

Something like Love

Modern Love

Charmed by the Bartender

Hooked by the Boxer

Mad about the Banker

Single Dads Club

Real Deal

Dirty Talker

Sexy Beast

Hollywood Hearts

Mister Mom

Animal Attraction

Domestic Bliss

Bedroom Games

Cold as Ice

On Thin Ice

Break the Ice

Chicago Law

Smitten with the Best Man

Tempted by my Ex-Husband

Seduced by my Ex's Divorce Attorney

Blue Collar Brothers

Flirting with Fire

Crushing on the Cop

Engaged to the EMT

White Collar Brothers

Sexy Filthy Boss

Dirty Flirty Enemy

Wild Steamy Hook-up

The Rooftop Crew

My Bestie's Ex

A Royal Mistake

The Rival Roomies

Our Star-Crossed Kiss

The Do-Over

A Co-Workers Crush

Hockey Hotties

Countdown to a Kiss (Free Prequel)

My Lucky #13 (FREE)

The Trouble with #9

Faking it with #41

Tropical Hat Trick (Novella)

Sneaking around with #34

Second Shot with #76

Offside with #55

Kingsmen Football Stars

False Start (Free Prequel)

You Had Your Chance, Lee Burrows

You Can't Kiss the Nanny, Brady Banks

Over My Brother's Dead Body, Chase Andrews

The Baileys

Lessons from a One-Night Stand (FREE)

Advice from a Jilted Bride

Birth of a Baby Daddy

Operation Bailey Wedding (Novella)

Falling for My Brother's Best Friend

Demise of a Self-Centered Playboy

Confessions of a Naughty Nanny

Operation Bailey Babies (Novella)

Secrets of the World's Worst Matchmaker

Winning my Best Friend's Girl

Rules for Dating Your Ex

Operation Bailey Birthday (Novella)

The Greene Family

My Twist of Fortune (Free Prequel)

My Beautiful Neighbor (FREE)

My Almost Ex

My Vegas Groom

A Greene Family Summer Bash (Novella)

My Sister's Flirty Friend

My Unexpected Surprise

My Famous Frenemy

A Greene Family Vacation (Novella)

My Scorned Best Friend

My Fake Fiancé

My Brother's Forbidden Friend

A Greene Family Christmas (Novella)

Lake Starlight

The Problem with Second Chances

The Issue with Bad Boy Roommates

The Trouble with Runaway Brides

The Drawback of Single Dads

The Complication with the Best Man

Plain Daisy Ranch

One Last Summer

The One I Left Behind

The One I Stood Beside

The One I Didn't See Coming

C.F.(Title to be Revealed)

Holiday Romances

Single and Ready to Jingle

Claus and Effect

Merry Kissmas

cockamamie unicorn ramblings

Were you surprised? We've never done a stop-the-wedding book, nor have we done one with a list. After all the books we've written, it's fun when you figure out something new to try, and adding those two elements to Conor and Eloise's story made it so fun to write!

We're not sure when the idea of Conor stopping a wedding was thought of to put in this series. Maybe after Rowan and Kyleigh's book, but it wasn't going to be Eloise until we were plotting Henry and Jade's book. This idea came because we wanted the girls to be as tight of a group as the guys. Plus, if you know us, we love to surprise you!

Originally, Eloise was just going to be Conor's roommate because she had nowhere to go. Things would obviously progress, but something in our gut said we needed more. So, we decided to add the list to keep things interesting. At first, it was going to be a sexual list to fulfill that Conor would gladly agree to help Eloise out on, but we felt some time needed to pass for Eloise before she jumped into bed with Conor. They needed to grow closer. That's how we decided on the list of thirty things to do before you're thirty. Maybe look for that other list in our P. Rayne pen names books. LOL

There's so much that did changed from original conception to publication in this book. Eloise's grandparents were going to be a bigger problem for her and Conor. Tristan was going to try to win her back. The distance was going to be a problem once Conor started his season. If you clicked the bonus to see their bucket lists, that changed a lot and what would be incorporated into the story. The stalker girl was going to kidnap Eloise... there were many things thrown into our brainstorming/plotting session. Maybe one day, we will record one of these for all of you to see. LOL

As with every book, there were a lot of changes, but we feel as if their journey ended up just as it should—at the altar. I think we all know those couples where someone was dating someone else for a long time, they broke up, and the person ended up married six months later because they met someone else and just knew. Conor and Eloise just knew they were each other's person from the moment they met.

As always, we have a lot of people to thank for getting this book into your hands...

Nina and the entire Valentine PR team. The organization, the promotion, the way you keep us on point with deadlines. We appreciate you SO much!

Cassie from Joy Editing for line edits who once again accepted a rush from us, allowed us to split into parts because we booked a deadline in December—again—no matter how many times we say we're not going to do this!

Ellie from My Brother's Editor for line edits and proofing. We give you barely any time, but you always come through.

Hang Le for the discreet cover and branding for the entire series, which is always top tier. Your talent and eye are unmatched.

Simone at Buerosued for our illustrated cover. Your work is amazing and we're so happy to be working with you on this series. We love Conor and Eloise's pose! You always pick a better one than we do. LOL

All the bloggers who choose to read us when you have so many options out there. We're appreciative and honored to be on your list of must-reads and love reading all your reviews, edits, and more.

All the Piper Rayne Unicorns who support us every day, all day. We'd be lost without you answering our polls and telling us what you love and hate. We strive to give you the best Piper Rayne experience, and we can't say much else except that you're fantastic and unmatched!

You, the reader, reading this now in real time, who has an abundance of books to choose from—thank you for picking up one of ours. We hope you enjoyed the story and want to continue the series.

And... drum roll... you're finally getting the story you've been waiting for—Tweetie. And that's about all we're going to tell you right now! :P

xo,
Piper & Rayne

about piper & rayne

Piper Rayne is a *USA Today* Bestselling Author duo who write "heartwarming humor with a side of sizzle" about families, whether that be blood or found. They both have e-readers full of one-clickable books, they're married to husbands who drive them to drink, and they're both chauffeurs to their kids. Most of all, they love hot heroes and quirky heroines who make them laugh, and they hope you do, too!